Praise for *Hearth Fires*

"Leave it to Dorothy Keddington to bring two people from completely different worlds into a luscious world of their own. *Hearth Fires* is ample proof that she is the master of romantic suspense. It is a book to savor late at night, when you really need a hero." —Ka Hancock, best-selling author of *Dancing on Broken Glass*

"*Hearth Fire*s is full of the same heart-pounding romance, suspense, and twists that make all of Dorothy Keddington's books shine. Like her previous novels, *Hearth Fires* does not disappoint. With its page-turning plot, and characters you will think about long after you've finished reading, this book will leave you happy and satisfied." —Mindy Holt, ldswomensbookreview.com

"Long-time fans and first-time readers alike will quickly fall in love with *Hearth Fires*. Dorothy Keddington masterfully combines intrigue, romance, and gentle humor. She creates characters that come alive. You will love them, cry with them, and fear for them. Keddington's beautifully descriptive style and ability to create a powerful mental image will have you rooting for Mackenzie and falling in love with William. It doesn't matter if your taste in books is mystery, romance, crime, or even *Architectural Digest*. *Hearth Fires* has it all. This book offers readers a wonderful literary buffet, with a bit of 'happily ever after' for dessert. This is truly a story that will have you saying, 'Just one ~~~~~ ~ter!'" —Jenny Craghead, teacher, Carden Memorial Sch

"In *Hearth Fires,* Dorothy J⌐⌐⌐⌐⌐ ⌐⌐⌐⌐⌐ hand and welcome you into the lives ⌐ ⌐⌐⌐⌐ u will make fast friends will Mackenzie and w⌐⌐ pulled into a breathtaking whirlwind of danger, suspense, a⌐⌐ ⌐hanting romance." —Lori Snider, www.reading-with-kids.com

"In her new novel, *Hearth Fires,* Dorothy Keddington has woven a tapestry with words. Her delightful descriptions evoke images much like painting a canvas upon our minds. Storybook cottages, cypress-lined shores, and picturesque ranches with orange-gold sunsets come to life in her words. Dorothy's vivid characters mingle amid adventure, danger, and romance, while the mystery grips and pulls you into the story, holding you captive until the last word. The flames of *Hearth Fires* will warm you even on the coldest of nights." —Vachelle Anderson Johnson

HEARTH FIRES

DOROTHY KEDDINGTON

CURRAWONG PRESS

For Sylvia Butterfield,
a dear friend, fabulous teacher, and wonderful whip-cracker

Currawong Press
110 South 800 West
Brigham City, Utah 84302
http://walnutspringspress.blogspot.com

Cover design by Tracy Anderson (www.TracyAndersonPhoto.com)

ISBN: 978-1-59992-894-4

This is a work of fiction. The characters, names, incidents, and dialogue are products of the author's imagination and are not to be construed as real, and any resemblance to real people and events is not intentional.

Acknowledgments

Gratitude and praise is heaped upon the talented heads of the wonderful Fort-Nightly Group—Carol Warburton, Ka Hancock, and Lou Ann Anderson—faithful friends and fellow writers who have shared, cared, and been totally fair with me through many years of our creative endeavors.

Many thanks to Wade Butterfield, who generously gave of his time and expertise to educate and enlighten me concerning police policy and procedure.

My gratitude and admiration is given to Linda Prince, for her superb editing and patience with a writer who loves to bend the rules.

And finally, to all those friends, family, and readers who have encouraged and awaited this novel—thank you, and I hope *Hearth Fires* is worth the wait!

Prologue

Blackmail and extortion. The words settled uncomfortably in Vince Dicola's mind as he sat eating greasy fries and an even greasier burger in the booth of an all-night diner. Might as well call it what it was, he thought. Blackmail and extortion.

Vince poured more ketchup on the fries and scowled, shoulders hunched, elbows on the table, wondering what they wanted this time. He didn't need this. It was going on ten o'clock, and he'd already put in over nine hours today. Just when he was wrapping things up, thinking about a microwave dinner and a can of beer in front of the TV, the call had come. Terse instructions for a meeting with the time and place and little else, but he knew that voice and he hated it.

He glanced at his watch and felt his gut tighten. Someone would be here soon. Brock or some other bozo working for Sarcassian. Vince stared down at the burger with sudden distaste, took a gulp of coffee, and gave a tired nod to the tired server who appeared at his table, wanting to know if everything was all right. No, everything was not all right, Vince thought morosely. The past two years had been pure hell. The divorce. Ulcers. Getting passed over for promotion in the department. Then that anonymous phone call offering him a tantalizing tip about a huge drug shipment. Dates and names of suppliers and dealers. All that was his if he would be willing to do a small favor in return. Nothing dangerous or illegal, they'd assured him. Just a simple matter of looking the other way.

The decision was a no-brainer. He had no problem rationalizing the slight discomfort to his conscience by assuring himself that the potential good from such an offer far outweighed the negatives. And for a while, it seemed he might be right. The bust was successful. Arrests were made. Over sixty kilos of "coke" were intercepted and destroyed. And Vince finally got some of the recognition he deserved.

Yet somehow that one favor wasn't enough. It wasn't long before other demands were made, always in the form of requests, but Vince knew what they really were, and he didn't know how to back out. After a while, backing out was no longer an option. Especially when the bitter taste of his betrayal was sweetened with generous amounts of cash and other, more sensual benefits.

A big man dressed in jeans, a leather jacket, and a tight black T-shirt slid onto the seat opposite Vince and offered a smug "Evening, Lieutenant. It's been a while."

"Not long enough." Vince met the big man's eyes with a cocky show of anger and bravado he was far from feeling.

Brock Symonds was exactly the kind of guy he'd spent the past fifteen years of his life trying to put behind bars. Brock was nothing more than a well-paid, sadistic gofer whose idea of right and wrong began with the questions "What's in it for me?" and "How much?"

"We have a little problem we'd like you to help us straighten out," Brock was saying.

"What kind of problem?"

"A legal matter."

Vince popped a cold fry into his mouth. "Sounds like you need an attorney, not a cop."

Brock glanced around the nearly deserted diner, then leaned across the table. "What we need is for a certain judge to dismiss the case against the daughter of an associate of mine. And we think you can help."

"Come on, Brock. Get real," Vince snorted, his mouth curling into a derisive smile. "Since when would any judge listen to a cop? If I so much as suggest that he should mess around with a case, the guy could have my job."

"I don't think so." Brock sat back against the booth and said casually, "The judge I'm referring to happens to have a nasty little cocaine habit. And with elections coming up, if certain facts were made public, trust me, it'd be his job, not yours that'd be hosed."

Dicola glanced down at his uneaten dinner. "But why me? I still don't know why you think he'd listen to me."

Brock made no attempt to hide his smirk. "Who better to remind the judge of his civic duty than a fine, upstanding officer of the law."

"I don't know. It still sounds risky."

"You worry too much, Lieutenant. Oh, there's something I forgot to mention. You see, this isn't the first time the judge has accepted a small offering to keep his bad habits out of the public eye." Brock reached into his jacket pocket, took out a fat envelope, and tossed it on the table next to Dicola's plate. "I brought along a little offering for you as well. That is, if you're interested."

Vince stared at the envelope for a long moment, but both he and Brock knew the decision was made. Slipping the envelope into a pocket of his coat, Vince said quietly, "So what do I have to do?"

One

Houses hold secrets, much like people. A well-maintained exterior can conceal flaws as well as heartaches, but once inside, there is usually a feeling, a lingering echo of the lives and events that have gone before. It's difficult to explain, especially to someone with a rational, modern mind, but as far back as I can remember, this awareness of old houses has been part of me. As a child, I instinctively knew whether a home was happy or sad—or empty, like the one I grew up in. Discovering the secrets of a dwelling is not as easy as discerning its emotions, especially when those secrets are carefully guarded.

And what secrets do you hold? I wondered, looking at the storybook cottage that sat smiling in the mellow gold of a September sun. Seeing the home for the first time, it was difficult to imagine anything dark or furtive in its history, especially with those diamond-paned windows winking a sleepy but inviting hello. I smiled back, feeling the cottage's fairy-tale charm tug at my sensibilities until imagination and fancy were set free.

What would it be like to live in an enchanted cottage by the sea? All in a moment, the latent part of me that longed to believe in fairy tales and happily-ever-afters pictured myself working in the garden, hands wrist-deep in warm, dark earth, planting promises for spring.

And there would be someone wonderful to meet under that rose-filled arbor. Someone whose footsteps along the stone path would make my heart beat a little faster, and whose presence would fill the home and my life with quiet joy and completeness.

I closed my eyes, trying to insert a particular face into the scene, and found myself jerked rudely back to the present. This was not my home. Nor was I part of a fairy tale, but a mere ten minutes outside of Carmel, California. And I had a job to do.

As a contributing editor for *Hearth & Home* magazine, it was my pleasant but often stressful task to produce an article for each bimonthly issue on the topic "Then & Now." Two months ago found me in an old fishing village on the coast of Maine, interviewing the owners of a delightful bed-and-breakfast that served as a colonial way station during the Revolutionary War. Before that, I had written about the resident ghosts as well as the present-day owners who inhabited an antebellum mansion in the Old South.

My current project was a feature article on California's charming storybook homes, a unique style of architecture that developed during the early decades of the twentieth century. Some said the style had its roots in the film industry, that it was a byproduct of the glamorous era of silent-film stars and movie moguls. Others felt it came from Europe, with borrowed elements of country French, English Tudor, and German folk architecture. Whatever the source, these whimsical homes had been rediscovered in the twenty-first century, and the magazine had flown me to San Francisco for a two-week stay to do research, interview owners, and photograph prime examples.

Five years ago, I never dreamed my love of history and old houses would result in such an enjoyable career. The only downside, if it can be called one, is the fact that my mother's name and reputation was a key factor in my landing the job. Mother is an ultrasuccessful interior designer with a moneyed, jaw-dropping clientele. One would think that having my name linked with hers would be a source of pride rather than resentment, but there's a strain of stubborn independence in me that prefers to blaze my own trails, rather than take a ride on my mother's fashionable coattails.

Mother firmly subscribes to the old adage "It's not what you know, but who you know," and in my case, a not-so-subtle suggestion to her dear friend, the magazine's editor-in-chief, resulted in my initial employment. Just thinking about it still rankles. To hear Mother talk, my position with one of the nation's foremost home magazines was entirely her doing. That may be. But getting a job and keeping a job are different things altogether, and I made up my mind at the outset that the byline of Mackenzie Graham would stand on its own merit, and not because I am Vanessa Graham's daughter.

The current project was very much my own brainchild and received enthusiastic endorsement from Allison Meyers, the magazine's West Coast managing editor. Fortunately for me, she had long been enamored with storybook style and was more than eager to lend her support. It was Allison who arranged today's interview and photo session with Judge Peter Wolcott and his wife Dana, the owners of the charming home I was seeing now. According to Allison, the cottage had a history as fascinating as its architecture. The original owner was a silent-film star with all the attendant Garbo-esque glamour and allure. The current owners were well-respected residents of picturesque Carmel-by-the-Sea, and Allison made it very clear how important it was to make a favorable impression on the good judge and his lovely socialite wife.

With my own roots planted in Chicago's semi-industrial soil, I am admittedly unaware which individuals occupy the higher rungs of California's social ladder. Nor do I really care. Thanks in part to my mother's lifelong obsession with it, social strata does not impress me. Still, knowing how important the assignment was to Allison and the magazine, I couldn't help feeling an added weight of responsibility. One of the magazine's staff photographers would come at a later date to do a final photo session, but it was my job to interview the Wolcotts, get a general feel for the home, and do a preliminary photo shoot.

Where to begin? Everywhere I looked there was beauty begging to be photographed. I drew an excited breath, my professional self dissolving into childish delight, not unlike Snow White when she spied the Seven Dwarfs' fanciful dwelling deep in the heart of the forest. Unlike Snow White, I fished my handy digital camera out of its case and quickly adjusted the settings. Before announcing my arrival, I simply had to get a few shots. Those curving, half-timbered walls with ivy trailing down the sides . . . the dark-paneled door with its oversized hardware . . . the rolled eaves and that distinctive, sea-wave-shingled roof . . .

Ideas and angles for the article began humming an evocative melody in my mind. The cottage was reminiscent of those found in Arthur Rackham's and Edmund Dulac's classic fairy-tale illustrations. I might be able to use that. A few old illustrations paired with some contemporary photos. An image from the story of Rumpelstiltskin suddenly came to mind. Seeing this present-day storybook cottage basking in the dappled sunlight of an autumn afternoon, I wouldn't be at all surprised to find a mysterious little man inside spinning straw into gold. I smiled then at the foolish direction my thoughts had taken. It was highly unlikely that Judge Peter Wolcott bore any resemblance to Rumpelstiltskin. Nor was his wife a fairy-tale maiden in distress.

No more flights into fancy. Putting my imaginings away along with my camera, I approached the front door and gave a few sharp raps with the brass knocker. Silence was the only answer. I waited a moment, enjoying the drowsy hum of bees amid the roses, then pressed the doorbell. A faint chorus of chimes sounded within the house, but brought no response. Puzzled, I glanced at my watch. My appointment with the Wolcotts was at two o'clock, and it was now three minutes before the hour.

That someone was at home I had no doubt. Off to the left, perhaps ten yards from the house, a narrow drive led to a two-car garage. The structure was much newer than the cottage, but its design resembled that of an old-fashioned gatehouse and was perfectly in keeping with the home's whimsical elements. Not so, the two cars parked in front. Both vehicles were black, shining and new—one a sleek Mercedes, the other a BMW. If his taste in automobiles were any indication of his income, perhaps the good judge had found a modern-day method of spinning straw into gold.

I pressed the doorbell once more for good measure and tried to smooth a few wrinkles from my linen slacks. A pair of jeans would have survived the warm two-hour drive from Palo Alto much better, but today's meeting required my best professional "uniform"— cream-colored slacks and jacket with a silky camisole in my favorite shade of teal. I gave a flyaway strand of hair a quick swipe and tried to ignore the nervous little pulse beating in my throat. What was wrong with me? I'd done my homework and knew I was well prepared for the interview. So why the sweaty palms?

The faint shadow of a memory stole into my thoughts, gradually becoming clearer, like the opening of a door sheds light into a darkened room. I saw myself, a child of eight or nine, opening the door to admit another judge, one of my mother's "important clients." I don't remember the purpose of his visit—picking up carpet or fabric samples, perhaps. The reason hardly matters. But I can still remember the man's expression as he looked down at me with slightly raised brows, a faint frown of distaste marring his distinguished features.

In that moment, I knew a kind of judgment had been made—one in which I'd been found somehow lacking. Before I could say or do anything, my mother appeared in the doorway behind me, hastily greeting the judge and inviting him inside. There was a marked change in the man's expression as his sharp-eyed glance shifted from me to my lovely mother.

"So this is your daughter," he'd said politely, but with a critical edge to his tone. "She certainly doesn't resemble her mother."

His careless comment cut me to the quick, yet even as a child, I knew it was true. Tall and slender, with smooth sable hair, ivory skin, and blue-violet eyes, when Vanessa Graham walked into a room, people instantly took notice, while I resembled my father's side of the family, sturdy Scots that they are. Thankfully, my figure lost its sturdiness around age thirteen, but my hoped-for growth spurt ended when I reached a scant three inches above five feet. I frequently took comfort in the fact that Mother once said my eyes were my best feature, an unusual blue-green with flecks of gold. Grandfather Graham was fond of telling me that I had his mother's eyes—Great-Grandmother Mackenzie, after whom I was named. But when one adds to the picture chestnut hair that refuses to be tamed and fair skin that will never in this life experience a tan, it isn't difficult to understand why my mother should be such a daunting figure. Still, you'd think at age twenty-eight I'd stop comparing myself to her.

I sighed and straightened my shoulders, mentally shrugging aside the past with practical thoughts of the present. If Judge Wolcott and his wife were anything like other homeowners I'd interviewed, they'd probably be so excited about seeing their home on the pages of a national magazine, they wouldn't really care how I looked or what I was wearing. That is, if the Wolcotts ever answered the door.

Glancing about, I noticed a flagstone path leading to the north side of the house and wondered if Mr. and Mrs. Wolcott might be somewhere around back where they couldn't hear the doorbell or my knock. I waited a moment more, then ventured along the narrow pathway.

The home had been built near the edge of a thickly wooded ravine and was set well back from the main road. No sounds of traffic intruded on the drowsy, midday silence, nor were there any close neighbors on either side. The grounds were a seamless blend of wild, natural habitat and beautifully maintained gardens.

The fairy-tale feeling of the place persisted as I followed the path down an embankment bordered with gnarled oaks and yews. Seeing clumps of waist-high azaleas, I found myself wishing the photo shoot could have taken place in the spring when they were in full bloom. And yet September's Midas touch had its own kind of beauty. Ferns grew thick and wild under the trees, their curling brown edges making a rusty carpet of yellow and green, while patches of sunny goldenrod and purple asters sang sweet autumn songs. I took out my camera to capture a few shots of deep blue hydrangeas and fiery orange lilies against a crumbling stone wall.

Somewhere below, I heard the musical murmur of water. Nothing fast-tempoed enough to be a stream; a small brook or fountain, perhaps. Camera in hand, I followed the sound and discovered the path's gentle descent had changed to stone steps. These led down to a secluded courtyard sheltered on two sides by ancient oak trees. In the center of the courtyard, a fountain of natural stone and stucco rose from a small circular pond, complete with creamy white water lilies.

I smiled, half expecting to see a princess sitting beside the pond with her golden ball, and the Frog Prince watching her from beneath a lily pad. The spell of enchantment hung in the air like the gossamer threads of a spider's web. When a shaft of sunlight caught the fountain's spray in a rainbow kiss of jeweled color, I couldn't help myself. Switching the Canon to its rapid-fire setting, I took a series of shots—the pond and fountain, the gnarled oaks, and the flower-bedecked courtyard. In the midst of this, three men moved into the scene. The camera automatically recorded their entry and actions before I had time to change the setting or react to their presence.

The next instant I was grabbed roughly by the arm, and a man's guttural voice demanded, "What the hell do you think you're doing?"

With a startled cry, I turned to see a pair of angry, dark eyes in a swarthy face whose intent seemed only slightly less than murderous. If Rumpelstiltskin was the mythical inhabitant of the storybook cottage, this man was the monstrous ogre straight from his forest lair. Barrel-chested, with a muscled neck and beefy shoulders, the man towered over me by more than a foot. Unlike an ogre, he was dressed in black leather and denim that smelled of sour sweat and stale smoke.

"I asked you a question," he growled, tightening his hold on my arm. "And you better have a good answer."

The lethal expression in those dark eyes rendered me momentarily speechless. All I could do was stare dumbly, my breath caught in a paralyzing knot of fear. The next moment I was yanked down the stone steps to the courtyard below. My attempts to free myself were basically useless and only resulted in sharp pain from his vice-like grip. Heart pounding, I stumbled after him to where the three men stood, staring at me with frowning suspicion.

One was tall and slender with wire-rimmed glasses bridging a prominent nose and clever brown eyes. His brown hair was thick and sprinkled liberally with gray. Dressed in tan slacks and a tweed sport coat, he had the appearance of a middle-aged Ivy League scholar. The man beside him reminded me of a well-dressed pit bull. No more than medium height, but broad of shoulder with a muscular build, he regarded me from small, shrewd eyes set in a square-jawed face. His immaculate gray suit and black silk shirt fairly screamed money, as did the gleaming presence of gold on his wrist and the rings on both hands. Yet, strangely, the expensive clothes and jewelry lent no respectability to his hard-edged features. Just the opposite.

The third man was a sorry contrast in appearance and dress. Pudgy and balding, he had bags under his eyes and a paunch that hung over his belt. His wrinkled brown suit had definitely seen better days, and there was a dark stain on his tie. Standing beside the Pit Bull, the man looked sorely out of place and more than a little uncomfortable.

As we approached, the Ivy Leaguer shoved a thick envelope into his jacket pocket and demanded, "What's going on? Who's this?"

"I found her hiding up there in the bushes taking pictures," the Ogre announced, scowling at me from beneath bushy black brows.

The tall man blanched slightly at this, while the others looked nervously away.

"I wasn't hiding," I flung back, still trying to free my arm from the Ogre's grasp. "And I have every right to be here."

"What right would that be?" the scholarly man questioned in chilly tones.

"I'm an editor for *Hearth & Home* magazine, and I have an appointment at two with Judge and Mrs. Wolcott."

The man straightened, his eyes darting to the well-dressed pit bull, then back to me. "I'm Judge Wolcott. And you are—?"

"Mackenzie Graham. And if you'll call off your guard dog, I'll be happy to show you my ID." My voice was cold with control, but inside I was shaking with reaction.

The judge said nothing to this, but the Pit Bull gave my burly detainer a tight-lipped nod. The Ogre reluctantly let go of my arm and stepped back, his dark eyes still full of suspicion. Who did he think I was, for pity's sake, the queen of the paparazzi?

Ignoring him, I removed the camera strap and put the Canon back in its case, then took out a business card and shoved it at the judge. Peter Wolcott gave the card a cursory glance and regarded me with an expression that was only faintly apologetic.

"I did knock," I inserted into the awkward silence. "And when no one answered, I thought perhaps you or Mrs. Wolcott might be around back."

"My wife isn't at home," he informed me. "And there must be some mistake. I knew someone from your magazine would be coming to photograph our home, but I have nothing on my calendar for today. As I said, there's obviously been a mistake."

My lips parted, but I had no reply, especially when the judge's tone strongly implied the mistake was mine. Sloppy Joe and the Pit Bull had turned away to stare out over the wooded ravine, clearly wanting to distance themselves from an awkward situation, while the Ogre remained close by, arms folded across his burly chest.

"Well then, I apologize for intruding on your time and privacy," I said, managing a tight smile.

"And I'm sorry if we frightened you," Judge Wolcott responded, more warmly this time. "We've had a little trouble lately with prowlers in the area, and I'm afraid Brock here overreacted."

I ignored blockhead Brock, smiled sweetly at the judge, and accepted his placating lie without comment. Inwardly, I seriously doubted the man's property suffered from a rash of twenty-eight-year-old female prowlers who arrived at midday with camera in hand.

"I don't know how or why I was given the wrong time for the appointment," I told him, "but you can be sure I'll call my managing editor and let her know about the mix-up. I believe she's an acquaintance of yours—Allison Meyers?"

Judge Wolcott moistened his lips. "Allison . . . yes, yes, of course. I'm sure there's a good explanation. Probably just a simple oversight."

Then why do you still look so uncomfortable? I wondered. Like a child whose hand is caught in the cookie jar. And why am I standing here feeling like an intruder instead of being invited inside? The answer was like a douse of ice water poured over my heated thoughts. *Because I am an intruder. They don't want me here.* A prickle of fear shivered through me, but I tried to shove it away with a polite albeit stiff smile.

"Someone from the magazine will be in touch with you or Mrs. Wolcott about rescheduling," I told the judge, ignoring the others. "And again, I'm very sorry to intrude."

"Please don't give it another thought—Ms. Graham, is it? Would you like me to walk you to your car?" His attempt at politeness was unraveled by the tight threads of tension pulling at his voice.

"No need. I've kept you long enough."

As I turned to go, Judge Wolcott gave me a parting smile that never quite reached his eyes. Making my way up the stone steps, I felt four pairs of eyes on me the entire time. It took considerable effort to keep my pace casual and unconcerned, when every instinct was urging me to run. I didn't feel completely safe until I was inside my car with the doors locked, heading down the long drive toward the main road.

Behind me, the cottage basked innocently in the afternoon sun, but for me, the fairy tale was definitely over.

Two

The more distance I put between myself and the Wolcotts' disenchanted cottage, the braver and angrier I became. What on earth was that all about? Since when does a district court judge need to engage a muscle-bound thug to protect his property? For that dark-eyed ogre to insinuate I was spying on the Wolcotts strongly suggested there might be a reason why someone would want to do just that. My anger flamed anew when I thought of the way I was manhandled and dragged down the hillside. At the time, I was too shaken to say or do much of anything. But now, going over the incident with some helpful hindsight, it seemed more than a bit odd that it was the Pit Bull who'd given the authoritative nod to release me, rather than the judge. Peter Wolcott's attempt to diffuse the situation had been halfhearted at best. In fact, he'd been quick to place the blame on me or the magazine. Keeping me on the defensive had been deliberate. Why?

I was certain I'd been given the correct date and time for the appointment. Allison had been very clear about the particulars. So why was Mrs. Wolcott not at home, and who were the judge's surly visitors? Thinking back, the whole experience bordered more on threatening rather than uncomfortable. But that was ridiculous. There was absolutely no reason why I should be considered a threat, or threatened.

I released a tense breath and relaxed my white-knuckled grip on the steering wheel. I might not have a plausible explanation for the incident, but one thing was certain: I'd better call my managing editor and let her know what happened. Allison wouldn't be at all happy, but there was no point postponing the inevitable.

I slowed the car and glanced around for a familiar landmark or highway sign, suddenly realizing I'd been driving with no real sense of direction or conscious thought. Just driving. To get away. Thankfully, I still had enough presence of mind to know I was headed north on Highway 1, somewhere near Carmel. Moments later I came to a junction, glimpsed a sign for Ocean Avenue, and impulsively turned left.

As promised by its name, Ocean Avenue led me due west, past Carmel's quaint clusters of hillside homes and the business area of town, toward the blue Pacific. I opted not to take a scenic road skirting the beach, but parked off the street in a public wayside with twisted old cypresses and walking trails. Switching off the ignition, I released a long sigh. I needed to walk. And think. But first, the bad news.

I took my cell phone from my handbag, put in the magazine's number along with Allison's extension, and turned on my most cheerful voice. "Hi, Allison, it's Mackenzie. Could you check on something for me?"

"Sure. How did your session go at the Wolcotts'?"

"It didn't happen." Before she had time to explode, I went on quickly, "Mrs. Wolcott wasn't at home, and the judge—well, he had visitors and clearly wasn't expecting me."

"What? Are you serious?"

"Very serious. He insisted he didn't have anything on his calendar for today. The situation was more than a little awkward. I told Judge Wolcott that I'd look into the matter and have someone from the magazine give him a call."

I heard her muttered expletive followed by a grieved sigh. "Hold on a minute, will you, while I do some quick checking to see whose head needs to roll."

"Will do."

Put on hold, I stared out at the ocean, watching the endless roll of the waves, building, swelling, then breaking in a white froth of pure power.

"Mackenzie, are you there?"

"I'm here. Whose head is on the block?"

"Definitely not yours or the magazine's. The appointment with the Wolcotts was made for today at two. I have Dana Wolcott's cell number. I'll call her now and see if I can tactfully find out why she blew us off."

I gave a short laugh. "Good luck with that."

"Don't worry. I'll smooth it out somehow and we'll reschedule."

"Thanks, Allison."

"No problem. How's the house by the way?"

"Fabulous. Pure fairy-tale charm."

My voice was less than enthusiastic, and Allison was quick to pick up on it.

"Look, this wasn't your fault, so don't beat yourself up about it. You hereby have my permission to get yourself a huge Pepsi and take the rest of the afternoon off." She chuckled and added slyly, "But if you're up to it, you could always drive around Carmel and do a little research on some of Hugh Comstock's storybook homes."

"I think I could manage that. After the Pepsi, of course. Thanks again, Allison."

"Don't mention it. I'll be in touch."

I put my cell in my handbag and leaned back against the seat, feeling better by the minute. I'd feel even better after that long cold drink. But first . . . I stared out at the Pacific with its inviting swath of creamy white sand, and knew I needed a walk even more. I'd been in California nearly five days without taking a single walk by the ocean. Pathetic. There were times when my Spartan work ethic got totally out of hand. I took off my jacket and placed it over my handbag and camera case on the floor of the passenger seat. Then, on impulse, I retrieved the camera and slipped the strap over my head. That ocean was much too gorgeous to ignore. Getting out of the car, I gave the key fob a quick click and headed for the beach.

The wayside's groomed walking trails ended in a stretch of sandy dunes covered with ice plants. I picked my way down, slogged across the soft sand, and reached the hard surface of the slick a few yards from the water's edge. The ocean was loud today, with breakers hitting the land in a pounding roar before retreating with a liquid hiss. The breeze was fresh and clean, with only a hint of brine. Off in the distance around a gentle curve of land, I could see Pebble Beach, the playground of the rich. But here, the sand and sea and sky were free for all to enjoy.

I contented myself with taking a few shots of the seaside panorama, then took off my sandals and rolled my pants up calf-high. The sand felt firm and cool under my bare feet, the sun warm on my shoulders. Unpleasantness was carried away as easily as a gull's feather on the breeze.

There were others on the beach enjoying the warm September sun and cloudless sky. Two mothers with their young children and all the attendant paraphernalia—towels, pails and shovels, sunblock and sunglasses, bottled drinks, books and snacks. I smiled and walked past, not minding that my own life was momentarily free and uncluttered. Three joggers—two men and a slim young woman, all in biker shorts, tank tops, and baseball caps—breezed by me. Then a pair of Dobermans raced past in a canine blur of black legs and lithe bodies, their entire focus on retrieving a ball thrown into the surf by their teenage masters.

Glancing up, I saw a monarch butterfly floating overhead, its black and orange markings vivid against the blue. I paused, content to watch the butterfly's gentle passage toward land, and felt the last bit of tension inside me dissolve. No need to think or worry about the Wolcotts. Just enjoy.

Coming toward me across the sand was an older couple walking hand in hand. Gray-haired, tanned, and fit, the man glanced down at his wife with an affectionate smile. She returned his smile and leaned in closer so they were walking shoulder to shoulder, their heads nearly touching. A simple gesture denoting years of caring and companionship. *That's what marriage should be,* I thought. A smile. A touch. And that lovely, warm belonging.

The woman glanced up then and gave me a friendly nod. I smiled back. What was there about walking by the sea that erased the barriers between people, effortlessly turning strangers into friends? One rarely saw such camaraderie between people walking city streets. Was it the ocean, its awesome size and power a potent reminder of man's puny presence in the larger scheme of things? Or was it the simple lack of boundaries, political and cultural, that was felt more keenly at land's end? Whatever the reason, I felt refreshed and renewed as I turned and headed back across the sand.

I had just passed the dunes when the rhythmic sound of the waves was supplanted by one singularly jarring and man-made. Someone's car alarm had gone off. I thought little of the irritating noise until I reached the walking path and stopped to put on my sandals. Could it possibly be? The sudden tightening in my chest told me that it could, and my steps quickened. The alarm grew louder as I neared the wayside. Other than a few vehicles parked across the street, my rented Chevy was the only car close by. Grabbing the keys from my pocket, I gave the alarm button a quick punch, and the noise instantly stopped. Silence settled in the air as I glanced around, seeing no one. Then, hurrying toward the car, I gasped and stared.

The window on the passenger side had been smashed in, leaving a gaping hole, and chunks of glass splayed around the curb. I yanked open the door, preparing myself for the worst. My jacket had been tossed aside, but amazingly, my handbag was still on the floor mat. I picked it up and made a heart-pounding inventory of the contents. Wallet, cash, credit cards, all there. I stood for a moment, gratefully clutching the purse and staring at the smashed window. Had the thieves been interrupted? Obviously the break-in had been a smash-and-dash sort of thing. Then it hit me what was missing. My camera bag with all its contents was gone.

I took some steadying breaths. Better the loss of two lenses and some spare memory cards, than a twelve-hundred-dollar Canon. Hands shaking, I removed the camera strap from around my neck and put the Canon in my handbag. Why would someone steal the camera bag and leave the purse? My stunned brain had no answers, and the sudden weakness in my legs had me leaning against the side of the car for support. I knew I ought to call someone. Probably, the local police should be notified, and then I'd have to make yet another call to Allison Meyers.

A patrol car arrived some ten minutes later, but there was little the officer could do other than take my name and basic information. He was as puzzled as I that the camera bag had been stolen, while my purse was left undisturbed. After the report had been filled out and the standard lecture delivered about leaving valuables in the car, the officer was on his way and so was I.

The sun was still shining, the ocean still as blue and beautiful, but all in a moment my afternoon had gone from promising, to perplexing, to downright unpleasant. Now, instead of enjoying a leisurely drive around Carmel, I had the necessary task of turning in a damaged rental car. This might or might not entail driving back to the San Francisco airport where the rental agency was located. Hopefully, there would be another location near the Residence Inn in Palo Alto where I was staying. Either way, the afternoon was basically shot.

In my present mood, I rejected the idea of calling Allison yet again to tell her about the break-in. That could wait. But there was another phone call that wouldn't. Corbin Corelli, one of the magazine's staff photographers, had been assigned to work on the article with me. He'd suggested a casual dinner date for tonight to go over plans and ideas, although those dark eyes and that melting voice suggested a good deal more. Dark eyes, dark hair, and a killer smile, I might add. Corbin was on hand when I first met Allison and other members of the magazine staff in San Francisco. He'd listened to my presentation on storybook homes with unwavering and I have to admit very flattering interest. When Allison announced that Corbin and I would be working together, the smile and look he'd given me was enough to melt several glaciers, let alone the heart of a mere woman. His confidence might be a scant level below cockiness, but somehow I didn't mind. I liked his eyes, his smile, and the acerbic wit that peppered his conversation. Truth be told, there was a lot to like about Corbin Corelli, and thoughts of our working together held very pleasant possibilities. As did our dinner date for this evening.

I glanced at my watch, doing some quick mental calculations on time and distance. Corbin was planning to pick me up at six, and even if commute traffic cooperated, I'd be lucky to make it back to the Residence Inn by that time. If I had to drive to the airport and turn in the rental car, it would take even longer. Better call him now and ask if we couldn't meet at the restaurant at seven instead of the inn.

I brushed some stray chunks of glass off the car seat and reached for my cell, then realized that although Corbin had my number, I didn't have his. Great. Now I'd have to call the magazine office and work my way through the wonders of half a dozen recorded messages before reaching a bona-fide human being. And to make matters worse, I still hadn't had that Pepsi.

I was driving past Sand City when I spotted a convenience store and gas station just ahead on my right. I braked and pulled off the highway. One large Pepsi coming up, and then the phone call to Corbin. I grabbed my purse and got out of the car just as a black BMW zoomed past. There were two men in the car, and one of them glanced my way as the automobile sped by.

Brief though it was, the sight of dark hair and hard-bitten features sent my stomach into a tailspin.

Three

I watched the BMW speed past, trying to convince myself it couldn't be the same car. But what if it was? That didn't necessarily mean Brock and the Pit Bull were following me. The explanation could be as simple as the fact that we were both headed in the same general direction. Even so, my steps quickened along with my breathing as I hurried into the convenience store for a fountain Pepsi and a little normalcy.

Sitting in the parking area, sipping my soft drink, I kept one eye on the highway as I worked my way through the Gordian knot of the magazine's recorded phone menu. I didn't know which relieved me most—that I finally got Corbin's number, or that the black BMW did not return. Corbin's voice, warm and understanding, did wonders for my edgy nerves.

"Do you like Chinese?"

"Love it."

"How about P.F. Chang's? There's one not too far from your inn, near the Stanford Shopping Center. I could meet you there at, say, seven fifteen?"

"Sounds perfect."

He gave me directions to the restaurant and I hung up, savoring the anticipation in his voice. Yes, life was definitely worth living. And miracle of miracles, when I called the car rental agency, their representative graciously offered to deliver another car to the Residence Inn, saving me a lengthy drive to the airport.

My drive back to Palo Alto was uneventful, although a bit noisy with the wind whistling through the car's broken window. Once, I thought I caught sight of a black car some distance behind me, but I firmly dismissed the notion that it might be the same one. Black BMWs were not exactly a rarity in northern California, and there was no point getting paranoid over an unpleasant experience.

—∞—

I bit into my second delicious lettuce wrap and enjoyed the equally delicious sight of Corbin Corelli sitting across the table from me. The expression in those dark eyes said quite plainly that he, too, liked what he saw, and I was glad I'd had time to shower and change into a pair of dressy black pants with a silky turquoise top. Dessert arrived long before the main course as I savored the pleasant parfait of compliments Corbin inserted into our conversation. Praise for my writing and articles progressed to comments on my hair and eyes. Burnished copper . . . midnight blue . . . Very nice, even if they did sound like the names of paint samples.

Our conversation was a comfortable blend of business and generic pleasantries until Corbin gave me a searching look and said, "So, are you currently involved with anyone?"

The bluntness of his question took me by surprise, but I hesitated only slightly. "No. Not now."

"What happened?"

I shook my head. "Do you mind, I'd rather not discuss it."

He smiled, not put off in the least. "In other words, it's none of my business."

"Well, that's one way of putting it."

"And I see it differently. I mean, we could go on discussing the article, or the weather, and waste a perfectly good evening. Or we could forget about business and enjoy getting to know each other."

When I didn't reply, Corbin went on with a confident smile, "You intrigue me, Mackenzie. You're obviously intelligent and good at what you do, but there's something else—something I can't quite put my finger on. I have the feeling you're a woman of many layers. Can you blame me if I'd like to do a little exploring and find out what they are?"

I cleared my throat and took a sip of water. "You're very direct, aren't you?"

"Very," he agreed. "And observant. It's one of the qualities that makes me such a good photographer."

"What about modesty?"

"Highly overrated," he said with a laugh. "I have little use for it. Give me up-front honesty any day. The camera doesn't lie and neither do I." He poured a little more wine into his nearly empty glass and savored a healthy swig. "Sure you wouldn't like some wine?"

I smiled and shook my head. "No thanks. I don't drink."

"Not even a little wine?"

"Not even wine."

He gave me a long, melting look over his wine glass. "Like I said, a woman of many layers. You realize, Mackenzie, that most men would take one look at you and toss out some stale, practiced line about how beautiful you are. But not me."

"Does that mean I should forget about the 'burnished copper' bit?"

He laughed and leaned forward, dark eyes gleaming. "Far from it. I find you very attractive. But not in the usual way. You're completely opposite from the average California girl."

"Maybe because I was born in Illinois."

"No, you weren't," Corbin contradicted, but softly, his voice a husky purr like a jungle cat. "It's like you were born in a different time, or century—like those storybook homes we've been talking about. You're going to have to let me photograph you while you're here." He reached for one of my hands and lightly caressed the palm.

I glanced down, feeling the heat rise in my cheeks. "Maybe we should talk about you for a while. This is getting to be a little embarrassing."

"Why? Whoever you were involved with before must have told you—"

"You know, I'm a little uncomfortable with the whole 'being involved' business," I said, withdrawing my hand. "People can be involved in a lot of things, like a football game, and politics, or . . . or a traffic accident. I was not just involved. I was in love with someone and, well, it didn't work out."

"Okay, so I'll ask you again. What happened?"

I glanced away from his probing look and realized my nails were making creases in the tablecloth. "I—we—didn't want the same things."

"So what did you want?"

I tried to brush Corbin's question aside with a halfhearted laugh. "You don't want to know."

"I wouldn't have asked if I didn't want to know. But if you'd rather not tell me, that's okay."

I looked into his dark eyes, trying to see whether the honesty he subscribed to was really there or just a clever line. "All right. What I wanted was marriage, children, and a home. In that order."

Corbin straightened and his expression changed from one of gentle teasing and flattering interest to a sort of grimace. "In other words, commitment."

I couldn't help smiling. "You say that as if it were something terrible—like someone committing a crime or being committed to a mental institution."

He had the grace to look a bit sheepish and tried to salvage the awkwardness of the moment with some bad humor. "Marriage, mental institution—same thing." When I didn't laugh, he cleared his throat and added, "Look, I'm just trying to see both sides and understand where your guy was coming from. You have to admit that commitment is something—well, something huge. What exactly did he want?"

"He wanted me to move in with him. Or vice versa."

Corbin spread his hands in a gesture that said plainly, "So what's the problem?" His words followed suit. "That doesn't sound so unreasonable."

"No, not unreasonable at all," I answered, unable to keep a tinge of sarcasm out of my voice. "It keeps everything very simple and selfish and temporary. Move in, move out, and move on. Isn't that how it works?"

Corbin stared at me. His mouth moved, but no words came out.

Not surprisingly, our conversation returned to safer, more generic topics after that. We said our good nights at the restaurant, and I drove back to the Residence Inn with only my frustrated thoughts for company.

Honesty. Right. That wasn't all he wanted. And I was an idiot for thinking he might be different from any other so-called modern male. Hopefully, tonight's little discussion wouldn't put too much strain on our working together. But one never knew. I had effectively shut the door in his face for anything more than a casual working relationship. And it wasn't the first time. Three years had gone by since my break-up with Todd Latimer. Three years, with only a few scattered, casual dates that held no possibility of progressing to anything beyond that.

In contrast, it hadn't taken Todd long to find someone who was more than willing to go along with his loose requirements for a relationship. In fact, the last I heard, there had been two significant someone's in his life—each one very happy to move in, and after a time, move out and on to the next. No thank you. The initial hurt and loss I'd experienced after our break-up was long gone, replaced by relief and a renewed determination that I wanted nothing to do with the transient aspects of so many modern relationships. Maybe Corbin was right. I did belong in another century.

By the time I reached the inn, my frustration had morphed into simple fatigue. All I wanted was to climb into that wonderful, soft bed and sleep.

The night was black and starless, with a gauzy curtain of clouds obscuring the moon's thin crescent. Thankfully, the parking area at the inn was well lit, and several cars were parked in the surrounding spaces. This didn't stop me from taking a cautious look around as I got out of my car. No BMWs, black or otherwise. I put my silly fears to rest, took the key card from my purse, and climbed the outside stairs to the second floor. Knowing I'd need relative quiet to work, Allison had reserved a small suite at the inn's far end, away from the pool and indoor spa. A thick border of oaks blocked most of the noise from the nearby highway as well as offering a pleasant view.

I slid the card into the slot, waited for the light to flash green, then turned the handle and went inside. A gasp caught in my throat when I flipped on the lights, and my entire body went rigid. Clothes, shoes, and other belongings were strewn every which way, on the floor, chairs, and bed. Drawers were open, their contents spilled. Chair cushions had been tossed aside. Notebooks, photos, and papers littered the carpet. My searching eyes flew to the small table where I'd been working the night before, and I felt a sick wave of loss. My laptop was gone, along with who knew what else. I backed away from the chaotic invasion, made my way down the stairs on shaking legs, and headed for the office.

The person on duty was a young Hispanic woman with a helpful smile and a thick accent—Rosa, according to her name badge.

"My room's been broken into," I panted. "We need to call the police."

"Something ees broken?" she repeated, confusion clouding her dark eyes.

"No, not broken. Burglarized. You need to call the police—911, comprende?"

She nodded, wide-eyed, and picked up the phone. It dawned on me then that I could have avoided the explanations and saved precious time by calling the police on my cell. That is, if I'd been thinking at all, which I wasn't.

I listened as Rosa began a halting explanation, then reached across the desk and took the receiver out of her hand. She stared at me, too surprised to object. "Hello, this is Mackenzie Graham. I'd like to report a burglary." I was amazed how calm my voice sounded.

Detective Wade Evans from the Palo Alto police department arrived less than fifteen minutes later. Sandy-haired and square-jawed, Detective Evans was an easy six feet of solid male authority. My taut nerves began to relax the moment he entered the inn. As we made our introductions, there was something about his soft-spoken manner that didn't quite add up to the usual image of a street-wise city cop. For one thing, I'd been expecting a uniformed officer, not someone dressed in khakis and a sport coat. There was nothing soft-spoken about the gun at his hip, however.

Detective Evans must have read the questions in my eyes, because he said, "The officers normally on patrol are tied up with a nasty wreck over on the boulevard. I happened to be in the area and offered to look into things."

He took a small, leather-bound notebook from his back pocket and jotted down some basic information. Then, after speaking to Rosa in fluent Spanish for a few moments, he turned to me. "All right, Miss Graham, let's check out your room."

"Was the door locked or open when you arrived?" he asked as we climbed the stairs.

"Locked. I have no idea how they got in."

"They have their ways. I'll have a little chat with housekeeping when we've finished here."

I handed him the key card, and he stood for a moment in the doorway, surveying the disaster scene with keen-eyed interest.

"What did you do when you saw the condition of the room?" he asked. "Did you go in?"

"No. No, I went straight to the office."

"So you don't know what, if anything, was stolen?"

"My laptop was on the table when I left this morning. I did notice that it was gone."

"Laptops are always a good item on a thief's list," he said as we walked in. "But if it was in plain sight—on the table, like you said—there'd be no need to tear the place apart. From the looks of things they must have been after something else. Any ideas?"

"Not really."

While Detective Evans made a brief inspection of the room, I snatched up a bra and two pair of panties off the floor and shoved them under the rumpled bed covers. He made no comment, but the slight twitching of his mouth said my actions hadn't escaped his notice.

"Do you have anything else of value besides the laptop?"

"No."

"No cash?"

"I had my cash and credit cards with me."

"What about jewelry?"

I shook my head. "I never bring anything expensive when I travel. Just a few bracelets and earrings."

"And are they here?"

A quick inspection of my suitcase proved that the small makeup bag containing my jewelry was intact.

"Everything's here," I told the detective with a puzzled sigh. "I still can't believe it. Twice in one day is a bit much."

The sandy brows lifted. "Twice?"

"My car was broken into this afternoon."

"Here? At the inn?"

"No. It happened at a beach wayside in Carmel." I sank down on the side of the bed. "Believe me, this has not been one of my better days."

"I can see that." Evans replaced a chair cushion and sat down, resting one long leg across his knee. "Let's talk about your day."

I stared at him, more than a little surprised. "What do you want to know?"

The detective met my gaze with a steady look. "It's possible the two incidents are totally unrelated, but I'm not a big believer in coincidence. From the looks of this mess, the thieves were definitely after something. Otherwise, why not just grab the laptop and get out?"

I nodded uneasy agreement to his reasoning as he went on, "So let's start at the beginning. What were you doing in Carmel?"

I gave him a brief explanation of my assignment for the magazine without going into the unpleasant details of my meeting with Judge Wolcott. "There was a mix-up in the date and time of my appointment," I told him. "So I decided to stop at a wayside for a walk on the beach. I wasn't gone long, maybe twenty minutes. No more than half an hour. When I got back, someone had smashed in the car window on the passenger side."

"What did they get?"

"My camera case."

Evans stared at me. "That's all? Just the case?"

I nodded. "My purse was sitting on the car floor, and the contents were untouched. I had my camera with me, so all they took were some lenses and a few memory cards."

Evans' expression was slightly incredulous. "I don't get it, but you are one lucky lady."

"Right now, I don't feel so lucky." I said, glancing around the room.

He gave me a sympathetic smile and pocketed his notebook. He took a small card from his jacket pocket and handed it to me. "I don't think there's any point in sending someone over to dust for prints, especially if the only thing stolen was the laptop. But after you've had time to check your belongings, if you discover anything else that's missing, you can reach me at this number."

"Thank you."

He stood, then asked as I followed him to the door, "How much longer will you be in California?"

"Another ten days or so."

"And you'll be staying here at the inn?"

"Yes, but after tonight, not in this room."

"I don't blame you," the detective said. "Sorry I couldn't be more help. If you have any questions or concerns, give me a call."

Any sense of security or safety I was feeling left the moment he did. I slid the dead bolt into place, but it didn't help. Who was I kidding? There was no way I could stay here tonight. Not in this room. Or even the inn. I stared at the invasive scene, fighting back useless tears. Even the room's silence felt alien and threatening.

I swallowed hard and slumped down on the edge of the bed, then took my cell phone from my purse.

"Hello, Allison. It's Mackenzie . . ."

Four

It was a novel experience waking up in a rose-covered hatbox. I stretched and turned over, staring at the papered ceiling and walls. Roses, roses, everywhere, from the twining branches of bud and blossom in the wallpaper, to the huge Damask roses splashing across the bedspread, and Victorian prints of old roses on the walls. Sunlight streamed through diamond-paned windows, warming the sight of a crystal vase on the bedside table, filled with fragrant tea roses in palest pink and lemon yellow.

I sighed and snuggled deeper into the pillows, enjoying the cool breath of morning air wafting in from the partially open window. Such luxury. To be safe and rested in this lovely, flower-filled room.

Allison had come straight to the Residence Inn after my distress call the night before. She was matter of fact but kind, insisting I leave the disaster area until morning. After I gathered a few personal things for an overnight stay, we were on our way. I think I must have been slightly dazed with shock or reaction, as well as fatigue, because I was scarcely aware of the drive to the Meyers' home in an upscale neighborhood of older homes and huge trees.

As she ushered me inside, I must have been making some sort of apology, because Allison just laughed and said briskly, "Don't be an idiot. I'm glad to have the company. Ron's out of town on business, and I hate being alone at night."

Safety and security returned in abundance as we sat in her cheerful Country French kitchen drinking herbal tea and eating cinnamon toast. There was nothing timid or halfhearted about Allison's decorating scheme. When she did country French, she did it with a vengeance, using a palette of bright yellow, blue, and white. *Mother would probably hate this room,* I thought, glancing at walls papered in sunny yellow with sprigs of blue and white flowers. Curtains in a bold yellow-and-white check framed the window. The antique table and chairs were painted white, the seats covered in the same fabric as the curtains. Behind me, a wonderful old hutch displaying blue and white crockery filled one wall.

I smiled and sipped my tea, feeling totally bathed in warm, safe sunshine despite the dark night outside. Yes, Mother would hate this room. She would take one look at Allison's happy use of color and décor and give it that slightly pained, superior expression only Mother could give. Nor would she hesitate to express her displeasure.

It struck me then that not once during the day's difficult events had I thought of calling my parents. Sadly, it wasn't distance or the obvious fact that I was a twenty-eight-year-old adult that prevented me from doing so. Rather, it was because I knew, and had known for a very long time, there was no comfort to be found there.

I took another sip of tea and told Allison, "I love this room."

After the second piece of cinnamon toast, I found I was able to talk quite calmly about what had happened. It was over, and I was safe. Tomorrow I would have the unpleasant task of buying a new laptop along with some camera lenses, but there was no point in worrying about that now.

Allison and I talked a while longer, and the conversation turned to more personal things. She told me a little about her husband Ron—that he was husband number two, and they had been married for five amazing years, seven months, and thirteen days. I smiled, enjoying the glow of happiness on her face, as well as her voice as she talked about him. For the most part, I was content to listen, my initial impressions of Allison Meyers, capable businesswoman, enlarging to include Allison Meyers, wife and mother. Anyone meeting her for the first time would never suspect what a soft heart lay beneath that cool, crisp exterior. A youthful forty-five, with short hair colored a determined shade of brown, and pointed, almost sharp features, Allison gave the outward impression of being a woman who was very much in charge of her life as well as the magazine's.

Yet, here I was, listening to her motherly worries and woes about her brilliant son who was working too hard in medical school at Stanford, and her daughter, who wasn't working hard enough at some ridiculously expensive art school in New York.

I'd liked Allison well enough at our first meeting, but during our talk over toast and tea, I felt the more formal roles of employer/ employee shift and soften into friendship. When I could no longer cover my yawns, she laughed and apologized for keeping me up so late, then took me upstairs to the guest bedroom which her husband had fondly labeled "the hatbox." I was asleep mere moments after my head hit that heavenly pillow.

Now, with my body rested and my mind calm, I could ponder the previous day's events with some objectivity not colored by stress or fear. The incident at Judge Wolcott's fairy-tale cottage, the theft of my camera case, the break-in and theft of my laptop. Were these merely a series of unfortunate incidents, a simple string of bad luck, or could they be a related chain of events? Detective Evans' comments inserted themselves chillingly into my thoughts—that it might be something more than a simple burglary, that the thieves had been looking for something specific. All right, then. Dismissing coincidence and bad luck, let's assume the good detective was correct in his surmising.

What on earth did I have in my possession that was important enough to warrant two separate break-ins? I stiffened as my thoughts ceased their mental circling and centered on one simple object. My camera. Why else leave the handbag and all its contents? Why tear my room apart and steal just the laptop? The thieves must have been searching for the camera.

My heartbeat quickened along with my breathing as I got out of bed and retrieved my purse from the window seat where I'd left it the night before. Sitting on the edge of the bed, I scanned through the previous day's photos.

There they were. The judge, the Pit Bull, and Sloppy Joe. The camera's rapid-fire setting included a good deal more than scenic shots of the courtyard. Going through the frames of the judge and his visitors was almost like seeing a video recording of the scene. I stared intently at the unsuspecting trio. Even seen in miniature, their expressions were more than revealing. The Pit Bull, confident and clearly in charge, a thin smile parting his ugly mouth. The judge, wary and rigid, staring tight-lipped at an envelope in the Pit Bull's outstretched hand. Then, hesitantly, as if the envelope was something both deadly and precious, Peter Wolcott took it from the Pit Bull, all the while refusing to meet the man's narrow eyes. I zoomed in on the images of the envelope, but the contents were well sealed and unidentifiable. Then there was poor Sloppy Joe, hands in his pockets, glancing nervously from side to side, his chin jutting out in a small attempt at bravado.

The last still was tilted every which way, slightly out of focus, and cut off most of the judge's head. That one must have been taken when I was grabbed by Brock. The longer I stared at the series of pictures, the more I realized that what I'd stumbled into was far from a casual meeting. Clandestine, more like it. Little wonder my arrival was met with such suspicion.

My heart's pounding accelerated as I considered the ramifications of the incident. It was obvious, really. If my camera and laptop were gone, so was all the tangible evidence that these men had been at Judge Wolcott's home. But why should that be so important? I'd never seen any of the men before yesterday and didn't know a thing about them—not even their names, except for the judge and Brock. And for all I knew, that might not be Brock's real name.

I returned the camera to my purse, wishing I could go back to the safe scenario that the two break-ins were totally unrelated, that I didn't have enough information to make such rash assumptions. But my mind refused to cooperate. Like Detective Evans, I didn't believe in coincidence.

A light tapping sounded on the hatbox door, and the next moment Allison's dark head peeked inside. "Good morning. How did you sleep?"

I drew a quick little breath and answered, "Wonderful. Are you sure you didn't spike my tea with a little Tylenol PM?"

She laughed. "Wouldn't dream of it. How does French toast with fresh peaches and blueberries sound for breakfast?"

I smiled, tempted to ask if all the cuisine had to be French in keeping with the kitchen décor. "It sounds fabulous, but please don't go to a lot of work."

"Honey, I never go to a lot of work if I can help it. The French toast goes straight from the freezer to the microwave, and the fruit is Costco's finest. It only looks impressive."

"Then I'm duly impressed. I'll be down in fifteen minutes."

"Take your time."

We talked shop during breakfast, and Allison fielded a few phone calls—one from her husband, another from her daughter in New York, who was running short of funds as well as minutes on her cell phone. The last call came from Dana Wolcott. Allison gave me a knowing look as she graciously accepted Dana's apology for the mix-up the day before and assured her the magazine would be glad to reschedule.

"Tomorrow at four? That should be fine. Could you hold a minute while I double check the schedule?" Covering the mouthpiece, Allison turned to me and asked softly, "How about it? Do we need to juggle another appointment, or are you free?"

I nodded, hoping the sudden tenseness inside me didn't show. "Shouldn't be a problem."

Allison gave me a grateful smile and told Mrs. Wolcott, "Tomorrow at four will work fine. We'll look forward to seeing you.

Don't give it another thought. I understand." Allison raised her eyes and listened to what were obviously more apologies.

When she ended the call, I gave Allison a curious glance. "Were you referring to the royal *we,* or is someone else coming along?"

"Do you mind having some company?" she asked, pouring more syrup on her French toast. "Namely me?"

"Of course I don't mind, but I hope you don't feel like you need to run interference for me."

"Mackenzie, this has nothing to do with your ability to handle an awkward situation, which you've already done quite nicely, I might add. No, I'm just curious—and I'm dying to see that house."

I was curious too, albeit a good deal more about the owners than their lovely home. "You mean you haven't seen it? I guess I assumed that because you know the Wolcotts, you would have visited their home."

Allison shook her head. "Dana and I worked on a couple of charitable functions together, but we're not what you'd call close friends. Let's just say we inhabit different social circles. She and the judge have a beautiful town home here in Palo Alto. That I have seen. Their cottage in Carmel is more of a vacation home." Her mouth curved in a wry smile. "Wouldn't that be nice? Nothing fancy, mind you. Just a cozy little multimillion dollar cottage by the sea."

"Very nice," I agreed, mentally registering the fact that a clandestine meeting could take place in relative privacy in a second home that was not often used. "Maybe Judge Wolcott has found a way to spin straw into gold."

"What?" Allison's brow creased in confusion.

"Oh, nothing. It's just, when I first saw the cottage, it reminded me of those old fairy-tale illustrations by Arthur Rackham and Edmund Dulac. I was thinking that might be an interesting angle to pursue."

She nodded, eyes bright. "What sort of angle do you have in mind?"

As I'd hoped, her interest shifted easily from the Wolcotts to the article in general, and our conversation moved on to some creative brainstorming.

It was midmorning by the time Allison drove me back to the Residence Inn. It didn't take long for the two of us to restore order to the shambles of my room. I tried telling her that she didn't need to help me, that she must have a hundred other things to do. And she insisted it was no trouble at all, that it was the least she could do. As usual, Allison got her way, and I have to admit, I didn't mind the company. Her fussing and fuming about the burglary saved me from doing the same, and I knew that someone from the inn's management would soon be receiving a few choice words from her.

As far as I could determine, nothing other than my laptop was missing. I was picking up my notes and straightening the clutter on the table when it hit me. My backup CD of research and the rough draft for the article was gone. I rechecked the contents of my portfolio and the surrounding area. Gone. Even the blank CDs had been taken. With the laptop and CDs gone, weeks of painstaking work would have been lost if I hadn't saved a backup on my flash drive. Thankfully, that little item was still in my purse, attached to my key chain.

My heart beat faster. If I hadn't been so rushed to meet Corbin for our dinner date, I would have downloaded yesterday's photos onto the laptop and the thieves would have gotten exactly what they wanted. But they had to make sure. Something as small as a flash drive would explain the deliberate search of my belongings. Detective Evans was right.

"Mackenzie, is something wrong?" Allison's concerned voice broke into my thoughts. "You're looking a bit tense."

I hesitated, not sure how much to tell her. "I was just thinking of everything that's on that laptop. If I hadn't saved a backup on my flash drive, I would have lost weeks of research and pictures."

Allison's concern turned to cold fury. "While you finish up, I think I'll have a nice little talk with the management."

Hurricane Allison stormed out of the room, and I slumped down in a chair, staring at the bright autumn sunshine pouring through the window, my thoughts dark with worry.

Allison returned a few minutes later, a look of triumphant satisfaction on her face. "The management sends you their profound apologies," she informed me. "And they offered a complimentary larger suite to make up for any inconvenience. Sound okay?"

I put on a ready smile. "Very much okay."

The new suite was half again as large as my old room, with expanded kitchen facilities and a flat-screen TV. Even more attractive was the desk and chair, situated near a sunny window, that would make an ideal work station. After my belongings had been transferred to the new room, Allison and I took a few minutes to plan the trip to Carmel the following afternoon. Then I insisted she had done more than enough for me and needed to get on with her own day.

She hesitated in the doorway before leaving, her dark eyes soft with concern. "Are you sure you're okay? If I'd had a day like yours, I doubt I'd feel like smiling, much less working."

"I'm fine," I told her. "New car. New room. New day."

Allison shook her head at my response, adding in a gentle tone that was totally unlike her usual crisp self, "New friend?"

I've never been one who gives hugs easily, but it's not from a lack of caring. Just the opposite. My emotions run so deep at times, they have trouble making it to the surface in outward gestures others find so easy to give. Allison's words and the caring in her eyes couldn't be ignored or pushed away.

"Wonderful new friend," I mumbled gratefully and gave her a quick, hard hug.

"I think you ought to take it easy today," she advised. "Do you have anything so urgent that it can't be postponed?"

"Not really. There are a couple of houses in Oakland that I wanted to see, but first things first. I've got to buy a new laptop."

Allison grimaced. "That's right, you do. But call me later, okay? Maybe we could do lunch or something."

"Thanks, I will."

After spending less than a week in Northern California, I was far from confident in my ability to negotiate the intricate maze of its roads and freeways. Fortunately, the huge shopping mall near Stanford University was relatively simple to find. P.F. Chang's, where Corbin and I'd had our not-so-successful dinner date, was a handy landmark, located on a corner adjacent to the mall. And there were two parking terraces across the street from the mall itself.

Blame it on an active imagination, plus seeing too many detective shows where horrendous things happened in parking terraces, but I've never felt comfortable in those low-roofed, echoing concrete structures. Even in broad daylight they give me the creeps. And more than once, I could have used Hansel and Gretel's handy trail of breadcrumbs to discover my way out. Luckily, I found a convenient parking space on the second level, not far from the entrance. I made a quick note of the numbered area, then headed for the mall.

The morning was sunny and warm with the barest hint of a breeze. The huge outdoor shopping center had definitely been designed with California's mild climate in mind. Walkways and courtyards were beautifully landscaped, the flowers and trees as stunning in their own way as the posh displays in store windows.

I strolled past Bloomingdales, Cartier's, and Louis Vuitton outlets, thinking I probably should have asked Allison for directions to the nearest Walmart. Here I was, in the middle of Silicon Valley, with nary a computer store in sight. What I needed was a mall directory.

I made an abrupt about-face, thinking I might find a directory near the mall entrance, and my glance suddenly connected with the sharp-eyed stare of a tall man not ten feet away. Lank brown hair and a shaggy mustache made his narrow face appear even thinner. His clothes were casual but not unkempt. A short-sleeved T-shirt exposed a kaleidoscope of tattoos on both arms. A cell phone was held against one ear, and his deep-set eyes were staring straight at me. My heart gave a queer little jerk at the intentness of that stare and I turned away, focusing my own gaze on the stylish offerings in a nearby shoe store.

The man was a total stranger, yet the look in his eyes strongly suggested I was somehow familiar to him. More than familiar. His stare held a kind of watchful purpose, one that made me feel increasingly uncomfortable. My nerves began a disquieting little dance, and after giving the shoes and handbags in the store window another ten seconds of blind attention, I turned away and continued down the avenue in the opposite direction.

I drew a steadying breath, determined not to look behind me. Nerves. That's all it was. Nerves and a bit of overreaction after yesterday's unsettling events. Reaching an intersection between the mall avenues, I noticed a directory of sorts posted like a street sign, with numbers and arrows pointing the way to various stores. I paused to study the listing and saw an outlet called Sony Style. The name itself was rather ambiguous and could mean anything from computers and cameras to a high-tech beauty salon. Still, it was worth a try.

When I reached the end of the indicated avenue, Sony Style was nowhere in sight, but at least my nerves had calmed down, with irritation taking their place.

Somewhere behind me, I heard a child's mischievous laugh and a woman's scolding caution, telling him not to run. Seconds later, there was the startled *oof* from some kind of human collision, followed by a string of ugly expletives and the child's high-pitched wail.

I couldn't help cringing at the use of such foul language. Turning, I saw the source of the trouble. A blond-haired imp of a boy, no more than three or four, had collided with a toughly built man wearing sunglasses and a baseball cap. The little boy's ice cream cone lay on the ground in a chocolate glob, and the man's jeans bore messy evidence of the collision. The mother was busy making apologies for her son and offering the big man a handful of paper napkins.

He grabbed the napkins and swiped at the pant leg of his jeans, then glanced at the woman with an angry "Get your stupid kid away from me!"

Shocked into silence, she picked up the crying child and hurriedly walked away.

Mouth dry, heart pounding in my throat, I backed away as well. I knew that voice. The man's sunglasses and baseball cap had initially hid his face, but there was no mistaking the voice. It was him.

Recognition wrestled briefly with denial, but inside I knew it wasn't chance or coincidence that had brought the Ogre to a shopping mall nearly a hundred miles north of Carmel. The man was following me.

Five

What to do? Where to go? Fear and the instinct for flight raged inside me for a breathless moment before any kind of reason could take hold. Somehow, I managed not to turn and run. Walking doggedly on, I considered my options. The mall entrance was too far away to make a run for it. Besides, I didn't think Brock was aware I had recognized him—that I knew I was being followed. Better not do anything that would alert him to that fact.

I blew out a ragged breath and increased my pace, hoping to mingle with a trio of well-dressed women a few yards ahead. Before I could catch up, the women left the main avenue to head down a narrow side street. A few seconds of blind panic sideswiped my emotions as I wondered what to do, but I instinctively kept going rather than follow the women. A few feet farther on, I saw a clothing store that looked as if it might have some merchandise without designer labels and designer price tags, and made a beeline for the entrance. I seriously doubted Brock would be stupid enough to follow me into the store where he would be easily seen and recognized.

Rifling through a rack of tops and blouses, I cast a covert glance out the store window and spotted him across the way. Frowning, with a cell phone in one hand, he wiped at his ice-cream-stained pants with the other.

My fingers were cold and clumsy as I examined the tops, while my mind offered the desperate prayer, *Help me . . . help me know what to do.*

The answer, when it came, was beautifully simple. After selecting two tops and a pair of jeans, I asked a young sales clerk if I could try them on. She was only too happy to show me to the dressing rooms, which were located near the back of the store, safely out of sight. Once inside, I locked the door and sank down on the cubicle's small bench.

Setting the clothes aside, I searched in my handbag for the card Detective Evans had given me, then grabbed my cell phone and punched in the number.

I didn't realize I'd been holding my breath until I heard that competent voice. "Evans here."

"Detective Evans, it's Mackenzie Graham. I–I need your help."

"Who?"

"Mackenzie Graham. You came to the Residence Inn last night to investigate a burglary—"

"Oh, right. Stolen laptop. I take it you know something else that's missing."

"Yes, but that's not why I'm calling. I'm being followed."

"What? Are you sure?"

"Yes, I'm sure! The man following me is the same one who grabbed me when I was at Judge Wolcott's house."

"Grabbed you? You didn't say anything about that last night."

"I know—I know I didn't. At the time, I didn't think it was important. But I was wrong. Please, I need to talk to you."

"Where are you calling from?"

"I'm at the Stanford Shopping Center, in the dressing room of a clothing store."

"What about the guy that's following you? Where's he?"

"The last time I checked, he was waiting outside."

There was a short pause before the detective asked tersely, "Do you think you're in any danger from this man?"

"I . . . I don't know."

"Has he made any aggressive or threatening moves toward you?"

"No. "

"Good. Let's keep it that way. I'm just finishing up with an investigation, but I could meet you at police headquarters in, say, ten or fifteen minutes."

"You'll have to give me directions."

"The police department is in the big high rise on Forest Avenue. Do you know how to get there?"

"Not really. I'm sorry—" I broke off, hating the ragged sound of my voice.

"No problem. I'll tell you how to get there from the mall."

I grabbed a notebook from my purse and quickly wrote down the directions.

"Mackenzie, a word of caution. Stay in crowds whenever possible, especially when you're leaving the mall. Don't make it easy for him, okay?"

"Okay." My heart went cold just thinking of getting to my car in the parking terrace. "What if he follows me to the police station?"

"I'll be waiting for you out front," Evans said calmly. "That ought to discourage him."

I bought one of the tops, to justify the time spent in the dressing room as well as to show Brock that my actions were motivated by a woman's love of shopping, nothing more. That is, if he was still there.

And he was. As I left the store, I spotted him lounging on a bench across the way, his dark head bent over a newspaper.

Clutching my shopping bag and purse a little tighter, I began what felt like an endless journey through the mall. I kept my pace casual and unconcerned, yet I knew with every step and every heartbeat that he was there.

The noon hour was approaching, and the avenues of the mall were much busier than when I arrived. It wasn't difficult to mingle with the crowd—until I left the mall. Facing the street, I felt exposed and alone. I bit my lip, waiting for a break in traffic before I could cross the street to the parking terrace. Thoughts of those echoing concrete corridors sent waves of apprehension flooding through me. What if Brock had a weapon? What if he tried to force me into his car? Was I imagining it, or were there footsteps behind me, walking faster, coming closer?

Not only footsteps, but laughter, and busy, feminine chatter.

I glanced over my shoulder, relieved to see a happy group of young women approaching, packages and purses in hand. Judging from their age, late teens or early twenties, they were probably students from nearby Stanford University. The girls were dressed in uniform nonconformity—straightened, shoulder-length hair, tight jeans, and skin-hugging camis or T-shirts. We crossed the street together, with me following in the wake of their excited *you know*'s and *I mean*'s, all the way to the parking terrace.

Leaving the gaggle of girls behind, I sprinted to my car, climbed inside, and hurriedly locked the doors.

There was no sign of Brock as I left the terrace. Either he'd given up the chase or was headed for his own car. Clutching Detective Evans' directions in one hand, I drove away. I had no idea whether I was followed from the mall to the center of town. The initial feeling of panic was gone, replaced by a single goal: to reach the police station and Wade Evans. In spite of some lunch-hour congestion, I made it to Forest Avenue in good time and pulled up in front of the large high rise.

As promised, Detective Evans was waiting out front. He caught sight of me and quickly stepped forward. "Turn right at the next corner," he instructed, climbing into the passenger seat. "I'll show you where to park."

He said little until we'd left my car in the visitors' parking area and were headed for the building's main entrance. Then, giving me a sideways glance, he asked, "Were you followed on your way here?"

"I don't know. Possibly."

"Do you know what he was driving?"

"Yesterday it was a black BMW. Today, I have no idea."

The sandy brows lifted. "Yesterday?"

"That's right."

Evans gave me a pointed glance, but said nothing more until after we entered the building and were headed for the elevators.

"I share office space with several other detectives," he told me. "If you'd prefer someplace more private, we can talk in one of the interrogation rooms."

"Thank you. That would be better."

Evans pressed the up button beside the elevator, and moments later the doors opened with a metallic whisper and whoosh. Two men were inside—a uniformed officer and Sloppy Joe. Same wrinkled brown suit. Same tired expression.

Our eyes met, and he had to have seen the shocked recognition in mine. His registered bland curiosity at first, wondering I'm sure, why I looked so startled. Then his expression tightened and his glance slid away from mine to focus straight ahead.

Wade Evans exchanged casual greetings with the officer as we got on and acknowledged Sloppy Joe's presence with a nod and a respectful "Lieutenant."

The man nodded in return, but after that initial moment, refused to look my way. My palms felt clammy, and a frantic pulse hammered in my throat. I wondered if Detective Evans and the officer could feel the change in atmosphere—the charged awareness between the lieutenant and me that crackled in the air like an electrical current.

The elevator halted its ascent with an ungainly lurch. Sloppy Joe made his exit the moment the doors opened, brushing past us without a backward glance.

The officer gave Wade Evans a raised-eyebrow look. "Looks like Dicola's having a great day."

Evans grinned and shrugged. "So what else is new?" The two exchanged knowing looks before parting ways.

My brain was spinning as I followed the detective down a narrow hallway with rooms on either side. First the Ogre. And now Sloppy Joe. What kind of business would bring a police lieutenant from Palo Alto over a hundred miles south to Judge Wolcott's reclusive residence in Carmel?

Evans ushered me into a room sparsely furnished with a desk, three chairs, and two metal filing cabinets. He gestured to one of the chairs, seated himself behind the desk, and took out a notebook and pen.

"All right, Miss Graham. You told me on the phone that the man following you was the same one who grabbed you at Judge Wolcott's place. Do you want to tell me about that?"

There was professional politeness in his tone, but no real concern, and I thought I knew why. Young woman has a bad day. Her car is broken into. Then her apartment is burglarized. Now she imagines she's being followed.

I met his eyes, irritated by his casual posture, his attitude of patient forbearance. Even the way he was clicking the top of the ballpoint pen sent a clear message that he was a little bored with the situation, but willing to do his job.

My spine straightened against the hard back of the chair. "Last night, you said you thought the two break-ins might be related. That the thieves were after something specific."

He nodded, still clicking the pen.

I was highly tempted to grab the blasted pen and toss it across the room. Instead, I took my camera out of my handbag and told him with icy calm, "You were right. And I think I know what they were after. Yesterday I took some pictures at Judge Wolcott's home that may give us the answer."

Evans waited in polite silence while I went through the frames until I found the series of Peter Wolcott and his visitors. I selected one of the stills that showed the faces of all three men to good advantage, then set the camera on the desk in front of him.

"Take a look and tell me what you think."

Evans put down the pen and raised the camera. I have to admit there was real satisfaction in seeing his bland expression completely wiped away by open-mouthed shock. His staring eyes left the camera long enough to give me an incredulous glance, then returned to the image on the screen. Finally, he set the camera down with a muttered profanity and shook his head.

"There are several other stills if you'd like to see them," I said. "I happened to have the camera on rapid-fire setting at the time."

Evans shook his head again and said nothing for a long moment. Then he leaned forward and asked, "Do you know those men?"

"I've never seen any of them before yesterday, and Judge Wolcott is the only one I know by name." I paused, then added, "But the man on the left is the one we saw in the elevator. The one you called Lieutenant."

Evans acknowledged this with a quiet "Police Lieutenant Vince Dicola."

I waited a moment more before asking, "What about the man in the middle? You know who he is, don't you."

"Let's just say I know about him. Nicholas Sarcassian is a big-time investor who has an import/export business in San Francisco. He's also rumored to have dealings with illicit trade, drug traffic, and who knows what else."

It was my turn to gape at the detective in wide-eyed shock. I moistened my lips and slumped against the back of the chair.

Evans gave the picture another stunned glance, then set the camera down and picked up his pen. "Last night, I asked you to tell me about your day," he said quietly. "I'm asking you again—and this time, don't leave anything out."

Six

"We have quite an interesting scenario here," Evans said after I had related the events of the previous afternoon. "Sarcassian and his gofer—Brock, you said his name was—along with Lieutenant Dicola, all show up at Judge Wolcott's place in Carmel. Why? What kind of business would a scumbag like Sarcassian have with a circuit court judge? Or Dicola, for that matter? It doesn't smell right. From what little I know, Sarcassian's an ultracautious guy. The man likes to keep his hands clean and let others do his dirty work. He never would have agreed to the meeting if he didn't feel it was important—and safe. But what was Dicola doing there? He knows what Sarcassian is." Evans paused, then added with a bitter twist to his voice, "At least, I thought he did. And let's face it, there's no way Judge Wolcott would want to be seen with any of these guys."

Evans' look was sober as he met my eyes. "Then you show up, not only unexpected, but with a camera. It's no surprise Brock reacted with some strong-arm tactics. Witnessing their meeting was bad enough, but you have evidence it took place. I can see why these guys are worried."

I swallowed, my mouth dry. "It's not good, is it?"

"It's certainly not good for them, and whatever it is they're involved in—and it could be dangerous for you."

Inside, I think I already knew that, but hearing the words from this soft-spoken detective was chilling. A shudder went through me and I had to ask, "How dangerous?"

"That depends on what's at stake. We don't have all the pieces to the puzzle yet, but what we do know . . . " He whistled low, then shook his head. "Sorry. I don't want to frighten you unnecessarily."

"Don't worry about that. I'm already scared to death."

Evans fixed me with a steady look and the hint of a smile. "For the record, Miss Graham, I think the way you're handling all this is pretty amazing."

"Mackenzie," I said. "I haven't been called Miss Graham since college."

His smile broadened. "Mackenzie. Can I get you anything? Coffee? A soft drink? There's a pop machine down the hall."

"Not right now, thanks. I'd like to know what it was you thought might frighten me unnecessarily."

Evans leaned forward and faced me across the desk. "Okay. I don't like it that these guys know so much about you. You gave the judge your business card, which by now Sarcassian's probably made good use of. They have your cell number, where you work, probably an e-mail address. Right?"

I nodded, feeling fear's cold fingers touch my spine.

"So they follow you," the detective went on. "Getting the camera would take care of the evidence, and the car break-in was easy. Like you said, a smash-and-dash sort of thing. But they didn't get the camera. By now, Sarcassian, not to mention Judge Wolcott, must be getting pretty nervous. What if you download the pictures? What if somebody else, like your boss, sees them?

"So they broke into my room and stole the laptop."

"Right. And tore the place apart, looking for any other evidence—the camera, memory cards, or something small, like a flash drive. You have one, I assume?"

"Yes. The flash drive and my camera were in my handbag when I went to dinner last night."

Evans rubbed a thoughtful hand against his jaw. "So now they've made two attempts and failed both times. Not good for them, and definitely not good for you. Do you think you were followed to the Meyers' home last night?"

I thought a moment, then shook my head. "It's possible, but I don't think so."

"Why not?"

"Timing. I called Allison shortly after you left, and she came right over to get me. Whoever broke into the room and stole the laptop would need a little time to get into my documents and pictures." I paused, then added with some exasperation, "Believe me, there were a lot. I'm assuming they have someone who could figure out my passwords and get into my material."

Evans nodded. "Oh, yeah. That wouldn't stop them for long."

"But it would slow them down," I put in. "By the time they realized the pictures weren't on the laptop, I was at Allison's. We left my car at the inn, so even if they did risk coming back, I wouldn't have been there."

"I agree. But this morning, when you and your boss returned to the inn to clean up the mess and change rooms, someone must have been there, waiting and watching for the right moment, an opportunity . . ."

"An opportunity?" I repeated hoarsely.

"They still want that camera. And they need to know more about you—whether you're just a minor inconvenience, or a legitimate threat."

"Now you are frightening me."

"Sorry, Mackenzie, but there's no way I can downplay this. If Brock followed you to the mall, we have to assume that he or someone else followed you to the police station, and that raises all kinds of red flags."

"Someone else?"

"It'd be foolish to think Brock's the only guy working for Sarcassian. And since Sarcassian's put a tail on you, you can bet Brock's got at least one buddy around."

I sat very still, my hands in my lap, fingers clenched. "This morning at the mall there was someone else—a man, staring at me."

Wade Evans' serious expression relaxed and his mouth twitched into a crooked smile. "I think that's something you'd be used to. Men staring at you, I mean."

I smiled back, the unexpected compliment easing some of the tension inside me. "Thanks, but this was different."

"Different how?"

The detective's smile disappeared as I told him about the shaggy-haired man and how my unexpected about-face had caught his intent stare. "He was talking on his cell at the time," I said. "I know it doesn't sound like much, but there was something about the way he was looking at me—almost as if he knew me—that made me very uncomfortable."

Evans nodded. "So what did you do?"

"I–I turned around and went the other way."

"Did you see the man again?"

"No. It wasn't long after that, a few minutes at most, that the incident with Brock and the little boy occurred. I didn't recognize him at first—he was wearing sunglasses and a baseball cap—but there was no mistaking his voice." My own voice trailed away as fear returned, making me shudder. I met the detective's eyes and said miserably, "I . . . I don't know what to do."

Wade Evans got up and came around the desk to stand beside my chair. "I'll do everything I can to keep you safe. Under ordinary circumstances, I'd go straight to Lieutenant Dicola and fill him in on the situation. There's no way I can do that now—not until I know how deep he's in with that scum Sarcassian." Evans broke off, his pleasant features tight with worry. "When you saw Dicola on the elevator, did he recognize you?"

"Not at first, but . . . yes, yes, he recognized me."

Evans swore under his breath and ran a hand through his sandy hair.

"That complicates things, doesn't it?" I said grimly.

"Not much more than they already are, but I'm sure seeing you must have been quite a shock. Dicola's got to be feeling pretty nervous right now, wondering why you're here and what you're telling me." Evans leaned against the desk, a frown narrowing his sandy brows.

"Will this—this whole affair get you in trouble?"

"That's not your problem. I can handle Dicola," he said tersely. "But in order to get the kind of protection you need, I'll have to go over his head and talk to the chief. Unfortunately, he's out of town until tomorrow or the next day. "

"So what can we do?"

"For now, you need to stay out of sight, somewhere safe, until I can get hold of the chief and make arrangements for your protection. And there's no way you'll be driving to Carmel tomorrow to interview the Wolcotts."

"What am I going to tell Allison? I can't just back out of an assignment without giving her some kind of explanation. She was going to go with me tomorrow."

"No good," he said with an adamant shake of his head. "I admit you'll have to tell her something, but Carmel is out. And you can't go back to the Residence Inn. From now on, you can't be alone. Period." He thought a moment, absently tapping his pen on the desk. "Do you think your boss would be willing to let you stay with her— not long, just for a couple of hours—until I can get you some real protection?"

"Yes, I think so. We'd talked about having lunch together."

"Why don't you give her a call and confirm that, then I'll drive you over to her place."

"What about my car and my things? Could we stop at the inn first?"

Evans shook his head. "We can't risk going back. Sarcassian might have someone watching the place. And don't worry about the car. I'll have someone return it to the rental agency."

All I could do was nod, feeling slightly overwhelmed with it all.

"And if you'll trust me with that memory card, I'll make sure it's put somewhere very safe."

I picked up my camera and opened the compartment holding the memory card. "It's all yours."

Wade took the card and tucked it into his shirt pocket. "Thanks for the trust."

"Actually, it's a relief to be rid of it. Please remind me what I'm supposed to do now besides becoming invisible."

"Invisibility's not a bad idea," he said. "Especially if I'm going to get you out of here without Lieutenant Dicola being the wiser."

I heard the anger building in the detective's voice, saw it spark in the mildness of his eyes, to be released as a fist came pounding down on the desk. "If there's anything I hate, it's a dirty cop, he ground out."

I bit my lip, not knowing what to say as Evans wrestled with the ugliness of the situation. The next moment he was shrugging his anger aside with a determined lift of his broad shoulders and a steadying breath.

"All right," he said. "This is the deal. If anybody asks, you came to see me because you had more information about last night's break-in. I don't know anything about what happened at the Wolcotts', or those pictures. If Dicola thinks I'm just doing my job, following up on a simple burglary, it might buy us some time." Wade's expression hardened as he admitted, "Believe me, I'd love to tell that piece of trash exactly what I think of him, but that wouldn't do either of us any good."

"And Allison? I'm still not sure what to tell her. She's bound to be curious why a police detective is escorting me to her home."

"I realize that, but for her sake as well as yours, she needs to know as little as possible."

"What if that's not good enough? I haven't known Allison long, but I do know she won't buy flimsy excuses or fabrication."

Evans acknowledged my concern with a tight nod. "Then tell her whatever you think she needs to know. I'll leave that up to you. Just make sure she understands the trip to Carmel is out."

"All right."

He moved to the door and held it open for me.

"And if Lieutenant Dicola sees us?"

"Like I said, Dicola's my problem. You came to the station to talk to me about the break-in. End of story."

Thankfully, there was no sign of Lieutenant Dicola as we left the building and drove away in Evans' unmarked car. Nor were there any black BMWs tailing us across town. A quick call to Allison confirmed she was available for lunch and eager to go over some new ideas for the article.

I put my phone back in my purse, still uncertain how I was going to break the news to her that we wouldn't be going to Carmel the next day. Maybe I'd have to become violently ill between now and then.

The detective glanced at my tense expression and said in a gruff voice that I'm sure was meant to be comforting, "Hey, Mackenzie, try not to worry. As soon as I get hold of the chief, we'll get you some protection. It'll be fine."

I stared ahead and said quietly, "I hope so."

When Evans pulled up beside the Meyers' home, Allison was on her hands and knees in the rose garden beside the drive. She glanced up and stared at the unfamiliar car with a curious frown. Then, seeing me in the passenger seat, she smiled and waved. I waved back, knowing her curiosity must be at a peak, with questions brewing in that clever mind of hers.

Detective Evans leaned across the seat to put a hand on my arm as I reached for the door handle. "I'll call you as soon as I've talked to the chief. Hopefully, it won't be more than an hour or two. Just stay put and out of sight until then."

"All right, but I still don't know what to tell Allison."

Evans gave me a slow smile. "You'll think of something. You could always say we've got a hot date tonight."

The flushed color in my cheeks did not go unnoticed as the detective drove away and I headed up the walk where Allison knelt amid the roses. Her thinly arched brows were arched even higher, and her lips were curved into a knowing smile as she looked up at me.

"Well, well, well. Who's the guy?"

I couldn't help smiling. "Detective Evans investigated the break-in last night, and I . . . well, I just thought I should tell him about the other things that were stolen."

"Mmm-hmm." Her brown eyes sparkled. "I didn't know Palo Alto's finest made house calls."

I shrugged and sat on the lawn beside her. Plucking some blades of grass, I said, "Well, I had a problem with my car, so he . . ."

"Out of the kindness of his heart, gave you a ride to my place," she finished, rolling her eyes. "Come on, Mackenzie. You can do better than that. I couldn't help noticing the way he was looking at you when you got out of the car. I think the good detective has more on his mind than filling out police reports."

"You could be right," I said, thinking I might as well encourage the direction her thoughts were headed. "He did say he might call me later."

Allison gave me a triumphant I-told-you-so look, then added with all the subtlety of a bulldozer, "I wonder what our handsome photographer would say about the competition?"

"Corbin? Why would he—? How do you—?"

Allison responded to my string of incomplete sentences with a laugh. "Honey, being happily married does not make one blind, deaf, and dumb to the rest of the male species. Corbin is outrageously attractive, and he knows how to turn on the charm. The minute you arrived, I could tell he was on the prowl. Fresh meat in the jungle."

I had to laugh, grateful for the change of subject and her false assumptions about Wade Evans. Perhaps I wouldn't have to go into any detailed explanations after all. "Well, after last night, I think he'll be prowling somewhere else."

Allison put down the trowel and fixed me with a probing look. "What did happen last night, if you don't mind my asking? And if you do mind, that's too bad."

"Nothing happened," I said flatly. "That's just it. We had dinner together, but the evening ended much sooner than he'd planned."

Allison flashed me a pleased smile. "Good for you, girl."

The cell phone lying beside her in the grass erupted in a sultry tango, and she pulled off her garden gloves to pick it up. "Speak of the devil," she said after checking the caller ID.

"Hi, Corbin. How's it going? Are you going to have the layout for the Simmons piece ready by tomorrow?"

I paid little attention to her conversation, content to absorb the calming warmth of the sun and the intoxicating scents of the garden. Moist earth, sweet roses, and heavenly purple heliotrope.

"That's fabulous," Allison was saying with satisfaction. "When do I get to see it?" She listened a moment more, then shot me a significant glance. "Mackenzie's with me right now. I'd like her to see the photos. Why don't the three of us meet somewhere for lunch. Say, Le Croissant's in half an hour? Right. We'll see you there."

My fingers clenched around a fistful of warm grass. Now what was I supposed to do? I couldn't very well expect Allison to alter the plans without giving her some kind of explanation. *Think, think.* Telling her as little as possible no longer seemed a viable solution. The ready excuse of pleading a headache briefly crossed my mind, but besides sounding flimsy, the idea of staying here alone until Detective Evans arranged for my protection was more than a little unnerving. Wade had told me to stay put, but he'd also cautioned me not to be alone. If I went to lunch with Allison and Corbin, we'd at least be in a public place. If necessary, I could always call Wade and have him pick me up at the restaurant.

Allison gave me a quick glance. "Mackenzie, is working with Corbin going to be a problem for you? Because if it is—"

"No, no of course not." I tried to shrug away my concerns with a smile, but my lips felt stiff and the smile forced. "Where did you say we're going for lunch? Detective Evans said he might get in touch with me this afternoon."

Allison's dark eyes danced with enjoyment at my assumed predicament of juggling the attentions of two handsome males. "Le Croissant. It's a fabulous little French place that has the most incredible salads, and they make all their own bread and pastries."

I tried to insert some enthusiasm in my voice. "It sounds wonderful. Am I dressed too casually?"

She gave my jeans and peasant-style top an approving glance. "Honey, I'm sure Corbin will think you look good enough to eat, no matter what you're wearing. Come on. I need a few minutes to clean up, and we'll be on our way."

Allison kept up a cheerful round of chatter on the drive to the restaurant, inserting some gentle teasing amid the more mundane business matters. I paid little attention, more concerned with checking the side mirror for a black BMW that might be following. After ten minutes on the road, I had to admit the busy streams of traffic on the boulevard seemed completely normal. Allison's driving was as competent and assured as she was. I blew out a small sigh, trying to ease the tenseness inside me.

"Mackenzie, is anything wrong?"

My eyes left the mirror to discover her probing look of concern. "No, not a thing," I said, forcing a smile. "I was just noticing those flowering bushes along the median. I've seen them before, but I can't remember the name."

"Oleander. The entire plant is quite poisonous, you know."

"That's right. I remember reading about oleanders when I did an article on Georgia's 'painted ladies.'"

"Are you sure you're all right?" She gave me another quick glance. "You seem—well, you're not usually so tense. Did Corbin . . .?"

"No, honestly. Corbin's not a problem. I've got a bit of a headache, that's all. I guess I'm hungrier than I thought."

"We'll be at the restaurant in about ten minutes," Alison said, then added with a smile, "If you think you can last that long."

"Not a problem."

Allison squinted and adjusted the car's visor. "Well, I'm not going to last another minute without my sunglasses. I'm always forgetting to put them on. Could you get them for me? They're in my purse on the floor."

I leaned over and reached into the large leather bag by my feet. The next moment, the car was rocked by a strange explosion. I jerked up as the vehicle careened wildly, and saw Allison slumped forward on the steering wheel.

"Allison!"

I tried to reach out to her, tried to grab the wheel, but the car was like a mad animal, raging out of control. Time itself seemed caught in a terrifying vortex, and I was trapped—trapped inside a metal body of screaming tires and shrieking steel. The momentum slowed as the vehicle skidded into the barrow pit and scraped its way across a guardrail before colliding with the immovable barrier of solid concrete.

The airbags inflated with bruising force, and there was a hot hissing from the beaten car. The silence, when it came, was nearly as deafening as the sounds of the crash.

Stunned and shaken, I drew a careful breath, thinking for a blessed moment. *I'm breathing . . . I'm alive.* That much registered to my shocked mind before the horror set in.

"Allison?"

I turned my head to see her limp body face down against the deflated airbag, blood bright red in the darkness of her hair.

Seven

Outside the crushed car I heard the blur of running feet and frightened babble of voices. Someone asked, "Are you all right?" while someone else shouted in a strange echo, "Call 911! Somebody call 911!"

"Are you all right?" the question came again, this time from a woman's shrill voice. I tried to answer, but my mind couldn't find the words with the strident sounds of the crash still echoing in my head. Pain knifed through my ribs when I tried to move, and breathing became a brutal exercise in agony.

A man peered through the smashed window on the driver's side, and horror gripped his features.

"My friend . . ." I got out between short, tight breaths. "She's hurt."

He backed away, gasping, and I suddenly realized why. There was blood everywhere—splattered on the windshield, the dashboard, my clothes, my hands.

"Allison," I mumbled, trying to reach her in spite of the pain, but I couldn't move. The passenger door was crushed against the concrete barrier, and my seat belt was jammed tight. I felt a moment's terror at the thought of being trapped in the mangled car, and as my breathing escalated, so did the pain in my chest. I closed my eyes to the blood and horror and tried to focus on breathing instead. Just breathing . . . and silently praying for help.

I have no idea how much time passed before the highway patrol and paramedics arrived. It could have been minutes or hours. Time for me was measured by Allison's stillness and the painful effort of my own breathing. When sirens intruded on the stillness, I knew help was at hand.

"My friend . . . my friend's hurt!" was all I could say.

"Don't worry. We'll take good care of you and your friend."

Strong arms eased Allison out of the wrecked metal and cut me loose from the seat belt's stranglehold. I let out a cry as pain shot through me.

"Easy now, we've got you."

Male voices, competent and calm, issued instructions all around me. I looked for Allison, caught a glimpse of serious-faced paramedics bent over a gurney, and felt a heavy dread deep inside. Then the voices became a whirling echo in my head and everything faded away.

Consciousness returned and sharpened into focus as I lay on a gurney in a hospital treatment room. Flannel blankets wrapped me in a warm cocoon, and somewhere nearby I heard the steady beeping of machines. My right hand felt strangely heavy and cold. I shifted my gaze from the ceiling to see IV tubing going from a needle in my hand to a plastic bag hanging from a metal pole.

"Hi there, missy. My name's Emily. I'll be taking care of you."

The voice was close by and sounded like warm butter. I turned my head to see a buxom black nurse wearing blue scrubs, standing beside the gurney.

"How do you feel?" she asked.

"My face hurts."

"I'm not surprised. Those air bags are a blessin' and a curse. You're going to have one doozy of a shiner, and the right side of your pretty face has some superficial burns. Nothing too serious, though," she pronounced with a smile as warm as her voice.

Nurse Emily proceeded to take my vitals, all the while asking a series of basic kindergarten questions. Did I know my name? What day was it? When was I born?

I answered mechanically, then asked, "My friend Allison . . . how is she?"

"The doctors are with her. Now hang on to me, and I'll help you sit up. We've got to get you out of those clothes and into a gown. Then I'll take you down to Radiology."

I took hold of her arm, unable to prevent a gasping cry as pain stabbed through my chest and side.

"Easy now. Just take it slow," Emily advised, helping me sit up.

I drew some tentative breaths, shuddering at the sight of my bloodstained blouse and jeans. The blood brought back all the horrible images and sounds of the crash, and suddenly the room was spinning around me.

"Put your head down, honey," the nurse instructed. "I don't want you to go fainting on me. Take some slow, deep breaths."

I did as she asked, and after a moment, the dizziness receded.

"Feeling better?"

I nodded. "A little. Where's Allison? Can I see her?"

"Not yet" was all the nurse said, but something in her voice filled me with dread.

"Is she all right? I need to know how she is!"

"What you need is to take it easy and get out of those clothes," Emily ordered. "The doctors are taking good care of your friend."

She proceeded to help me out of my jeans, blouse, and bra, and into a shapeless cotton gown of hideous light-blue paisley.

"I'd love to know who designs these things," I mumbled as she deftly tied the gown in the back, preserving a portion of my modesty.

"It wasn't Calvin Klein, that's for sure." She chuckled. "Now sit tight, missy, and I'll get you a wheelchair."

Briefly put, being X-rayed was not a pleasant experience. Breathing was not a pleasant experience. To make matters worse, as Emily wheeled me back to the treatment room, nature was making an insistent call in other areas. I blessed the nurse a thousand times over for her matter-of-fact approach to life's urgent little necessities, as well as her strong arms and capable assistance in the bathroom. By the time I was back on the gurney with a flannel blanket tucked around me, I felt as if I had successfully climbed Mount Everest.

Moments later, a soft tap sounded on the door and Wade Evans stepped inside the room. I was so glad to see him, I couldn't stop the tears that suddenly stung my eyes.

Emily shot him a frowning look, then gave a brusque nod of acceptance when he parted his jacket to show her the badge on his belt.

"When you're finished, I'd like to ask Miss Graham a few questions," he said.

"Is that all right with you, honey?" Emily asked.

"Yes, it's fine."

Ignoring the detective, the nurse fixed me with a probing look. "How's your pain level on a scale of one to ten?"

"Six or seven, maybe." I grimaced as she raised the head of the gurney and adjusted the pillows at my back. "Okay, make that eight."

She took a syringe from a supply tray and injected some medication into my IV. "The doctor's ordered some pain medication for you. You'll start feeling better any time now."

"Will it make me loopy?"

"Sometimes loopy is good," Emily said and turned to Wade Evans. "Try to keep it short," she told him with the steely authority of a drill sergeant. Patting my arm, she added, "Dr. Taylor will be in to see you in a few minutes."

"I heard about the accident on the scanner," Wade said after the nurse had gone. "When the report came in, I kept hoping it wasn't you, but my gut told me otherwise." He shook his head, mute apology in his eyes.

"No one will tell me about Allison. Please, do you know how she is?"

His mouth tightened. "She's in surgery."

I waited, trying to read something—anything—hopeful from the grim set of his features. "Please," I murmured again, "I need to know how she is."

Wade stepped closer and gave my arm an awkward pat. "I'm sorry, Mackenzie, but it doesn't look good. The bullet entered just below her right ear, and the exit wound is—" He broke off and gave a helpless shake of his head.

I stared at him, my mind reeling. "A bullet? Allison was shot?"

"The investigating officers didn't realize it was a shooting at first," Wade said quietly. "For all they knew, the accident was just a matter of the driver losing control. It wasn't until one of the paramedics got a closer look at her head injuries that they realized she'd been shot." He paused. "The bullet came through the passenger-side window. I don't know how it could have missed you. Do you remember anything—did you see or hear anything at all?"

I drew a shaky breath, trying to think. "I was bending over to get something out of her purse . . . Allison's sunglasses . . . and there was this strange sort of explosion. Then, suddenly, the car was out of control, and . . . and she was slumped over the steering wheel—" I broke off as hard tremors of realization shook me from the inside out. "It should have been me, not Allison!" I pressed balled fists against my eyes, feeling the hot sting of tears. "That bullet was meant for me, wasn't it? Wasn't it!"

"Mackenzie, look at me!" Wade grasped my hands firmly in his, forcing me to meet his eyes. "Don't go there. It won't do Allison any good to blame yourself."

"Who else can I blame?" I choked, tears blurring my vision of his face.

His grip on my hands tightened. "Listen to me, Mackenzie. If we're talking about guilt and blame, then you better give a lion's share to me. I knew you were in trouble, but I had no idea the situation was so critical. I thought I had time to get you some protection. I was wrong. I never should have left you." He let go of my hands to grab some tissues from a box on the supply cart and gave them to me. "If you want someone to blame, put it on whoever fired that shot. Better yet, blame the guy who ordered the hit."

I wiped my eyes and looked up to find the detective's serious gaze on my face.

"Look, I know you've been through a lot, but there are some things we need to deal with, and we don't have much time."

"What do you mean? What kind of things?" I asked, beginning to feel slightly fuzzy around the edges.

"I'm talking about what could happen when Sarcassian finds out you're alive."

Part of me registered what he was saying—that the danger was still present and very real—but suddenly it was difficult to worry too much as my pain levels were floating away on a cloud of drug-induced euphoria.

"Mackenzie, do you know what I'm saying?"

"Yes, yes, I know." I sighed and murmured against the pillow, "The nurse was right. Loopy is good."

Evans leaned closer, his voice urgent. "Mackenzie, listen to me! We don't have much time."

I sighed and asked, "Time for what?"

"To get you out of here. To do that, I need you to trust me."

"I trust you."

"Enough to do exactly what I say?"

Something in his voice, a heightened urgency, filtered through the haze. "What do you want me to do?"

"The first thing we've got to do is get you out of the hospital and somewhere safe before Dicola or Sarcassian have a chance to come up with plan B. And I can't be involved. At least not directly."

"Then what can we do?" I tried to focus on what he was saying, but I was feeling so relaxed, all I wanted to do was close my eyes and sleep.

"My brother's been visiting me this past week," Wade said. "William's an attorney and he's agreed to help. He knows about the pictures and pretty much what's happened. I've asked him to take you someplace safe. He's on his way to the hospital now, and I want you to go with him."

"But I don't know your brother," I said, my voice sounding slurred.

Wade cracked the first smile I'd seen since he entered the treatment room. "That's okay, I do. Will's a great guy, even if he is my brother."

"I don't think I like attorneys."

"Sometimes they come in handy," Wade said, still smiling. "Will you do it? Will you go with him? I promise he'll keep you safe."

Before I could answer, a vibrating buzz sounded somewhere close by. Wade reached for the cell phone attached to his belt. His response was a swift "Right. I'm on my way."

"Sorry, I've got to go," he told me in a rush. "But William'll be here soon." And with that, the detective hurried out of the room.

Nurse Emily returned moments later to check my vitals and start another bout of kindergarten questions.

"My birthdate hasn't changed since the last time you asked," I said.

She ignored this and commented with a frown, "Well, your blood pressure has. It's up a bit. So's your pulse."

No surprise there, I thought, considering all that Wade Evans had told me.

"Is there anything I can get you?" she asked.

I wanted to ask her about Allison, but suddenly I was afraid of what she might tell me. I swallowed and said thickly, "Something to drink."

"Sure thing, honey. I'll get you some juice and crackers."

"Thank you." I turned my face toward the wall, not wanting her to see the tears that were threatening.

"Dr. Taylor's on his way," she said softly and left the room.

The tears refused to be kept back any longer. They coursed down my face in a silent stream as I prayed for the woman who had taken a bullet meant for me.

Sometime later, I heard the soft *whoosh* of the door opening and wiped clumsily at my tear-stained cheeks. "Dr. Taylor?"

"No," answered a male voice from the doorway. "It's William."

My half-drugged eyes took in the broad-shouldered figure of a man somewhere in his mid-thirties. Dark brown hair. Rugged jaw, and a firm mouth framed by a goatee and mustache. Amazing eyes.

"You don't look like a lawyer," I said as he approached the gurney. What kind of attorney wore faded blue jeans and a v-necked T-shirt that clung to his muscular chest like a second skin? "How do I know you're really Detective Evans' brother?"

The man flashed me a grin. "Good question, Miss Graham. I'll be happy to show you some ID."

With effort, I stared at the driver's license and credit cards he took from his wallet, all bearing the name William T. Evans.

"Satisfied?" he asked, a smile playing around his bearded mouth.

I nodded and mumbled, "You have creases in your cheeks," then cringed. "Sorry. I didn't mean to say that . . . I think it's the pain medication."

"No need to be sorry." He returned the cards to his wallet.

"Are you really Wade's brother?"

His lips twitched. "Yes, I'm his brother."

"You don't look like a lawyer." I sighed and put a hand to my forehead. "I said that already, didn't I?"

He nodded.

"Wade said I could trust you."

"And you can. We need to get you out of here. Can you walk on your own?"

"I don't know . . . I'm waiting for Dr. Taylor."

Right on cue, a brisk knock sounded and a lanky physician with charts in hand entered the room.

"Ms. Graham—Mackenzie—I'm Dr. Taylor. We have the results of your X-rays." The physician gave Wade's brother a questioning, official look. "And you are?"

"Mackenzie's fiancé. I hope you have some good news for us."

It's a good thing I was drugged. All I could do was stare at my newly acquired fiancé in a semi-stupor as he reached over and took my hand.

"Fairly good news," Dr. Taylor said, approaching the gurney. "Other than some deep bruising and trauma to your rib cage and right shoulder, there are no broken bones or internal injuries. That doesn't mean you should try and run a marathon any time soon."

William released my hand and stepped aside as the physician put a stethoscope to his ears and leaned over me.

"I know you're uncomfortable," Dr. Taylor said, "but I need you to turn on your left side, so I can listen to your lungs. That's it." He untied the back of my gown and put the stethoscope through the loose opening. I couldn't help jerking a little at the touch of cold metal against my bare back. "Take some deep breaths," he instructed. "Good. Again. All right. You can lie back now and I'll take a listen to your heart."

I did as he asked, feeling too woozy and uncomfortable to be embarrassed by William's presence as the physician moved the top of the gown off my shoulders and put the stethoscope to my chest.

Dr. Taylor straightened, put the instrument around his neck, and nodded. "Your lungs are clear and your heart sounds good. Your injuries could have been much worse, but you've still suffered some serious trauma. Now I need to examine your right side and shoulder. This might be a bit painful, so take some nice deep breaths and try to relax."

I stared at the wall as the doctor moved my gown aside to put probing, professional hands on my injured side. When his fingers found a tender place near my rib cage, I couldn't prevent a sharp gasp.

"Sorry," he said, never pausing in his examination.

I cringed and bit down on my lower lip to keep from crying out.

"It's okay. I'm here." Warm fingers took my hand in a firm grip. "Just hang on to me."

I opened pain-clenched eyes to see Wade's brother standing beside the gurney, his gray-green eyes offering silent sympathy. His hand held mine and those amazing eyes never left my face until the doctor finished his examination. Then, giving me a little smile, William released my hand and proceeded to retie the back of my gown. The gentle touch of his fingers against my skin produced a reaction far different from the physician's probing hands.

Dr. Taylor made some notations on the chart, then handed me a small slip of paper. "I've written a prescription for some pain medication, and I want you to take it easy for a few days. Plenty of rest, and no bending or lifting. And don't be surprised if that injured side is looking pretty colorful by tomorrow." Turning to William, he added, "Take good care of her."

"I will. Very good care," William said, extending a hand to the physician.

Dr. Taylor's professional mien lapsed slightly as he shook William's hand. "I don't think I need to tell you that after what happened today, you're very lucky to have a fiancé."

"I know that," William assured him and sent me a warm look.

I was too stunned by this interchange to make any sort of reply. Thankfully, I didn't really need to.

Dr. Taylor issued a few more *do*'s and *don't*'s, which I promptly forgot, politely asked if I had any questions, and left the room before I could think of any.

The moment the physician had gone, William turned to me. "Do you think you can walk, or shall I get you a wheelchair?" There was the same urgency in his voice that I'd heard in his brother's.

"I might need a wheelchair . . . but I can't leave. Allison's still in surgery. I–I need to know how she is."

"There's no time for that."

I stared at him. "What do you mean?"

"I mean we have only a small window of time before they find out you're still alive. Lieutenant Dicola won't have any trouble getting the facts about your condition, and when he does, you can bet he'll pass that news to Sarcassian. We've got to be long gone before that happens."

Fear forced its way past the morphine like the current of an icy river, and for a moment, I couldn't speak. When words finally came, my voice sounded pathetically small. "But . . . what can we do?"

William leaned closer and put a hand on my shoulder, his eyes meeting mine with complete assurance. "Leave that to me. Okay?"

Nurse Emily chose that moment to trundle back into the room, carrying some plastic-wrapped crackers and a paper cup filled with orange juice. Her dark brows lifted at the sight of the man standing beside the gurney.

"Well, well. More visitors."

"Yes," I said before she could protest. "This is William, my fiancé."

Eight

Wade's brother stood politely aside while the nurse checked my vitals. The task done, Emily handed me a paper cup of juice, then adjusted the drip on my IV.

"Well, missy, I can see you're in good hands," she pronounced, giving me a wink. "Unless there's something else you need, I'll be back in a while to see how you're doing."

I took a grateful sip of juice. "Thank you."

The moment she left, William moved swiftly to the door, opened it a crack, and glanced out. "Be back in a minute," he said softly. He was gone barely that, returning with a pair of blue scrubs and a surgical cap under one arm, pushing a wheelchair with the other. He answered my questioning look with a brief "Time to go."

"But how?" I raised the hand with the IV tubing. "I can't very well drag this along."

"No problem. I'll take care of it."

"You—?" I broke off in a surprised croak as he pulled his T-shirt over his head and tossed it on the gurney beside me.

I knew I was staring, but I couldn't help it. Not even a healthy dose of morphine could diminish my reaction at seeing his muscular chest and torso with its trail of dark hair. The jeans came off next, and this time I did glance away.

In seconds William had donned the blue scrubs. Then he turned to me. "Okay, let's get this IV out."

I cringed and swallowed. "Have you ever done this before?"

"No, but it can't be that hard." He shrugged and concentrated on peeling off the tape that held the needle in place.

"I don't think I want to watch."

William grinned and the creases appeared on either side of his bearded jaw. "Suit yourself, but once the needle's out, I'll need you to apply some pressure with this." He handed me a sterile pad off the supply table. I took it and looked away.

"All done," he said moments later. "Keep that pad on and give it some pressure while I try to get this drip to stop squirting."

"There's a clamp," I told him. "Up higher. Use the clamp . . ."

Between the two of us we got the squirting under control. William found a bandage and placed it over the sterile pad, then blew out a slightly ragged breath. "You okay?"

I nodded, trying not to smile.

"Let's get you into that wheelchair and out of here."

"Like this?" I fingered the cotton gown. "What about my clothes?"

"Your clothes are a bloody mess." He grabbed my shirt and jeans off the chair where the nurse had left them, and tossed them into a garbage bin.

"Here. You better put this on." He handed me the surgical cap. "That hair of yours is much too noticeable."

Even though the gurney was raised and pillows supported my back, trying to lift my head to put the cap on was painful and more than a little awkward.

"Hang on to me and I'll help you sit up." William leaned closer, extending a muscled forearm for me to hold on to, while his other arm went around my back. "Okay, easy does it."

My ribs and shoulder shouted a painful protest as I pulled myself up. The next moment the room was swimming around me, and my head felt too heavy to hold up. With a moan, I sought the nearest refuge available—William's neck and chest.

"Sorry," I mumbled against the warmth of his throat.

"Don't be. Just keep your head down and take some slow, deep breaths."

When I did, I found myself breathing in the clean, masculine scent of his skin. The dizziness passed, leaving in its wake a heady awareness of him and our closeness. I could feel the pulse beating in his throat and taste his skin beneath my lips. Lifting my head, I met his eyes. Deep set and an incredible gray-green, with a fringe of dark lashes.

"Better?" he asked softly, one arm still around my back.

"Better."

He took the cap from me and without another word, lifted the hair off my neck and began tucking it into the elasticized cap. I glanced down, my awareness shifting from the warmth in his eyes to the touch of his fingers against my skin.

We both started as a buzzing vibration sounded somewhere nearby. William let go of me to reach for the cell phone attached to his belt. A frown narrowed his brows when he checked the caller ID.

"What's up?" He listened a moment and the frown deepened. "We were just leaving. Yeah, I know. Thanks for the heads up. I'll call you later."

"Was that Wade?"

He gave a brief nod, and the grim look to his mouth started my heart pumping double time.

"Is something wrong?"

"Dicola's on his way to the hospital."

I stared at William, my lips parted.

"Come on. Let's get you into that wheelchair."

Leaning into his arms, I let him help me off the gurney and into the chair. William took one of the flannel blankets, shoved it in my lap, and grabbed a pillow. "Here. You might need this." He tossed a hurried look around the treatment room. "Did you have anything else with you?"

"My purse and my shoes."

His quick glance found the plastic bag that held my belongings. He stuffed his T-shirt and jeans into the bag, set it beside me, then snatched the prescription off the supply table.

"Better not forget this. When the morphine wears off you're going to need it."

He opened the door, then held it with his back and turned the wheelchair around. "Keep your head down," he instructed. "We don't want anybody getting a good look at you."

"What if someone's watching?"

"All they'll see is an orderly wheeling a patient down the hall. Nothing unusual about that."

"And Lieutenant Dicola?"

"To hell with Dicola," William said and started down the hall.

I caught a brief glimpse of a wide hallway to my left leading to double doors and the main area of the emergency room. William steered the wheelchair in the opposite direction where an overhead sign had arrows pointing to Radiology and an exit. I felt the firm pressure of his hand on the cap.

"Head down," he ordered under his breath.

I did as I was told.

Moments later, we were heading across a walkway toward a parking area. It seemed strange and slightly surreal to be outside the hospital, with the sun shining and the sky a cloudless blue. The breeze was warm and soft against my face. I took in the manicured strips of lawn and the orderly line of trees bordering the parking area. Everything looked so normal. So safe.

Then my gaze encountered a hedge of scarlet oleanders, and I heard Allison's voice telling me about the deadly blossoms only moments before the crash. I put a hand to my eyes, as if blocking out the sight could somehow erase what had happened. Inside, I knew I would never see oleanders again without thinking of Allison.

The wheelchair left the walkway, jolting onto the asphalt of the parking area, and I bit back a small cry.

"Sorry, we're almost there," William said.

I glanced around. "You parked in the physicians' area."

"It was handy." He maneuvered the wheelchair to the passenger side of a dark brown Range Rover. After casting a quick glance around, he grabbed his car keys and wallet from the bag holding his clothes and my things. "Let's hope Dicola parks near the main entrance to Emergency. What does he look like, by the way?"

"Sloppy Joe," I said, gripping William's arm for support as he helped me out of the wheelchair.

"Come again?"

"Pudgy, balding, wrinkled brown suit."

William nodded, some of the strain leaving his face as he looked at me. "Got the picture. Okay, in you go."

He handed me the pillow to protect my right side, then leaned across me to buckle the seat belt. The flannel blanket was tossed in the back seat, along with the plastic bag. His movements were quick and precise, but not frantic, the tight line of his mouth the only evidence of his inner tension.

Leaving the wheelchair propped against the curb, he ran around the car and climbed in.

"So far so good." He shoved the key into the ignition. "Better keep that cap on and your head down until we're clear of the hospital," he cautioned when my hand moved to my head.

"Sorry."

"It's okay. You're doing fine." His hand pressed mine for the briefest of moments, then all his concentration was focused on leaving the hospital grounds.

"Dicola?" I asked after a moment, suddenly realizing I'd been holding my breath.

"No sign of him."

Neither of us spoke until the hospital was well behind us. Once we were on the freeway, William glanced at me and asked, "How're you doing?"

"All right, I guess. Can I take off the cap now?"

He smiled, reached over to pluck the cap off my head, and tossed it onto the seat behind us. Strangely, I didn't feel the need to ask him if we had made it safely, or even where we were going. His smile and the hint of a twinkle lighting his eyes was enough to tell me I was safe.

"I think I'd like to sleep now."

William nodded and said gently, "You go right ahead."

It was pain that finally woke me. A heavy, thick pain emanating from my rib cage that pounded through me with every breath. I shifted position with a moan. When I tried to open my eyes, I discovered my right eye was nearly swollen shut, and the entire side of my face felt raw and stinging.

"William?"

Through the pain, I felt the warm pressure of his hand on my leg. "Hang on a few more minutes, and we'll stop to fill that prescription."

"Where are we?"

"Gilroy."

"Where's that?"

"Roughly eighty miles south of Palo Alto."

"That far? How long have I been asleep?"

"A little over an hour."

I grimaced and adjusted the pillow at my side. "I feel awful. And I'm sure I look even worse. I can't walk into a pharmacy like this."

"I know. I've been looking for one with a drive-up window for the past ten minutes."

I bit my lip and instinctively reached for his hand, as if his warmth and strength could somehow take away my body's pain.

William gave my hand an encouraging squeeze and said, "Hang in there, Mackenzie," then swore under his breath. "You'd think there'd be at least one Walgreens in this city."

"It's okay," I mumbled, the sound of my name on his lips filtering through the pain in a way that was amazingly pleasant.

Minutes later, William pulled up beside the drive-up window of a Walgreens pharmacy. He reached into the back seat for my purse and handed it to me.

"They'll need some ID. Better get out your driver's license. And for the record, I'm Dr. Evans, your fiancé. We're on our way home from the hospital—never mind which hospital."

I handed him the license, trying to smile, but it felt more like a grimace.

The white-coated technician at the window was young, no more than her midtwenties, with straight brown hair and colorless features. She took the prescription, along with the ID, and gave me a frowning glance.

"This window is for pick-ups," she began primly.

William nodded and gave her a warm smile. "I appreciate that, but we've come straight from the hospital, and I need to get my fiancé home. Since there's no one else waiting, I'd be real grateful if you could help us out."

Even in my present state, I could see the young woman was not immune to that voice and that smile. Rosy color touched her pale cheeks as she told him, "It'll be just a few minutes."

Not ten minutes later, I was clutching a small plastic container of potent pain relief and we were on our way.

"Could we stop for some bottled water?" I asked, anxious to get the pills into my system.

William gave me a close look. "When was the last time you had something to eat?"

"I don't know. This morning, I guess, at Allison's."

"Then we need to stop and get something."

I gave a little groan of protest. "I'm not that hungry."

"Sorry. I know you're hurting, but you'll feel a lot worse if you take those pills on an empty stomach." Glancing ahead, he said, "There's an In & Out Burger on the next block. How does that sound?"

Just the thought of a hamburger and fries made my stomach cringe. Right now, nothing sounded good.

"Come on, Mackenzie," William said in a lighter tone. "No one should leave California without having an In & Out burger."

I stared at him. "Am I leaving California?"

He nodded. "As soon as possible."

"Where are we going?"

"Somewhere safe," he answered. "That's all you need to know for now."

Nine

In spite of my grumbling, I had to admit William was right. The hamburger tasted delicious, and the ice-cold Coke was pure heaven. I managed to eat half the burger and a few fries before he gave his approval to take the Percocet. Some thirty minutes later, my pain had subsided to a tolerable level, and I felt my bruised, beaten body start to relax.

We were on a freeway, heading roughly southeast. Beyond that, I had no idea where we were or where we were going. Somewhere safe, William said. That I should trust this man who was little more than a stranger seemed slightly amazing. But I did.

I adjusted the pillow at my side and shifted position, watching him as he drove. His hands on the wheel, the strong curve of his wrist meeting tanned forearms. Somehow, it was difficult to picture those strong hands rifling through law books and legalese. I couldn't quite make the image work. Nor could I see him in the courtroom, wearing a dark suit and tie. He was soft spoken like his brother, and at times I detected what might be described as a Western drawl in his voice. The man was an enigma, albeit a very attractive one. I could see a slight resemblance between him and his brother, but in most ways, they were more different than alike. Wade's sandy hair and light-blue eyes were an obvious contrast to

William's darker coloring. Wade was probably taller by an inch or so, yet William seemed stronger, tougher somehow. And while I would never diminish Wade's capabilities as a police detective, there was something easygoing, almost boyish about his manner. Not so William. Quiet confidence and rugged strength fairly oozed from those chiseled features.

William chose that moment to send me a sideways glance. "You doing okay?"

I nodded and closed my eyes before further questions could follow.

When I awoke, darkness had fallen and pain was rising inside me once again. I shifted position, feeling stiff all over, and glanced out the window at a dark desert landscape with the promising glimmer of lights in the distance.

"I . . . uh, would appreciate a rest stop."

William nodded, stretching his shoulders. "We need to stop somewhere for the night anyway. We're just about to Barstow."

"How close is 'just about'?"

He glanced at me with an understanding grin. "Five or ten minutes?"

"If you make it five, I think I'll survive."

Six minutes later we were pulling up in front of the Holiday Inn Express, and barely two minutes after that, William had registered for a room and was sprinting back to the car.

Dry desert air blew through the thin cotton gown as he helped me out of the car. The night breeze was far from cold, but I couldn't help shivering. Without a word, William took the flannel blanket from the back seat and wrapped it around my shoulders. I leaned heavily on his supporting arm as we went inside.

I gave only a passing glance to the generous-sized room with its two queen-sized beds and headed for the bathroom.

"Will you be able to manage okay?" he asked hesitantly.

I waved aside his offer of help and shut the bathroom door firmly behind me.

A few moments later my bladder and I were feeling much relieved, and I was grateful the dizziness hadn't returned. Washing my hands, I risked a furtive glance in the mirror and gasped at the sight of the pale-faced witch woman who stared back at me. The right side of my face was scraped a raw, angry red, and my eye was wreathed in a mottled mixture of purple and black. Traces of dried blood still streaked my neck and throat.

I shuddered and gripped the sides of the basin. Pain or no pain, I was getting in the shower. Now.

It was more than a bit challenging, trying to wash my hair without twisting or bending, but the fresh, herbal scent of the shampoo and the sudsy rivulets running down my face and body were more than worth the effort. I stood under the steaming spray for a good ten minutes, letting it pummel me into warm, weary submission. After toweling myself dry as best I could, I stared at the hated hospital gown hanging on the rack. There was no way I could manage doing those ties in the back. I'd just have to wear it with the ties in front. The blasted thing was practically big enough for two people. I draped another towel across my shoulders, since my hair was still damp and my energy nearly spent. Feeling infinitely cleaner, if not better, I left the bathroom to find William sitting on one of the beds, talking on his cell.

"We're fine. No problems. And Mackenzie's been a real trooper." He glanced up to give me a brief smile. "It's Wade," he said softly, but there was worry and something else in his eyes.

I moved stiffly to the other bed and sat down, watching his face and waiting.

"Yeah . . . don't worry, I will. Give me a call tomorrow morning, okay? And watch your back."

William set the cell phone on the lamp table between the beds and met my anxious look with one of quiet concern.

"Is Wade all right?" I asked.

"He's fine."

"But you told him to watch his back . . ."

William gave a short nod. "He couldn't get hold of Chief McIntire. He and other police officers from around the state are in Sacramento meeting with the governor on immigration and other issues. That means Dicola's in charge of the investigation until the chief gets back, which won't be until the day after tomorrow. Wade can't insist on getting hold of McIntire without arousing some suspicion and Dicola wanting to know why. It's a good thing we got you out of that hospital when we did." William's voice was calm and matter of fact, but his eyes were still troubled.

"Did Wade say anything about Allison?"

When he didn't answer, my heart began a hard pounding and I felt my throat tighten up. "William?"

He gave a helpless shake of his head and leaned forward to take one of my hands. "Mackenzie, I'm so sorry. Your friend didn't make it."

"No—"

"I'm sorry," he said again, "but they couldn't save her. She died in surgery."

I looked down, unable to speak, my heart hurting inside my chest, and hot tears slipping down my face.

"Wade heard about it on the news. There wasn't a lot of information given, only that there was a shooting on the Bay Shore freeway with a fatality."

"A fatality," I choked. "They make it sound so . . . so impersonal."

"Allison's name was withheld until her family can be notified," William said quietly, "but Dicola knows you're alive. And that means Sarcassian knows you're alive."

I put a hand over my mouth, trying to stifle a sob. "It–it's not fair."

"Guys like Sarcassian don't know the meaning of fair," William said, anger heating his voice. The next moment his anger shifted to concern. "You're shaking. You need to get in bed and get warm."

"I–I know, but I can't lie down. Ev–everything hurts too much."

All I could do was sit there shaking while William hurriedly got some extra blankets and pillows from the closet and arranged them into a backrest against the headboard.

"Keep this one against your side," he said, handing me one of the pillows. "Okay, easy does it now."

I closed my eyes to the pain and what he might or might not be seeing, and let him help me into bed. When I was duly covered and propped in a semi-sitting position, he leaned over me with a worried expression.

"How does that feel? Any better?"

I nodded and drew some careful breaths, feeling the shaking subside as warmth took its place.

He put a hand on my damp hair. "There's a restaurant next to the motel. Will you be okay while I get us something to eat?"

"I'm not hungry."

"I know, and I understand, but you've got to eat something. And you're probably overdue for a pain pill." He went into the bathroom and returned with a glass of water and a small tablet. "You might as well take this now. I'll be back with dinner in a few minutes."

William handed me the pill and the water, and I gratefully downed the medication. "Thank you."

"Any requests for dinner?"

I shook my head, fighting the tears that still threatened.

"I'll be back soon," he said and left.

Dinner consisted of scalding peppermint tea, a cup of chicken-noodle soup, and saltine crackers. I dutifully ate what he gave me, too tired to do otherwise, and it wasn't long before a merciful numbness set in, assisted I'm sure by the potent pain medication in my bloodstream.

William checked the late news on several channels, but there was no information about the shooting other than the details Wade had relayed earlier. Listening to the commentator toss out the bare-bone facts of the incident, I felt as if it had happened to someone else. That it couldn't be true. That the entire day must be a bad dream and Allison was still alive.

The newscaster concluded by saying there were no witnesses to the shooting, and no evidence to indicate it was gang related. It appeared to be an act of random violence.

Violent, yes, I thought, but there was nothing random about it.

William took the remote and switched off the TV. "I'm going to grab a quick shower." He pulled the scrub top over his head and tossed it onto the bed. "We'll need to be on the road first thing in the morning, so you should try to get some sleep."

I glanced up at him, feeling the shock and horror of the day fade into weary gratitude for everything this man had done. "I don't know why you're doing all this," I began, "but I want to thank you."

"No problem," he answered in an easy, offhand manner.

"But it is," I insisted. "I'm a major problem for you and Wade, and I know it. I just don't know what to do about it."

The tight line of William's mouth softened as he looked down at me. "You don't need to do anything. Just try to get some sleep," he said and switched off the lamp.

There in the darkness, I tried not to think, tried to push away reality and all that had happened. My body's pain had subsided into a tolerable ache, but the pain of knowing Allison was dead—dead because of me—refused to relinquish its hold on my mind and heart. Was it only this morning, mere hours ago, that we had laughed and talked over breakfast in her sun-filled kitchen? Laughed, talked, and made plans for the day. Images of the living Allison clashed and collided with the horror of the accident. Allison on her knees in the garden, surrounded by roses and the fragrance of living things. Allison, slumped face down on the steering wheel. The blood, and that terrible stillness.

I shuddered, trying to push the images away, to empty my mind of the guilt and aching loss, but they refused to leave. I couldn't even cry. The pain inside was too deep for tears.

I was still awake but feigning sleep when William came out of the bathroom. Through half-shut eyes, I watched his dark form move across the room and climb into bed.

"Mackenzie?"

His soft voice reached out to me through the darkness, but I kept my eyes shut and my breathing measured and slow. Sometime later, his deep, even breathing told me he was asleep.

I was awake for a long while, listening to the sounds of the night—William's steady breathing, the bleak whistle of the wind, and the distant rumble of traffic from the highway. Sleep finally came, but it brought no rest. My dreams were brutal and blood-drenched, my mind replaying nightmare images of the accident. Once more I was trapped in the crushed car, with Allison's limp body just out of reach. Staring at me through the splintered glass of the windshield was the Ogre, an ugly smile on his face. I tried to call for help, but no words came out, only meaningless moans.

The sound of my voice crying her name finally woke me, but the dream was still there, dark and deadly, pressing down on my chest. Then another voice reached my ears, and I came fully awake, panting, with cold sweat on my body.

"It's all right. I'm here."

Turning toward the voice, I felt something solid and warm against my cheek. William was beside me, one arm coming round my shoulders, the other pressing my face close to his bare chest.

"Allison," I got out. "I tried . . . I tried, but I couldn't help her . . ."

"I know you did. What happened wasn't your fault."

"It was my fault! She's dead because of me. It should have been me."

"Don't say that—"

"Why not? It's true. Allison has a family—a husband who loves her, and . . . and children. If I'd died, it wouldn't matter."

I felt his sudden stillness, then one of his hands stroking my hair. "Don't you have a family?"

I couldn't answer. Not when everything hurt so much and thoughts of my own family caused even more pain.

He was silent for a long moment, just holding me, until my breathing calmed. "It does matter," he said finally, and there was absolute assurance in his voice.

"What does?"

"Whether you live or die. Mackenzie, listen to me. I know you're hurting and blaming yourself, but what happened isn't a case of either/or. That if Allison had lived, you should die. Or that her life is more important than yours. I'm sorry your friend died. But I'm not sorry you're alive—which, as far as I'm concerned, is nothing short of a miracle. The men who killed Allison need to be stopped, and you can help. Believe me, your being alive will help."

Hearing the soft, sure sound of his voice, feeling the warmth of his chest beneath my cheek and the strength of his arms around me, the horror of the dream began to fade, and guilt's crushing hold slowly eased its grip.

"Are you okay? Can I get you anything?" he asked.

"Just . . . stay with me."

For the briefest moment, I felt the touch of his lips against my forehead. "No problem."

Ringing, jarring and insistent, brought me out of sleep. There was a moment of drowsy confusion when I wondered where I was, until I opened one eye and saw the man beside me. Consciousness, flooded with a goodly amount of self-consciousness, had me quickly adjusting the gaping hospital gown as William eased himself off the bed, switched on the light, and reached for his cell phone.

"Wade? What's up?" William stretched his shoulders and ran a hand through his tousled dark hair. His brows narrowed as he listened. Then he swore under his breath.

I straightened with a grimace. "What is it? What's happened?"

"Dicola's got the media involved," he answered tersely and reached for the TV remote. "Wade? Call me back in fifteen. If I can't get the story on cable or a local station, I'll need you to fill me in on the details. Right."

William tossed his cell phone on the bed with barely restrained anger and turned to me. "Wade says there's a van from KGO-7 news outside the police station, and Dicola's scheduled some kind of interview with reporters. If we can't pick it up here, Wade'll call us back."

I shivered and pulled the bedcovers around my shoulders, waiting in silence while William did some frustrated channel surfing, finally finding a Los Angeles-based channel that was halfway through its morning news broadcast. We listened to a few minutes of national news intermixed with commercials, and William was about to switch off the TV when the newscaster, an attractive woman with a stylish sweep of blonde hair, cut short her report of California's current budget woes with "This just in from law enforcement agencies in Santa Clara County. Police have issued an all-state bulletin for a missing person, twenty-eight-year-old Mackenzie Graham."

My jaw dropped as I saw my face filling the screen from a photo that was used with my byline for the magazine.

"Ms. Graham, who disappeared yesterday afternoon from Stanford Hospital's emergency room, was an associate of Allison Meyers, the victim of a fatal shooting on the Bayshore Freeway," the woman continued. "Palo Alto's police department has asked for the public's assistance in locating Ms. Graham, who may be suffering from a head injury and other trauma. Reporter Kevin Marcroft from KGO-7 News is live on the scene with Lieutenant Vincent Dicola."

William and I exchanged a quick look, and the camera shifted to a street scene in front of the large high rise in downtown Palo Alto. There, standing next to a spiky-haired reporter, was Sloppy Joe, his jowly face wearing an official frown of concern.

"Lieutenant Dicola, what can you tell us about Ms. Graham's disappearance?" the reporter asked.

"We have reason to believe that Ms. Graham was taken out of the hospital by a dark-haired man claiming to be her fiancé."

"Do you think there's a connection between her disappearance and the shooting death of her business associate, Allison Meyers?"

Sloppy Joe presented his best stone face to the camera. "That isn't known at this time. Naturally, we're investigating any and all leads. Our first concern is for Ms. Graham's safety and well-being."

William shook his head and muttered, "Like hell it is."

"Do you suspect any foul play connected with the woman's disappearance?" the reporter continued, pressing the angle.

"I can't comment on that," Dicola answered. "I will say it's vital we locate Ms. Graham as soon as possible."

The camera shifted from Sloppy Joe to the reporter, who announced in a bland voice, "Mackenzie Graham is five foot three, with reddish brown hair and blue eyes. Anyone having information about her disappearance or whereabouts is asked to contact their local police department or this station."

William angrily punched the remote with his thumb, turning off the TV, then reached for his cell. "Wade, it's me. Yeah . . . we got the story on a channel out of L.A. Dicola sure didn't waste any time."

I released a shaky breath as shock and fear joined my body's pain. Seeing my face, William reached out to give my shoulder a gentle squeeze before asking his brother, "How much do you think Dicola knows or suspects? Has he questioned you about Mackenzie's visit to the station?" He listened a moment, his lips tight, then gave me a nod. "No surprises there, but you need to be careful. Better go along with whatever he wants until Chief McIntire gets back. I'll call you this evening after we're settled."

"What's happened? Is Wade in trouble?" I asked after William ended the call.

"No, he's fine. Dicola had more questions about your visit to the police station and the accident, but we expected that. Wade played it innocent and safe."

In spite of William's reassurance, I was sick with worry. After getting stiffly out of bed, I made my way to the bathroom and splashed handfuls of warm water on my bruised face. I felt worse than useless. I was rapidly becoming a liability to the two men who were trying to help me. Holding on to the basin, I tried to think what to do, but my mind couldn't come up with any answers, especially when pain was demanding all my attention. I closed my eyes, clutching the sink as if it were a lifeline, and tried to concentrate on taking one breath at a time.

By the time I left the bathroom, William had shed the scrubs and was dressed in his own clothes, a look of grim determination hardening his features.

I felt a sudden stab of worry. "What else did Wade say? Is there something you're not telling me?"

William shook his head and let go a disgruntled sigh. "Mackenzie, I've already told you what Wade said. He knows what he's doing. You don't need to worry about him, so don't get all uptight."

"Stop telling me not to worry, and— and how to feel! After what's happened, I have every right to . . ." My words trailed away as I broke out in a clammy sweat and my knees began to buckle.

William was at my side in an instant, taking firm hold of my arms. "You need to lie down before you fall down," he said gruffly and steered me towards the bed.

"William, please listen to me—"

"I'll listen all you like, after you're in bed. You're white as a sheet."

"I'm fine . . . just a little shaky, that's all."

"What you need is some breakfast," he said as he helped me into bed.

I pulled the blankets around me and said crossly, "Why are you always trying to feed me?"

"Why are you always arguing?" he countered, his mouth turning up at the corners. "Anyone would think you were the attorney, not me."

I tried to think of an appropriate comeback, but my anger collapsed the moment I saw the teasing twinkle in those gray-green eyes.

"Okay. Talk." He sat down beside me on the edge of the bed. "What's bothering you?"

"What's bothering me? My picture is plastered on the morning news, the police think you're a kidnapper, and we have the whole state looking for us, and you ask what's bothering me?"

William acknowledged this with a brief shrug. "Look, I'm not trying to downplay the seriousness of the situation, but there's no point making it worse than it is."

"I'm not trying to make it worse. It's already worse! You heard what they said! Dicola and that reporter made it sound like— like I'd been kidnapped."

"I know, and that's exactly what Dicola wanted. He may be a crooked cop, but he's not stupid. And right now he's desperate. He's not only got to make it look like he's doing his job, but he's got to save face and keep Sarcassian happy. Getting the word out about your disappearance was a smart move, but it also tells me that he doesn't have a clue as to your whereabouts. And that's good news for us. What would you like for breakfast? I'm thinking an Egg McMuffin sounds pretty good, with some orange juice and hash browns."

"And I'm supposed to walk into a McDonald's looking like this?"

"No, you're supposed to sit tight and try not to worry so much," William said calmly. "I'll be back with breakfast in a few minutes."

I gave an exasperated sigh. "And then what? Someone's bound to spot us. This hospital gown is pretty hard to miss."

"I know, and that's about to change. Breakfast first, then I'll make a quick stop at the nearest Walmart to get you some clothes."

"But William—"

"No buts," he said matter-of-factly. "I was married once, about a million years ago, so I think I'm capable of picking out a few things."

I couldn't help noticing the slight bitter twist to his voice. "If you'll hand me my purse, I've got a little cash and some credit cards—"

"No credit cards. I'm not about to give Dicola any help in finding you."

"You're right. I wasn't thinking."

William's voice softened. "I'll be back soon. Don't answer the phone and don't let anyone in. Okay?"

"'Don't worry. Don't answer the phone. Don't let anyone in.' I think I've got all that. Anything else?"

"Nope. That'll do for now." He reached for his car keys and wallet then glanced at me, amusement and something else in his eyes. Standing over me, he made no move to go, his gaze steady on my face.

The intentness of that gaze brought warmth to my cheeks and I glanced down, twisting the sheets between my fingers. "I don't know how you can stand to look at me," I mumbled. "I look terrible . . . and I'm nothing but a nuisance and a burden."

"No, you're not," he said softly.

I stopped kneading the sheets and met his eyes. The amusement was gone, but not the warmth.

"You're not a burden," he said, then left, shutting the door behind him.

Ten

We had been on the road for perhaps an hour. Mile after mile of barren desert passed by, offering not even a faint promise of green, with nothing but dry washes, gray-white sand, and distant mountains, tawny brown. The sun had long since spilled its gold over the eastern mountains, and the desert was filled with light when it suddenly occurred to me that I didn't have the faintest idea where we were going. That we were heading east on Interstate 15 was obvious, but our final destination was still very much a mystery.

William and I were both too concerned about getting safely away from the motel in Barstow for any kind of discussion. After a quick breakfast, his trip to Walmart had resulted in a pair of gray sweat pants, a zip-up hoodie, and a baseball cap. All very comfortable and unobtrusively generic. My first inclination was to toss the hospital gown in the garbage with good riddance, but William wisely took it from me, along with the blue scrubs, and stuffed them both into the Walmart sack, stowing them safely out of sight in the back of his car.

There were few people about when we left our room, only a tired trucker and a young maid from housekeeping, her arms loaded with white towels. Neither one paid any attention to us, and I knew our exit had been accomplished with complete anonymity. Besides the new clothes, sunglasses helped hide the bruises on my face, and the baseball cap made my hair much less noticeable.

Now that we were safely away, the tight knot of tension inside me began to dissolve, with curiosity taking its place. Yet I found myself hesitating to ask questions, hoping William would offer that information.

The silence between us was not uncomfortable. I felt no need to make idle comments on the weather or the landscape. Breakfast and a pain pill had settled nicely, and I was blissfully relaxed, if not totally pain free. I reached into my purse for some lip gloss and applied it to my dry lips.

William's eyes left the road to give me an appraising glance and the hint of a smile as I dropped the lip gloss back into the purse.

"You look good, Mac" was all he said, but his voice and that slow smile were more than enough to raise my spirits. Far more so than Corbin Corelli's pathetic phrases about "burnished copper" and "midnight blue."

I was about to put my purse away when William gave it a sharp second glance and asked, "Do you have a cell phone?"

"Yes."

"Is it on?"

"Probably. I don't remember." I took the cell phone from my purse. "I don't have many bars, but it's on."

He gave the steering wheel a thump with this fist, made a quick check of traffic in the rearview mirror, and pulled off the freeway onto the road's shoulder.

"Can I see your phone?" he said, shoving the gearshift into park.

Mystified, I handed it to him. Without a word, William got out of the car and walked around back to open the hatch. The next thing I knew, he had come to the passenger side of the Range Rover, my cell phone in one hand and a tire iron in the other. I let out a startled gasp when he dropped the phone in the roadside gravel, gave it some crushing blows with the tire iron, and kicked the smashed remains off the highway into a patch of weeds.

He returned the tire iron to the back of the vehicle and climbed into the driver's seat. "I owe you a phone," he said.

I stared at him, mouth open, as he pulled the Range Rover back onto the freeway and accelerated. "You–you certainly do," I sputtered. "What was that all about?"

"We can't risk Sarcassian or Dicola tracking you through the GPS on your cell."

"Can they really do that?"

"It's possible, but I doubt they've had time."

William's words did little to reassure me. Seeing my worried expression, he said, "Dicola has no idea where you are, or he wouldn't have issued that all-state bulletin. Getting rid of the phone is just some added insurance."

"Was it necessary to be quite so forceful?"

William gave me a sideways glance, a smile touching his bearded mouth. "Maybe not. But thinking about what Sarcassian and Brock tried to do to you, and what they did to your friend—well, smashing something to pieces felt pretty damn good."

I shook my head, unable to keep back a grin. "I think I was wrong about something."

"What's that?"

"When I told your brother I didn't like attorneys."

William chuckled and gave me a wink. "Glad to hear it, Mac."

It wasn't long before the small town of Baker was behind us, scarcely more than a blink and brief oasis in the vast stretch of Southwest desert. Giant Joshua trees stood as shaggy sentinels along a few stretches of the highway, a welcome contrast to barren rock and dry lake beds of blistering alkali. Beckoning in the distance, shining mirages teased us with their illusive blue dance.

Morning moved into afternoon, with brief stops for lunch, gasoline, and restroom facilities. We drove past the decadent dazzle of Las Vegas without stopping, and I gave in to my body's need for sleep. When I awoke, the dull, monochrome tones of the desert were gone, replaced by colorful sandstone mesas that stood against the hard blue sky in sunset hues of vermilion, coral, and fiery reddish-orange. Rising like misty gray ghosts against the far horizon were mountains, layer after layer, peak after peak, with no end in sight.

"Where are we?" I asked, gazing about with an increasing sense of wonder.

"A couple of miles past St. George."

"St. George? Where's that?"

William glanced at me with that slow grin. "Southern Utah."

"We're in Utah?"

"We are. I own a ranch about forty miles northeast of here. It used to belong to my dad, but he had a heart attack a few years back and couldn't keep things up. I was able to buy the property, keep things in the family."

"So . . . we're going to your ranch?"

William nodded. "When Wade filled me in on your situation, there wasn't much time to come up with an elaborate plan or even get official help. We just knew we had to move fast to get you out of Sarcassian's reach. The ranch was the safest solution all the way around. It's not only two states away from California, it's also several miles from the nearest town—someplace where no one will know you." He gave me a quick glance. "I'm assuming, of course, that you don't have any long-lost relatives or close friends living in La Verkin or Rockville, Utah."

I smiled and shook my head. "My parents and an older brother live back East—Chicago and Philadelphia."

"That's good."

I hesitated a moment, then said, "I've been thinking about that news report with my picture. Do you think it made any TV stations outside of California?"

"I doubt it. The story's not something that would make national news." William gave me a close look. "But if you're concerned about your family finding out you're missing, I'm afraid that's pretty much a given. If not the police, then some guy working for Sarcassian will probably contact them, trying to find out where you are."

"Do you think they'll be in any danger?"

William shook his head and said firmly, "No, I don't. So don't go borrowing any more trouble than we already have."

I nodded and carefully shifted position, adjusting the pillow at my side. "This ranch of yours, does anyone else live there?"

"Nope. My folks have a little place in La Verkin, a few miles away." He gave me a sideways glance. "You're going to need some help for a few days, and that means I'll have to tell my folks pretty much what's happened. You can trust them not to say anything. And Mom will make sure you have what you need—meals and such."

"How long do you think I'll need to—"

"Stay at the ranch?" he finished. "It's hard to say. Part of that depends on Chief McIntire and what he decides to do when Wade tells him about Dicola and those pictures you took."

"Speaking of the pictures, I'm not trying to borrow trouble when I say I can't help worrying about something."

"What's that?"

"If it was a mistake to give Wade the memory card. I hate to think what might happen if Dicola or someone else finds out he has it."

William made no comment to this, and I couldn't see so much as a trace of worry on his face. All his concentration was seemingly focused on the road ahead and our passage through a rocky canyon where shrubby junipers clung precariously to the sides of steep sandstone cliffs.

I remained silent while he passed a large semi truck struggling up the grade, then burst out with "Aren't you concerned at all? Those pictures could put your brother in real danger!"

"They could," William agreed. "But Wade doesn't have the memory card. I do."

"You do?" I croaked.

"Who better than Wade's attorney to keep it safe? And for the record, my feelings about those pictures are the same as yours. I didn't like the idea of Wade carrying around a potentially lethal piece of evidence. Until we know more about what's going on and who's involved, that memory card is going to be locked up in the safe at my office."

I looked at him with sheer amazement, feeling a huge heap of worry lifted off my shoulders. "Thank you, William."

"You're welcome."

I settled back against the seat with a sigh and allowed myself to take in the stark beauty of our surroundings. Coral cliffs, juniper-dotted hills, and rising behind the cliffs, more mountains, ruggedly aloof and mysterious.

"This is the most amazing country," I said. "I've never seen anything like it."

"It is pretty spectacular. When you're feeling better I'll have to take you over to Silver Reef. My partner and I have a law office there—it's a fascinating old ghost town."

"You have your law office in a ghost town?"

He chuckled at my astonished look. "Sort of makes you wonder who my clients might be, doesn't it? Actually, it's my partner's office more than mine. He lives in the new section of Silver Reef. The place is a real anachronism. Geologically speaking, the experts believed it was impossible to find silver in sandstone, but Silver Reef proved them wrong. In its heyday, the mines were pulling out tons of it."

"What happened? Why is it a ghost town?"

"In the late 1880s, the price of silver fell faster than the stock market. That and when most of the mines stopped producing forced people to pull up stakes and move away. There's nothing much left of the town now. Ruins mostly. The old Wells Fargo building is still there. It's been turned into a museum and an art gallery. And there's a subdivision of new homes north of the old town. A lot of the owners, like my partner, are transplants from California—folks looking for a piece of the Old West and an escape from suburbia, but with all their creature comforts. The homes are an interesting mix, everything from Spanish haciendas and French chateaus to modern mansions." William glanced at me with a lift of his dark brows. "Who knows? With the kind of work you do for the magazine, you might find some good ideas for an article."

His words brought a sharp injection of pain into what had been a pleasant conversation. The article. Allison. Storybook homes. All the fanciful plans and ideas collided with grim reality, then collapsed into the empty grayness of grief. I shut my eyes, feeling the heavy return of guilt and loss.

The warm pressure of William's hand made its way past the hurt, his strong fingers enfolding mine. "I'm sorry. I didn't mean to be insensitive."

I just nodded, not trusting myself to speak past the lump in my throat.

"Tell me about Allison," he went on. "How long did you know her?"

"Not long."

"What was she like?"

He gave my hand an encouraging squeeze, and I began to find the words. Little things—her cleverness and brisk business self, along with the glimpse I'd had of her personal life, her home and family. Even though there was pain in the telling, it also brought a kind of release, changing the hard ball of hurt inside me to a softer, more bearable shape of sadness. Tears fell, but they were cleansing, not bitter.

Strangely, along with the death of a friend, I think I was also mourning the loss of the fairy tale and the desecration of the enchanted seaside cottage. The door to that storybook domain was forever shut to me now, and with it, the quaint charms of Carmel and coastal California. All these had been left behind, exchanged for a harsh landscape of red rock and mountainous desert. Yet I was not alone in this strange new journey.

William released my hand and turned right, leaving the interstate to head east across rolling hills of sagebrush. "It won't be long now," he said with a smile. "Another half hour or so and we'll be at Hearth Fires."

"Hearth Fires?"

"That's the name my great-grandparents gave to the homestead when they first came to southern Utah."

"I like it. Is there a story behind the name?"

"There is," William said, "but it'll keep till another time."

Another time. I smiled and contented myself with the promise in his words.

It was late afternoon, and the surrounding hills and valleys were drenched in the slanting gold light that photographers fondly dub "the golden hour." Gold was everywhere. In shorn fields where bales of alfalfa were drying into hay. In the sunflowers growing along the roadside, and trembling leaves of aspens on the far hillsides. Even the rocks themselves. The setting sun seemed to infuse its light into their stony surfaces, bringing the cliffs and canyons alive with jeweled color. Amber and amethyst. Ruby and topaz. I gazed from side to side in pure wonder at the startling richness of color in this rugged landscape.

Soon the towns of Hurricane and La Verkin were behind us, the ephemeral presence of chain stores and gas stations a weak contrast against the desert's ageless existence. A few miles past La Verkin, the highway narrowed to two lanes of rusty-red asphalt. Barren lava fields pitted the dry landscape on our left, while a strip of rangeland with the curving blue ribbon of a river spread out to the right. Much of the land was rocky and dry, with gray-green sage the only vegetation hardy enough to eke out an existence. But where there was water, either from the river or man-made irrigation, one saw life-giving green. Here, grassy pastures supported herds of cattle and horses, and green bands of willows and ancient cottonwoods lined the stream banks.

"What kind of cows are those?" I asked as we drove by a fenced pasture where some two dozen or more animals were grazing, their coats a glossy black.

"Black Angus," William said. "And most of them are steers, not cows," he added with a crooked grin.

"Steers or cows, they really are beautiful. Like black satin against green velvet."

He glanced at me with an indulgent smile. "Nice" was all he said, but it was more than enough to spark a pleasant warmth inside me.

A few miles farther brought us to the town of Rockville, which was little more than a mile-long stretch of homes and stores tucked between the canyon's steep sides. Rising straight ahead, like ancient citadels of the gods, were massive sandstone cliffs, their rocky pinnacles and towers a flaming orange in the late-afternoon light.

"What is this place?" I murmured.

William caught my glance and nodded. "The entrance to Zion National Park is just a few miles up the road. Those cliffs you're seeing are all part of the park. The highest peak off to your left is Mount Kinesava."

"Amazing."

The presence of those giant citadels completely dwarfed the little town and captured all my attention until William turned right off the main highway to take a narrow road heading south. He slowed the Range Rover as we approached an old iron trestle bridge that spanned a small river. The bridge was barely wide enough to allow one-way traffic, but looked sturdy enough. A mile or so farther on, the road curved west, turning and twisting a rough passage between barren sandstone ridges on our left and the verdant fields and tree-lined river to the right.

As we approached a large, fenced pasture, I saw a dozen or more animals whose gender needed no clarification. The huge bulls, some black, others brown, and a few with mottled gray-and-white coloring, were grazing idly, paying little or no attention to us. William slowed the vehicle to maneuver around a pothole, and one of the beasts, a dirty gray with black rings around both eyes, lifted his head to give us an unflinching stare.

"Is that fence strong enough to keep them in?" I asked, looking at the flimsy strings of wire attached to worn wooden posts. William's answer of "Most of the time" was not at all reassuring.

"There've been a few times when one of them will get out," he admitted. "These are all rodeo bulls. The guy who owns them leases the pasture from me. He also has a couple of dozen horses that are used for bronc riding."

"So this is all your land?"

"It is," he answered, a smile touching his mouth as he glanced at the expanse of fields and pastures.

"I probably ought to give you fair warning," he said as we continued down the road. "The place isn't exactly ready for company. I went to California a week ago to take care of some business, as well as visiting Wade, so there won't be much food in the refrigerator. Tonight's dinner might be just a can of chili, but I'll drive in to town tomorrow to pick up some groceries and whatever else you need."

"It's all right. I don't want you to go to a lot of trouble." I glanced away, hating the fact that I was a burden to this man.

William slowed the Range Rover and turned down a dirt lane whose roughness played havoc with my injured side, no matter how I tried to brace myself.

"Sorry about that." He swerved to avoid another pothole. "We're almost there."

I grimaced and glanced ahead to see a stucco-and-stone house perhaps a hundred yards ahead, with a windbreak of sheltering cottonwoods. The home was reminiscent of those Craftsman-style bungalows ordered from Sears & Roebuck catalogs around the turn of the century, with its Prairie-style windows, expansive front porch, and large dormer window on the second floor. The front of the home faced east, with a stone chimney climbing its north side. Fruit trees and flower gardens adorned the sunny south side of the yard, while a short distance away, I glimpsed a barn and several corrals, all made of graying timber. Parked next to the house in the shade of the cottonwoods were two trucks, one a battered brown pickup, the other much newer and a shiny black.

"Looks like you'll be meeting my folks sooner rather than later," William said. "That's Dad's truck parked next to mine. He probably came out to check on the horses or some other excuse." Shaking his head, William added wryly, "It's been nearly three years since he and Mom moved to town, but Dad still has trouble letting go of the place. I can't say I blame him. This ranch has been Dad's life for over seventy years."

William parked beside the brown pickup, switched off the ignition, and came around to help me out of the vehicle. The long day's drive combined with my injuries made even the smallest movement a challenge, and I leaned heavily on his arm.

He ignored the concrete walkway leading to the front of the house in favor of a worn, grassy path that would take us to a side entrance. We hadn't gone more than a few steps when the screen door opened and a pleasant-faced woman in her late sixties or early seventies came out, wiping her hands on a dish towel. Short hair more gray than brown framed her pleasant face, but she had the youthful smile of a woman half her age. A pair of denim pants and a bright cotton blouse revealed a figure that was comfortably rounded, rather than matronly. She was followed by a man of medium height and build whose ambling gait was evidence he'd probably spent a good portion of his life on horseback. His tanned, rugged features were an attractive contrast to white hair that was still thick and wavy. Dressed in worn jeans, a plaid shirt, and a leather vest, he presented the perfect image of a gentleman cowboy.

"Wade called and let us know you'd be coming," the woman said, meeting us with a smile.

William kissed his mother on the cheek and sent a grateful look his father's way, before turning to me. "Mom, Dad, I'd like you to meet Mackenzie Jones."

I gave William a surprised glance at the sudden change of surname, but the silent message in his eyes prevented any comment I might have made.

"Mackenzie, I'm so glad to meet you," Mrs. Evans said warmly. "You can call me Mom or Jenny, whatever feels comfortable. I'm sure you must be exhausted after that long drive and . . . well, everything. Come on inside and I'll show you where you can freshen up. I hope you're hungry because I've got supper keeping warm on the stove."

"You couldn't have given us better news," William said. "I was just trying to prepare Mackenzie for a can of beans."

"Oh, I think we can do better than that," his mother told him with a chuckle.

William's father held the screen door open for his wife and gave me a courteous nod. "Tom Evans," he said, offering his hand.

"Mr. Evans."

"Tom," he corrected firmly. "Wade told us you've been havin' a pretty rough time," he added, neatly eliminating the need for explanations. I saw kindness and wisdom in the gray-green eyes that mirrored William's. Taking my hand in his big, calloused paw, he said, "Welcome to Hearth Fires."

I smiled my thanks and felt the warmth of William's supporting arm come around my shoulders as we stepped inside.

Eleven

It was a wonderful meal with ample helpings of home-cooked food and human kindness. I couldn't remember a time when I'd felt so surrounded by warmth and caring. I'm not sure what I'd expected, but one would think my arrival might be met with a degree of reservation, even suspicion, unannounced as it was and carrying the troublesome baggage of potential danger. Instead, I was made to feel as if my coming were a long-anticipated event worthy of celebration.

The four of us sat around a big oak table in a kitchen that held remnants of decades past, in spite of its modern amenities. An old cast-iron stove held a place of honor in one corner of the room, although its main purpose now was to display vintage crockery and potted plants. The tall wooden cupboards had to be original to the house, as was the shallow enamel sink with its old-fashioned faucet and hardware. The modern additions of a microwave and built-in ovens almost seemed like anachronisms in this homey ranch kitchen.

Jenny Evans dished out lavish portions of Swiss steak swimming in gravy, accompanied by red potatoes cooked in their skins. There were green beans, fresh from the garden, and sliced tomatoes that had never seen the inside of a store. Homemade bread slathered with butter and tangy apricot jam tasted more divine to me than the finest gourmet fare.

When I complimented Jenny on the jam, she said with pleasure, "It was a good year for apricots. Occasionally we'll get a late frost that kills the whole crop. But not this year. My daughters and I bottled eighty quarts, besides making six batches of jam."

I stared at William's mother in amazement, thinking of the work involved. "You bottle your own fruit?" I said, remembering Allison's laughing comment about peaches straight from Costco.

Jenny nodded. "But I don't do nearly as much now as when my children were small. Would you like another helping of steak?"

"No thank you, but it really is delicious," I assured her. "I've never tasted beef quite like it."

"That's because it's elk," William informed me. "Wade and I were lucky enough to get permits last year. You've never had elk before?"

"Apparently not," I said, enjoying the warmth of his smile. Before I knew it, his mother had dished a second helping onto my plate.

There was no discussion of the previous day's events during dinner. Jenny Evans was busy making sure everyone had enough to eat, as father and son shared a few local doings and legal tidbits. Despite some nagging pain and stiffness, I was grateful just to sit with a pillow at my side, savoring the meal and the men's conversation, along with a few insertions of Jenny's motherly concern.

"I've got some salve at home that'll help heal those scrapes and bruises on your face," she said. "I'll be sure and bring it by tomorrow."

"Thank you."

"Is your eye very painful?"

"Not really. I'm sure it looks a lot worse than it feels."

"Vern Jessup's mule jumped the fence and took off again," Tom Evans told his son. "You've never seen such a sociable animal. The mule wasn't trying to run away. Old Oscar just loves to go visiting.

Vern found him two miles down the road paying a social call to Earl Hansen's new filly."

William chuckled at this as his father went on, "Speaking of jumping the fence, what's happening with that latest case of yours? The one with the dispute over the buffalo and the dude ranch?"

"Nothing's been settled yet," William answered. "The hearing isn't scheduled until next month."

I gave him a curious glance. "You have a case about buffalo and a dude ranch?"

He leaned back in his chair and fixed me with that slow, easy smile of his. "I guess I forgot to mention it. I don't deal in criminal law. My practice handles property disputes and real estate. One of my clients owns a dude and cattle ranch a few miles outside Kanab. The man who bought the acreage next to his wants to turn it into a kind of a nature preserve for bison, or buffalo as we call them."

"And is that a problem?"

"It has the potential to cause a lot of problems," William said. "Buffalo can run faster than most horses and they can clear a six-foot fence without thinking twice. The owner would have to construct special fencing to keep them in, and even that might not be enough. Buffalo are notorious for going anywhere they want."

"Sort of like Vern Jessup's mule," Tom Evans filled in dryly.

William and his mother burst out laughing, and holding my side, I couldn't help joining in.

After dinner, while Jenny cleared the table and put away the food, William led me into the living room and insisted I rest in a big leather recliner while he and his father discussed more serious matters.

"How much did Wade tell you?" he asked his father.

"Pretty much everything. I haven't told your mother all the details, though. No sense getting her all worried about Wade." Glancing at me, he said with simple honesty, "I'm real sorry about your friend. That's a terrible thing to happen."

"Yes, it is."

"You and Wade need to get some high-powered help with this," Tom advised. "The whole thing sounds too big—not to mention too dangerous—for you to try and handle yourselves."

William nodded. "Wade's going to talk to Chief McIntire tomorrow—without Dicola's knowledge, of course. I'd better give Wade a call now, let him know everything's okay on this end."

"While you do that, I'll go see if your mother needs a hand." After giving me a courtly nod, Tom headed for the kitchen.

William reached for the cell phone at his belt, and as anxious as I was to know about the day's events, I suddenly found myself feeling like the proverbial third wheel and very much in the way.

In the middle of punching in Wade's number, William stopped and glanced up at me. It was almost as if he could read my thoughts. "Why don't we go in my office where I can use the speaker phone. You need to know what's happening as much as I do."

In years past, William's office had probably been the main-floor bedroom. Now it had bookcases filling one wall, a handsome L-shaped computer desk and filing cabinets on another, two brown leather chairs, and a strong Western flavor. Southwest prints hung on the walls, and on the desk was a stunning bronze sculpture of an Indian brave on horseback. William settled me in one of the chairs, took another for himself, then called Wade.

"Hi, it's me. Our lovely friend is here and I've got you on speaker phone. Is it safe for you to talk?" William sent a smile my way, and I made a brief and completely futile attempt to convince myself that the sudden warmth rising inside me was the effect of the pain pill I'd taken with dinner, rather than something far more potent.

"I just got back to my apartment, so we're good," Wade said. "Mackenzie, how are you doing? Is my brother behaving himself?"

Just hearing the calm steadiness of Wade's voice was infinitely reassuring. "I'm fine," I told him, "and William is—well, he's been very kind . . ." I trailed off, thinking that had to be one of the most pathetic answers on record.

"I appreciate you calling the folks and filling them in," William went on, hopefully attributing my lack of words to fatigue and a long day on the road. "That saved a lot of explanations on this end. Now tell me about your day."

"Like I said before, Dicola's pretty much running the show until the chief gets back," Wade said. "And let me tell you, the lieutenant's pretty uptight."

"Do you think he suspects you know more than you're telling?" William asked.

"I don't think so. But he had more questions about Mackenzie's visit to the station. Wanted to know why her car was left in the parking lot, and why I drove her to the Meyers' home."

William frowned at this and met my eyes. "So what did you tell him?"

"Just that she was nervous about being followed and too afraid to drive anywhere on her own. I told Dicola that I thought she was overreacting because of the break-in, but figured it would be okay to drive her to her boss's house, since I was headed in the same general direction."

"Sounds reasonable. Did he buy that?"

"I think so. He's read my report and accepted my explanation of why Mackenzie came to the station. As far as Dicola's concerned, the last time I saw her was when I dropped her off at the Meyers' place. Relax, Will. I've covered my bases. Besides, the lieutenant's got his hands full trying to follow the lead of the unknown fiancé who spirited Mackenzie out of the hospital."

"Wade, please be careful," I put in, feeling a chill of unease at the casual way he was discussing something that could easily become very dangerous.

"No worries," he told me cheerfully. "Especially now that you're safe."

"Mackenzie's right," William said, his expression sober. "Dicola's got a lot to lose, so keep a low profile, little brother. Do you know yet when the chief will be back in the office?"

"Probably sometime tomorrow afternoon."

"Try to stay out of Dicola's way until then," William cautioned. "Let him run the show, as you said. And keep your eyes open. What about the all-state bulletin? Does Dicola have any leads that you know of?"

"No, but he has traced the prescription to that Walgreens in Gilroy. The girl at the pharmacy gave him a detailed description of you, right down to the color of your eyes and the fact that you were wearing hospital scrubs. Her description of Mackenzie was pretty sketchy, with only a few details." Wade paused, then added dryly, "Pretty obvious what she was interested in."

William's tanned cheeks turned a shade ruddier and he said brusquely, "What about my car?"

"She had no idea what the make or model was, but she thought the color might be black or brown or maybe dark blue. Like I said, it's not hard to figure where her attention was."

"Well, that's one thing in our favor," William said, ignoring his brother's teasing comment. "Check back with me tomorrow night. Sooner, if you think there's a problem or anything we should know."

"Will do. See you, Mackenzie."

"Bye, Wade."

A frown narrowed William's brows as he hung up, and there was no mistaking the tightness of his mouth.

"What Wade told us—it is fairly good news, isn't it?" I asked.

"For the most part. I knew it wouldn't take Dicola long to trace the prescription."

"But something's worrying you."

William released a tense breath. "Not so much worrying as wondering what Dicola's next move will be. The pressure's on, that's for sure." He stood and offered me his hand, helping me to my feet. "Come on. It's been a long day and you're looking pretty beat."

"I don't know why I should be. I feel like I've slept more than half the day."

"After what you've been through, you need the rest. Doctor's orders."

We returned to the living room to find William's mother putting sheets and a blanket on the leather recliner.

"For tonight, I think you'll be more comfortable sleeping here, rather than one of the bedrooms upstairs," she told me. "William had some broken ribs a few years back," she added, sharing a knowing look with her son. "And if I remember right, going up and down those stairs caused you a lot of unnecessary grief."

"It did at that."

"Sleeping in the recliner will be just fine," I said, wondering how he broke his ribs.

Jenny fluffed a pillow and put it on the recliner. "Well, Tom and I better be heading home. I'll be back tomorrow around lunchtime with some groceries and a few things for you to wear. I just need you to write down your sizes for me. Wade said you had to leave all your clothes and belongings in California."

"Yes, I did, but you've already done so much—"

"Nonsense. It'll give me a good excuse to go shopping," Jenny said matter-of-factly, handing me a small notebook and pencil.

I sank down on the recliner, too tired to argue, and jotted down my sizes.

"Where's Dad?" William asked his mother.

"Probably out waiting for me in the car. You know your father. He gets restless if he has to sit in one place for too long."

I gave her the notebook and pencil, along with a weary smile. "Thank you for . . . for everything."

"You're welcome, dear. You get a good night's sleep now, and I'll see you in the morning." She turned to William, gave him a quick hug, and said in a whisper impossible not to hear, "You behave yourself, Son. Remember, I've raised you to be a gentleman."

Jenny gave me a parting wink as William took her by the arm with a firm "Good night, Mom," and steered her towards the kitchen.

I leaned back against the recliner with a sigh, wiggled my feet out of my shoes, and closed my eyes. The pain pill I'd taken with dinner was having a blissful effect, and I felt my mind, as well as my weary body, start to relax.

Sitting there in the quiet living room with its homey blend of old and new, I found my thoughts reflecting on the Evans family—their boundless kindness, along with the little courtesies. Jenny's teasing comment held more than a grain of truth. Even in the short time I'd known William, everything he said and did told me that he really had been raised to be a gentleman.

Perhaps it wasn't entirely fair, but comparisons between Jenny Evans and my own mother also came to mind. Jenny's selfless concern for others and her desire to please were a complete contrast to the way my mother's needs and wishes often took precedence over the needs of others.

I heard the throaty sound of a truck's engine starting up, then the crunch of tires moving over rough gravel to diminish in the night. An open window in the living room brought with it a night breeze scented faintly with hay. The silence was stunning and foreign, almost frightening in its scope.

My heart began a nervous little dance as I heard the back door slam, then William's footsteps moving through the kitchen to the hall. When he took the stairs to the second floor without coming into the living room, something inside me deflated like a tire with a puncture. I listened to the creak of floorboards overhead as he moved about. Wasn't he even going to say good night? I felt suddenly bereft, then cross that it should matter.

I clutched the arm of the recliner and stood with a grimace, needing a moment to deal with the pain before heading to the bathroom. I was too stiff and frustrated to do more than wash my face and run a comb through my hair. Holding a warm washcloth against my bruised cheek, I struggled with tumbled thoughts and emotions. I had absolutely no reason to be upset. The man had driven across two states, taken me to his home, and put his own life on hold just to help me. What more was I expecting, for pity's sake?

I drew a long breath and gingerly toweled my face. The fact that William hadn't bothered to say good night wasn't the real problem, only an uncomfortable reminder of how alone I was—in a strange place and a strange house, with the shadows of yesterday's terror pressing close around me. My logical mind knew I was safe—that Dicola and Brock and the pit bull Sarcassian had no idea where I was—but somehow, logical or not, my mind couldn't rid itself of those lingering shadows. Shadows that crept quietly into my thoughts, smothering the reason that was so easily accepted in daylight hours.

I'm safe, I told myself. And while William might be upstairs rather than nearby, he was at least within shouting distance. Armed with this assurance, I left the bathroom and made my way down the narrow hall to the living room where lamps were still burning.

My breath caught in my throat at the sight of William, in a T-shirt and pajama bottoms, making up a bed on the sofa next to the recliner. He straightened up and said simply, "In case you need something, or have any problems during the night, I thought it'd be better if I was close by."

All I could do was nod, my fears melting away in the warmth of his smile.

"Oh, and in case you'd like something other than that hoodie to sleep in, I brought you this."

"This" was the matching top to his pajama bottoms. I took it from him with a little smile. "Thank you."

"Need any help?" he asked with a lift of his brows.

"No thank you," I said sedately and made my way back to the bathroom.

I removed the hoodie and wriggled out of the sweat pants, then hung them both from a hook on the bathroom door. The pajama top was soft cotton, at least three sizes too big and smelled faintly of William's aftershave. I buttoned the front, reluctant to put the sweats back on. The night was warm and the pajama top reached almost to my knees. There was no need for modesty and comfort to be at odds.

When I returned to the living room, William was just finishing spreading out a blanket for his bed on the couch. He straightened up and glanced my way, and I had the pleasure of seeing his bearded jaw drop very nicely.

"Thanks for the pajama top," I said. "It's too warm a night for sweat pants and a hoodie."

William blew out a small breath and gave me an approving glance. "Much too warm," he agreed, his voice a shade huskier than usual. "Is there anything you need before I turn out the lights?"

"No thanks."

I eased myself onto the recliner by degrees, then pulled the cool softness of the sheet and light blanket over my legs, while William stood beside the sofa, still looking slightly dumbfounded.

"You can turn the light off now," I said.

"What? Oh, right."

In the ensuing darkness, I heard him blow out another breath. It seemed to take an inordinately long time before he was sufficiently settled.

Smiling to myself in the darkness, I waited until his restlessness had subsided before asking, "How did you break your ribs?"

"I was trying to break a horse, and he ended up breaking me," William said with a chuckle. "I was fourteen or fifteen at the time, and dumb enough to think I could teach that horse a thing or two, but it ended up the other way around."

Comforting silence settled around us. I shut my eyes and released a small sigh. There was no way fear's terrifying shadows could stay in the same room with Will Evans' strong presence.

Close by, his soft voice brushed the darkness. "Good night, Mac."

"Good night, William."

Twelve

When I awoke, sunlight warmed the walls of the room, and William was gone. I lay still for a moment, looking at the rumpled sheets and blankets on the couch and listening for some hint of his presence, but the house was silent. Gingerly, I eased myself off the recliner as pain and stiffness added their own potent greeting to the day. After a brief wash, and exchanging William's pajama top for the hoodie and sweat pants, I ventured into the kitchen, where the pungent smell of coffee lingered. Something acrid and slightly burnt lingered as well.

I smiled and picked up a note that was propped on the kitchen table beside a plate with two slices of near-blackened toast.

Good morning. There's orange juice in the fridge and coffee in the pot, but not much else. I'm outside, seeing to the horses. Sorry about the toast. I would have made more, but we're out of bread.

Will

Still smiling, I poured myself a glass of juice and crunched my way through a piece of toast, trying to convince myself that the pleasant warmth inside me was simply a response to William's thoughtfulness, nothing more.

I took my dishes to the sink, and from a partially open window felt the coolness of the morning breeze. Breathing in its freshness, I heard the unmistakable whinny of a horse. The sound drew me outside like a magnet.

Stiffness and pain were put aside as I embraced the miracle of the morning. Sounds, sights, and smells that were utterly unfamiliar to my urban senses offered a peaceful greeting. The dry crispness of the air, mellow sunlight on autumn fields, the warbling song of a meadowlark on a nearby fence post, even the breeze seemed to whisper peace, with the old house behind me offering its shelter and safety. I breathed it all in, wrapped the home's sturdy refuge around me like a garment, and offered a silent prayer of thanks.

I made my way across the back lawn, past some clotheslines and a flower garden where old-fashioned hollyhocks and sturdy zinnias were soaking up the sun, and headed toward the barn and corrals. A glossy brown horse pricked up its ears at my approach, but the barn appeared to be empty, and there was no sight of William.

Glancing around, I spied a worn path that led away from the corrals toward the belt of trees that hid the river from view. I had a sudden longing to explore the path and the river, but the pain in my ribs and shoulder was enough to discourage a lengthy walk. My exploration of the ranch would have to wait, yet I was reluctant to trade the freshness of the morning for the confines of the house. Leaning against the gray timbers of the corral, I let my glance wander instead, across the expanse of fields and pastures to the winding road we had traveled last night, and the rocky terrain to the south.

A rhythmic sound over my left shoulder had me turning toward the eastern fields, where I spotted a man on horseback. The rider must have seen me almost the same moment, because he urged the horse from its easy pace into a gallop.

It could have been a scene straight out of an old Western movie, where the cowboy hero rides up on his white horse, with his white hat and jingling spurs. The fact that the horse was a creamy tan with a black mane and tail, and William's cowboy hat was brown, did nothing to lessen my enjoyment of the moment. He rode well, with the ease of years in the saddle, and his horse gathered up the distance in long, easy strides.

Then, unbidden, a page from my past suddenly materialized in my mind, and I saw Todd driving up to my parents' home to show off his new red sports car. His arrival was accompanied by several honks on the horn and loud *vroom*s of the car's powerful engine. I could still see the way he caressed the steering wheel like a lover and leaned back against the leather seats, waiting, no, *expecting* me to favor him and the car with fawning adulation. And it wasn't difficult to give Todd the reaction he wanted. It was a beautiful car. He was a very attractive man. Together, they made a lovely couple.

Quite honestly, my response to Todd's macho entrance with his new sports car was nothing compared to the near primal stirrings I experienced as William drew closer. Watching him, I felt a queer tightening in the region of my stomach, and a sensual shiver ran up my spine. His white T-shirt clung to his muscular frame, and there was a fine glaze of sweat on his tanned neck and arms.

I blew out a shaky breath as William reined in the horse beside the corral and dismounted in an easy, fluid motion.

"Mornin'." The smile he gave me warmed his eyes as well as my cheeks.

"Good morning."

"How are you feeling?"

"Stiff, but better than yesterday."

"That's good."

After what seemed like an endless moment of just standing and staring, I turned my attention to the horse. "Your horse is beautiful. Will he mind if I pet him?"

"He'd be a fool if he did," William said and held the horse's bridle. "Go right ahead."

I put out a tentative hand, feeling a little nervous at the animal's nearness and size. "What's his name?"

"Strider."

"Oh . . . like *The Lord of the Rings*?"

Again that slow grin and those attractive creases in the corners of William's eyes. "Nope. With all due respect to Tolkien, Strider got his name because of his long legs and big stride. I've had him since he was a colt, and the name just seemed to fit."

I laughed and stroked the side of the horse's neck.

"If you like, when you're feeling up to it, we could go for a ride," William said. "I've got a pretty little chestnut mare that's almost the color of your hair. I think you two would get along real well."

"I'd like that very much," I said, feeling a return of that treacherous glow in the pit of my stomach. "But you need to know, I've never been on a horse in my life. Not even a pony ride at the fair."

William shrugged this aside. "No problem. I have a feeling you'll do just fine, but there's no rush. Whenever you're ready, just let me know."

While he unsaddled the horse, I said, "That sounds as if you think I'm going to be, well, staying here for a while."

William swung the saddle over a rail and led the horse into the corral before answering. After shutting the gate, he turned to face me. "I have no idea how long you'll need to be here. At the least, I'd say it'll be several days—maybe even a week or two." He paused, his gray-green eyes searching mine. "Do you mind?"

William's look and the question were equally disconcerting.

"I feel like I should be asking you that question," I said. "You're the one whose life has been totally disrupted because of me." I gave the rocks and dirt at my feet some serious attention, all the while feeling the steadiness of his gaze.

"Then go ahead and ask."

"What?"

"Ask me if I mind," he said softly, a smile playing around his mouth.

This time I couldn't look away. "Do you . . . mind?" I got out in a small voice.

William's smile deepened and he touched a hand to his hat in an easy gesture. "Let's just say I'd be real disappointed if we didn't have that horseback ride." He took my arm and we began walking back to the house.

"I need to drive in to Silver Reef sometime this morning," he said. "I've been gone close to a week, and my partner probably has a small mountain of work waiting." William gave me a sideways glance. "Will you be okay? Mom and Dad should be here around midmorning, so you won't be alone."

"I'll be fine," I assured him. *Except for the fact that I feel basically useless and completely unattractive.*

Those feelings escalated even more when William came downstairs after a quick shower and change of clothes. I was in my customary seat on the recliner, thumbing through the pages of *Western Horseman* magazine as he entered the living room. Except for his cowboy boots, the rugged rancher was gone and the confident attorney had taken his place, smelling completely wonderful and wearing a dark, pinstriped suit with a crisp cotton shirt. And here I was with a black eye, a bruised face, and my generic uniform of hoodie and sweats. Would this man ever see me looking anything less than terrible?

William gave me a brief smile and headed for his office, returning moments later, briefcase in hand. "I should be back sometime this afternoon. Is there anything you need before I go?"

"Not a thing," I answered in the most cheerful voice I could muster.

"I doubt anyone will call, but if the phone should ring, it'd be best if you didn't answer."

"I understand. I assumed the same rules would apply."

"Rules?"

"'Don't answer the phone, don't let anyone in, and try not to worry.'"

William's mouth twitched and he gave an approving nod. "Except for me, of course. See you this afternoon."

Tom and Jenny Evans arrived shortly before noon, arms loaded with groceries, and what William's mother described as "a few little things to tide you over." As promised, she also brought her wonder salve for my face. This was thick, greasy, and smelled suspiciously of cows, but would, she assured me, heal my face better than anything else on the planet. I reserved judgment on the smelly stuff and allowed her to administer a healthy dose to my scrapes and bruises.

Opening the sacks, I discovered that Jenny's idea of a "few little things" included an assortment of toiletries, a nightgown and underthings, a pair of jeans, some cotton capris, and two blouses. There was even a sturdy pair of walking shoes and half a dozen pairs of socks.

"This is wonderful, but it's far too much," I said, holding up a soft cotton shirt in apple green. "If you'll give me the receipts, I'll be glad to reimburse you."

"Don't you worry about it," she told me with a shake of her head. "We can take care of that later. I thought about getting you a couple of T-shirts, but figured it might be too uncomfortable having to pull something over your head."

I nodded my agreement, then picked up a bottle of mango-mandarin body wash and unscrewed the lid. "Mmm, very exotic."

"I couldn't decide between that one and the raspberry-vanilla bubble bath," she confessed, "so I bought them both."

"What's all this about mangos and raspberries?" Tom Evans asked, coming into the living room. "Sounds kind of fancy, if that's what we're havin' for lunch."

"Egg-salad sandwiches is more like it," his wife said with a laugh. "Could you start peeling the eggs, Tom? I want to put some more of my salve on Mackenzie's face, then I'll be out to help you."

"Sure thing, babe."

Jenny Evans turned back to me, a little frown of concern creasing the pleasant features of her face. "Are you all right, dear? Sometimes the salve might sting a little, at first."

I shook my head, blinking furiously at the sudden tears that filled my eyes. "It's not the salve—it's just . . . so much kindness."

She said nothing, just reached out to pat my hand.

William's parents left shortly after lunch, with Jenny giving me parting instructions to have a nice long nap and be sure to call if I needed anything. As much as I appreciated their company, what I needed most was a hot soak in a tub with an extravagant dose of bubble bath.

An hour later, with my hair washed and my body soothed by the benison of hot water, I was ready to try on some of the clothes Jenny had brought. I decided to forego the jeans for the capris and apple-green shirt. The clothes were comfortable, fit well, and were a welcome change from the gray sweat pants and hoodie. But there was nothing I could do to camouflage the bruising around my right eye, and the angry abrasions on the side of my face. Makeup and lip gloss helped in other areas, but I still felt like the Phantom of the Opera without his mask. Jenny had instructed me to keep a good coating of salve on my face, but somehow I just couldn't combine cow smell with the delectable traces of raspberry vanilla bubble bath.

Clean and refreshed, with my body's discomfort at a minimum, I settled myself in the recliner for a nap, but my mind refused to cooperate. I thumbed through half a dozen magazines then tossed them restlessly aside. Knowing I was safe, hundreds of miles away from Dicola and Sarcassian, couldn't remove the unsettled feeling of being in an unfamiliar place with nothing to do. I had no cell phone, no laptop—no tangible means to connect me with the busy, productive existence that had been mine a few days ago.

I tried watching TV, but my nerves couldn't tolerate the abuse of afternoon soaps and angry courtroom barrages, with so-called friends and couples hurling lies and accusations at one another.

Finally, I grabbed a pillow and abandoned the house for the front porch. Here, clay pots of pink and scarlet geraniums brightened the wide railing, and there was an old metal swing with floral cushions and an afghan tossed across the back. I sat down on the swing with the pillow at my side, trying to ease my restlessness with the peaceful sights and sounds of my surroundings. The afternoon was sunny and warm, the sky a cloudless blue. Across the way in a field, a few horses grazed, shaking their manes and tails against the occasional fly. The only sound in all the world was the rhythmic creak of the old swing. Back and forth. Back and forth.

I blew out a sigh and glanced at my watch. Two o'clock. This same time, only three days ago, I had arrived at the Wolcotts' storybook cottage in Carmel. It seemed more like three lifetimes ago. I couldn't help wondering what my life would be like right now if I hadn't taken those pictures. Granted, I still would have interrupted what was obviously a clandestine meeting, but without the pictures there would have been no need for break-ins, no attempts to steal my camera, or follow me. Allison might still be alive.

Allison. By now her husband and children must be making sad preparations for a funeral, and the entire magazine staff would be mourning her loss.

A painful hardness tightened my chest, and no matter how I tried to turn my thoughts in a different direction, they ran on and on, torturing me with cruel *might have been*s and *if only*s. Then, in the midst of my mental flagellations came a sudden realization. If I hadn't taken those pictures, if all the horrific happenings of the past few days could somehow be erased, I never would have met William.

I eased myself down on the pillow and closed my eyes, remembering the feel of his arms around me and his soft words of assurance. "It's all right. I'm here."

Clinging to that thought, I let go of the guilt and the pain, and slept.

Thirteen

When I awoke, shadows were lengthening across the lawn, and a cool breeze stirred the leaves of the old cottonwoods beside the house. Still hazy with sleep, I became aware of another sound, a vehicle coming down the road, the crunch of tires on gravel as it braked to a stop, then the slam of a car door. All drowsiness left me, and I pushed myself up from the swing and over to the porch railing just as William came around the side of the house. His suit coat was slung over one shoulder, and his shirt sleeves were rolled up, exposing tanned forearms. A glint of sunlight warmed the deep brown of his hair.

Seeing him, I felt a sudden rush of gladness and the nearly overwhelming desire to run straight into those strong arms. The desire startled me so much that I pulled back physically, as well as mentally, upsetting a pot of geraniums. Making a mad scramble for the pot, I barely managed to rescue it from tumbling off the railing.

William paused midstride and glanced up at me with a smile. "Now that's a sight worth coming home to."

His words swept through me like a song, leaving me momentarily speechless and utterly happy.

"Black eye and all?" I said, still clutching the geraniums.

"Black eye and all." He took the porch steps in one long-legged stride, moved the pillow aside, and sat down on the swing. "Besides, your eye's not really black," he said, a teasing twinkle in his own eyes. "It's turning a real nice shade of green. Sort of matches your blouse."

I couldn't help laughing. "Maybe that's what your mother had in mind when she picked it out."

William chuckled and patted the cushion next to him in a wordless invitation.

I put the geraniums back on the railing, feeling oddly breathless, then sat beside him, my thigh brushing against his, and our shoulders a mere touch away. We shared another smile and a quiet moment of awareness.

"You doing okay?" he asked tentatively.

I nodded, noticing a drawn look around his eyes and mouth. "I'm fine, but you're looking tired, or worried—I'm not sure which."

"A little of both," he admitted, leaning back against the cushions. "I had a long talk with Wade and Chief McIntire this afternoon."

My spine stiffened as I turned to face William. His gray-green eyes were sober when they met mine.

"The chief wants to see the pictures, and he wants to talk to you."

I moistened my lips. "I suppose that's to be expected. What did you tell him?"

"I told him that memory card wasn't going to leave my safe, and whatever he had to say to you, he could say just as easily to me."

The gruff protectiveness in William's voice did much to ease the worry inside me. "Somehow, I can't imagine Chief McIntire agreeing to those terms."

William gave me a tired grin. "And you'd be right, but after some healthy discussion we reached a pretty good compromise."

"Which was?"

"I told the chief I'd talk things over with you, and if you felt okay about it, we could make a recording for him with your statement about everything that's happened. Are you willing to do that?"

"Yes, of course."

"I also agreed to make a CD of the pictures and deliver it to Chief McIntire," William added quietly.

"You mean you . . . you're going back to California?"

"Tomorrow morning. I'll get an early flight out of St. George."

I leaned back against the swing, feeling a hollow sort of emptiness inside. "I–I suppose you couldn't just e-mail him the pictures?"

He shook his head. "It's too risky. Especially with Dicola and Sarcassian on the prowl."

I just nodded, saying nothing.

"The chief has known Dicola for a lot of years," William went on, "and up until now the lieutenant's had a pretty good record. I don't blame McIntire for wanting to see some proof. It's a real can of worms."

"Yes, it is," I said dismally, although at the moment I didn't give two figs for Lieutenant Dicola's record.

"Going back will also give me a chance to look over Judge Wolcott's upcoming court docket," William said. "I've been doing a lot of thinking about that meeting you interrupted, and there's got to be some kind of crooked connection between Wolcott and Sarcassian. Possibly something to do with an upcoming hearing or trial."

"William, is that safe?"

"Absolutely. The court dockets are all public records. I'm an attorney. There's nothing unusual about me wanting to check out a few things. I'd ask Wade to do it, but he's got his hands full right now. And the last thing I want to do is alert Dicola that Wade knows more than he's telling."

"I know, and I understand, but I can't help worrying—"

"About Wade?" William asked, a slight edge to his voice.

"About you . . . and your brother," I said softly, knowing my eyes said much more.

William's fingers lightly brushed my cheek. "I'll be fine—but thanks for the worry." He smiled. "Are you hungry?"

"Starved. Although after the lunch your mother fed me, I thought I'd never want to eat again."

He laughed, and I found myself watching for those creases in his cheeks. "I'm not much of a cook," he said, "but I thought I'd fire up the barbecue and grill us a couple of steaks. And we could put some potatoes in the oven. How does that sound?"

"Wonderful," I said, realizing a "couple of steaks" probably meant his parents wouldn't be joining us for dinner. The thought that William and I would have the evening to ourselves was far from unpleasant. Still, just to make sure, I asked lightly, "Will your parents be coming back? I was, uh, just wondering how many potatoes to cook."

William's mouth twitched and his eyes told me that my attempt at subtlety was a total failure. "Friday's their night to play canasta with some friends."

"Oh, that's nice." I rushed on, trying to cover a sudden feeling of shyness with silly, senseless words. "I used to play canasta with my grandparents, but that was so long ago, I've forgotten all the rules . . ." I glanced away from the amused warmth in his eyes and rattled on, "I think there's some lettuce and tomatoes in the fridge. I could make a salad—if you like salads."

"I like salads."

"That's good." I drew a shaky breath. "Will the steaks be elk or beef?"

Laughing, William got up from the swing and offered me his hand. "You'll just have to wait and see."

The steaks were grilled to perfection, but they could just as easily have been porcupine for all I cared. After my initial bout of shyness, conversation came easily, with William drawing me out in his easy, quiet way.

"I'm beginning to know a little about Mackenzie Jones," he said, "but I'd like to know a lot more about Mackenzie Graham. Tell me about her."

Instead of answering his question, I asked one of my own. "Why Jones? What made you choose that name?"

"It's a good Welsh name, like Evans." He fixed me with that direct look of his. "Besides, I had to lay claim to you somehow."

My heart performed an amazing double somersault and I glanced down, unable to think of a blessed thing to say.

"So tell me about your family," he went on. When I hesitated, he added, "Or your job. How did you come to be *Hearth & Home*'s most brilliant young writer?"

"I'm not their most brilliant writer," I said, flustered but pleased. "I'm only a contributing editor."

"With her own feature article in each issue. I googled you," he said, then added, "You're good, Mac."

I acknowledged his praise with a foolish smile and flushed cheeks. "Getting the job was part luck, and partly due to my mother's connections," I admitted, somehow not minding that he knew. "But I've always had a fascination for old houses—the styles, the architecture, and the history."

William leaned back in his chair, tanned forearms folded across his chest, his gaze warm on my face.

"My grandfather Graham was an architect, and when I was a little girl, we used to go for Sunday drives around the older neighborhoods of Chicago. And he'd quiz me about the houses we saw. Was that roof hipped or mansard? Was a particular home built in the Queen Anne style, or Eastlake, or colonial? He knew so much, but he always made me feel like I was the one coming up with all the right answers. And then, when it was time to go home, we'd stop somewhere and he'd buy me a strawberry milkshake as a reward." I smiled, then sighed, remembering.

"Is your grandfather still living?"

"No. He died when I was fifteen."

"And what kind of home did you grow up in?"

I hesitated a moment, knowing he wasn't referring to the architecture or style. "Several homes, actually," I said, avoiding the deeper meaning of his question. "We moved a lot when I was a child. Always up, to a bigger house and more prestigious neighborhood. My father's a broker in stocks and bonds. I suppose he must be very good at what he does. To be honest, I don't really know much about it. My mother is an interior designer and she's very highly thought of—very successful." I glanced down, hating the brittle sound of my voice.

"She and my father have always had a very busy social life. And their home is—well, it's pretty much a showpiece for her profession."

"Their home, not your home?" William said quietly.

"I've been on my own since college."

"And before that?"

I met his eyes. "Let's just say it can be difficult and a bit lonely growing up in a showpiece." Then, pasting on a quick smile, I shifted the subject to one less personal and a lot less painful. "The past few years, working for the magazine, I've had the chance to travel and see a lot of the country, but until now my assignments have never taken me west of the Mississippi." When he said nothing, just fixed me with a thoughtful look, I went on quickly and a shade too brightly. "What about you? After growing up on a ranch, what made you decide to become an attorney?"

"My dad always said it was because I liked to argue and have the last word. Mom insists it's my strong sense of justice—that I can't stand seeing someone being bullied or taken advantage of without wanting to step in and make things right." He gave an easy shrug of his shoulders. "They're probably both right. But we can talk about me another time."

He shoved back his chair, got to his feet, and offered me a hand. "As much as I hate to introduce anything unpleasant into the evening, we'd better get that recording made for Chief McIntire. You still feeling up to it?"

I nodded.

"All right. Let's go into my office. I want you to tell the chief exactly what's happened over the past few days, beginning with your arrival at the Wolcotts', and everything leading up to the accident. I won't prompt you or ask any questions. It'll just be you, okay?"

"Okay."

It was fairly easy at first, sitting in a comfortable leather chair, holding the palm-sized digital recorder. The events were still painfully clear in my mind. William sat across from me at his desk, listening, as he said, without comment or interruption. It wasn't until I got to the shooting and details of the accident that my voice faltered, then tightened up altogether. I cleared my throat and swallowed hard, determined not to cry and failing miserably.

William got up and came around the desk to take the recorder out of my hands. Without a word, he turned it off and set it on the desk. Then, helping me to my feet, he said softly, "Come here."

His arms wrapped around me, sure and strong. Tears slipped silently down my cheeks as he held me. "You don't need to go on," he said. "Not if it's too hard. If the chief wants to know more, he can read the accident report."

"No, I can do it."

"Are you sure?"

I nodded and drew a steadying breath. "I need to do this . . . for Allison."

He gave my shoulders an encouraging squeeze. "All right, then. Let's do it."

I sat back down, and William handed me the recorder. Leaning against the front of the desk, he gave me an encouraging nod.

"I was bending down, getting something out of Allison's purse—her sunglasses," I said, my voice tight but calm. "And there was a strange sound . . . sort of like a small explosion. Then the car was out of control. Allison was face down on the steering wheel and I–I couldn't reach her. The car finally crashed into the guardrail, and we— Allison and I were trapped inside until the paramedics arrived. I had no idea there'd been a shooting. It wasn't until Detective Evans came to the hospital that I found out Allison had been shot. I didn't see who fired the shot—everything happened too fast. I only know that bullet was meant for me."

I shuddered and handed the recorder to William.

"Good girl," he said softly. "You did great, Mac."

Fourteen

Spirals of dust hovered in the air above the road, catching the sun's gold for a few brief moments before dissipating in the dry air. William was gone, on his way to the airport in St. George. And I was alone. Jenny and Tom Evans would be arriving in a few hours, but somehow that thought did nothing to ease the lonely ache and strange restlessness inside me.

I left the porch to go into the house, determined to find something to occupy my hands, if nothing else. In the living room, the first things to meet my eyes were William's sheets and blankets, which lay in a tousled heap on the couch. A smile touched my lips as I untangled the mass of bedding and began folding the sheets, knowing he could just as easily have slept upstairs in the comfort of his own room. Instead, without a word of explanation, he'd chosen to remain close by. And to be perfectly honest, I probably should have worn the modest nightgown and robe Jenny had bought for me, instead of William's pajama top. But I didn't.

Remembering his soft "Good night, Mac," I held his pillow against me for a traitorous moment, then gave myself a brisk mental shake. This would never do. I was becoming positively maudlin.

What on earth was wrong with me? Ever since Will Evans had walked into that hospital room, my supply of caution and cynicism where men were concerned had become practically nonexistent. All it took was one of his slow smiles, the warmth in those gray-green eyes, or the way he called me Mac, and my protective barriers came crashing down like a child's clumsy tower of wooden blocks. And I had known this man how long—a grand total of four days? Actually, it was more like three and a half. Even worse.

I left the folded bedding on the sofa and went into the kitchen, determined to rein in my wandering thoughts. I gathered up our dishes, and before I knew it, my mind was moving over our conversation at breakfast—the way each of us made a concerted effort to keep things casual, with smiles and a layer of lightness covering the heavier issues that troubled us both.

At one point, William had commented on my serious expression and asked if I had any "words of wisdom" to share before he left.

My halfhearted answer of "Not really" was clearly unacceptable.

"I'm not letting you off that easy," he said. "Come on. An experienced writer like you should have plenty of pithy advice that'll help when I'm wading through all those court dockets."

"Wise and pithy," I said with a laugh. "I don't know if I'm up to that."

William just leaned back in his chair and folded tanned arms across his chest, a glint of humor and something else in his eyes. "I'm waiting," he said with mock patience.

"All right. It may not be very pithy, but here goes. When you're searching through those court dockets, try to remember that positive energy produces positive energy."

His dark brows lifted and his lips parted in a crooked smile. "Not bad. But doesn't that go against the laws of physics? You know, centrifugal and centripetal forces."

I shook my head. "I have no idea. I thought we were talking about advice, not physics."

"Positive energy, physics—same thing."

"I was never very good at physics," I told him, but William was not to be diverted from the subject.

"Think of it this way," he said, leaning toward me across the kitchen table. "I'm sure you know people whose energy is centripetal—always directed inward, toward themselves. They suck you in and drain you of your own energy. Then there are those who reach outward with centrifugal or positive energy."

I said nothing for a moment, thinking about the possible implications in his words. "After everything that's happened. I hope you don't think that I'm, well, one of those centripetal people."

William gave me a warm, steady look. "Not to worry, Mac," he said softly. "You are definitely a centrifugal experience."

A centrifugal experience. Who would have thought that all in a moment, physics would become one of my favorite subjects.

There was no lightness or words of wisdom when we faced each other on the front porch a short time later.

"Be careful" was all I could say.

William nodded and touched a hand to my hair. "I'll call you."

Then he was gone.

I sighed and reached under the sink for a scouring pad and some detergent, then took out my frustration on a greasy frying pan. When the kitchen was in spotless order, I returned to the living room, thinking I might find a book to occupy my time as well as my thoughts before his parents arrived.

Like many Craftsman-style bungalows built in the early decades of the 1900's, the home had attractive glassed-in bookcases on either side of the big stone fireplace. An eclectic mix of classics and novels that had been popular decades ago shared the shelves with current bestsellers, including a healthy selection of Louis L'Amour westerns and some courtroom thrillers by John Grisham. Knowing William's parents had lived in the home until three years ago, it wasn't difficult to discern which books had been theirs.

After glancing through some of the older novels, I took a worn copy of Thomas Costain's *The Black Rose* from the shelf and settled myself in the recliner. Ten minutes later, no fault of Mr. Costain's, I put the book aside in favor of taking a walk. The sun was well up as I left the house, and so was the temperature. I made it as far as the end of the pasture nearest the house and decided the horses huddled head to tail under some willows had the right idea. It was much too hot for a walk, and my injured side was still more painful than I'd thought.

Turning back, I paused to stare at the old ranch house, trying to get a feeling for the place. Only a few days ago, I'd been delighting in the charms of Judge Wolcott's storybook cottage, wondering what secrets it might hold. And there had been many—far more than I'd imagined. Now, posing the same question to this sturdy old bungalow, I felt rather than heard the answer: *Not secrets. Stories.*

In spite of the heat, a little shiver ran up my spine as I contemplated what stories Hearth Fires might have to tell. The next moment curiosity was abandoned in favor of going back inside and getting a cold drink of water. Thankfully, the home's thick outside walls provided excellent insulation against the heat of the day, and I realized any plans for a walk would have to be reserved for early morning hours or the evening.

I gulped down a glass of water and glanced up at the kitchen clock. Only ten thirty. Probably, William was still en route to San Francisco. He'd promised to call, but I doubted that would be much before evening.

Returning to the living room, I picked up the novel once more. My second attempt lasted five minutes longer than the first, before I set the book aside with a sigh. What on earth did people do all day in a place like this? Remembering what William said about the possible length of my stay only increased my frustration. I wouldn't last two days, let alone two weeks, without something productive to do.

I returned the book to its shelf, my gaze moving over a group of family pictures on the mantle. The photos spanned the generations as well as decades. Brides and grooms. Young men in uniform. An elderly couple posing proudly with sons and daughters on either side. Remembering William telling me he had been married once, "about a million years ago," I gave the wedding pictures a closer look, but he definitely wasn't one of the grooms.

Like the books on the shelves and the pictures on the mantle, the living room was a combination of things left behind and William's belongings. The old upright piano on a wall opposite the fireplace was probably the same vintage as the house, its mahogany surface still shining and well cared for.

I tested a few keys and found the tone to be rich and true. Glancing through the sheet music in the piano bench, I discovered a selection of popular songs, as well as some classical pieces by Chopin, Rachmaninoff, and Debussy.

Like Jane Austen's "accomplished woman," my mother believed piano lessons were an essential requirement for her only daughter. And much like Austen's Elizabeth Bennett, I considered my ability at the instrument adequate but was far from skilled. After reaching Thompson's Grade 4, I'd developed a real fondness for the piano, but Mother decided my progress did not warrant further lessons and made arrangements for me to take dancing lessons instead. This proved to be a complete disaster as I was too shy and self-conscious to join in with the other students. Angry and humiliated, Mother withdrew me from the class. Looking back, I realized my own feelings and interests were never considered—that I had nothing to do with either decision.

I set the classical pieces aside to thumb through a stack of old sheet music. Many of the songs went back several decades to the early twentieth century. I took a few pieces from the bench and sat down. It had been years since my fingers had touched the keys of a piano, and I was grateful there was no one to hear my initial attempts to play.

The subject of trails must have been a particular favorite with someone in the Evans family. I stumbled through "Twilight on the Trail," did somewhat better with "Blue Shadows on the Trail," and by the time I got to "There's a Long, Long Trail a Winding," found that my fingers and my mind were cooperating with each other.

I worked my way through some classic Cole Porter, apologizing to the old piano for an assortment of wrong notes. "Begin the Beguine" totally defeated me, but "Blue Moon" was definitely doable. Encouraged, I picked up the next piece in the stack. Its corners were dog-eared and the cover yellowed with time. I couldn't help smiling at the unabashed sentiment of the title: "The West, a Nest, and You."

How times have changed, I thought, playing through the melody with one hand. By today's standards the lyrics would be considered syrupy and overly sentimental. "The west, a nest, and you dear . . . oh, what a joy it'd be . . . a cozy little cottage, beside the western sea."

Sentimental, yes, but there was still something undeniably charming about the song. And some basic truths found in those simple lyrics. Decades later, people were still yearning for that special someone and searching for a "nest" or home where they belonged.

I began to sight-read the piece, enjoying the lilting melody set to an old-fashioned waltz. I was partway through the chorus when a strong tenor voice sang out behind me. I stopped with a jerk and turned to see Tom Evans standing in the doorway, a broad smile on his face.

"Don't stop now." He crossed the room to stand beside the piano.

"But I don't really know it. I was just—"

"You're doin' just fine." He gave me an encouraging nod. "Why don't you start the chorus again and we'll finish it together."

There was no way I could refuse the man. And I didn't do too badly. Tom's rich tenor caressed the melody and brought heartfelt meaning to the lyrics. When we finished, my eyes left the music to look into his weathered face. "That was beautiful. You have a wonderful voice."

He shrugged aside my praise. "It's a bit rusty at times, but I still love to sing. And that was my folks' favorite song. Mother used to tell me she had no intention of marrying my dad. In fact, she was engaged to marry some rich feller from St. George. But the night Dad sang that song to her sort of changed her mind."

"If your father's voice was anything like yours, I can understand why."

Tom Evans acknowledged this with an easy smile. "It's born in us, I think. Put a group of Welshmen together and before you know it, they'll be singing in four-part harmony."

I laughed, enjoying the crinkles that creased the corners of his eyes, seeing more than a hint of William's eyes and smile.

The next moment Tom's eyes grew soft with a memory. "It's been a good many years now, but I can still remember Dad singing that song to Mother the night of their fiftieth wedding anniversary."

"Fifty years . . . that's wonderful. How long have you and Jenny been married?"

Tom winked at me then turned his glance on his wife, who had just come into the room. "Jenny and I are still newlyweds. We just celebrated our forty-first anniversary a month ago."

Time passed more easily now that I was no longer alone in the house. And it seemed the Evans' visit would be more than a few hours. As we were eating lunch, Jenny informed me that William had asked them to stay at the ranch while he was away. Even though I'd been living on my own for several years, knowing I wouldn't be alone at night was infinitely reassuring.

"Since you're feeling a bit better, I think you'll be more comfortable sleeping in William's room," Jenny told me. "Tom and I always sleep in Wade's old room whenever we stay over, so it'll work out fine."

I nodded and thanked her, hoping my face didn't reveal the unsettling state of my emotions at the prospect of sleeping in William's bed.

After lunch, Jenny insisted I go upstairs and rest, and I was suddenly too tired to argue. Pain medication had eased my restlessness as well as my discomfort, and quite honestly, there was nothing else to do. Tom Evans had gone into town to take care of some errands, and Jenny was settled in the recliner, knitting a sweater for a granddaughter's birthday. It seemed everyone had something useful to do but me.

"William's room is the first door on your left," Jenny called after me as I headed for the stairs. "I've tidied up a bit and put your things on a chair next to the bed."

The stairs were steep, with a thin covering of worn carpet down the center. I paused halfway up, holding my injured side and breathing hard. By the time I reached the landing, I felt real sympathy thinking of William climbing these same stairs with broken ribs.

The door to his room was open, but I found myself hesitating at the threshold, my heart doing a nervous tap dance. During her tidying up, Jenny had pulled the blinds and closed the curtains, softening the glare of the midday sun to a pleasant dimness.

Like his office downstairs, William's bedroom and its furnishings had a strong Western flavor. The bed and bureau were sturdy mission oak, the walls and carpet a blend of muted earth tones. Hanging over the bed was a stunning painting of what had to be Zion Canyon on a glorious autumn day. I stepped inside, my gaze moving from the colorful cliffs to a framed black-and-white photograph on the wall nearest the window. In the photo, five children sat in stair-step fashion astride the broad back of a large draft horse. Two girls in pigtails were followed by three little boys sporting plaid shirts and big grins. I moved closer to get a better look at the children, seeing something of William's smile in the little boy closest to the horse's rump. I smiled, absently humming a nameless tune, fairly sure the youngest boy was Tom Evans.

In a corner near the closet, a rustic coat rack caught my eye. Fashioned of old metal horseshoes that had been welded together, the coat rack was unique as well as functional. A leather jacket hung from one of the protruding horseshoes, William's cowboy hat from another. I brushed my palm against the leather's softness, loving its musky smell, then traced the rim of his Stetson with one finger.

Doing so, I experienced an epiphany as disturbing as it was enlightening. I thought of the countless times I'd entered someone's home on assignment for the magazine. How I automatically made note of a room's style and furnishings, along with the small personal items that helped to reveal its owner. My eyes were quick to discern, yet always professional. Never probing.

Now, I had to admit there was nothing the least bit professional about my response to William's room or my desire to know more about him. I sat down on the bed with a little groan, kicked off my shoes, and tried to administer the comforting rationale that it was only natural to care a little because of the circumstances that brought us together. Danger could accelerate the tempo of any relationship. But the uncomfortable truth of the matter was that my feelings for William had already gone beyond the caring-a-little stage.

This was not good. Not good at all. Part of the problem was this place and having nothing to do. Being sensible would be so much easier if I had something constructive to do with my time and energies. And while I was at it, why not add pain medication to the list? Loopy sentimentality could always be blamed on medication.

In spite of this latest round of rationalization, my eyes continued their search. I really didn't expect to find a picture of William's ex-wife among the family photos on the mantle. But perhaps in the privacy of his room . . . The bureau top held no pictures at all, only a spare ring of keys, a pen, and two notepads. The dresser had a low stack of books, mostly nonfiction, and some fat manila folders that probably belonged in the office. Oh well. At least there was no ready evidence William was still pining over his lost love.

Still humming the same nameless melody, I took off my jeans, pulled back the bedspread, and eased myself down onto the bed. The sheets and pillowcases were cool and clean, and the faint fragrance coming to my nostrils was Downey fabric softener, rather than William's aftershave.

I settled myself on the pillow, wishing his mother hadn't been quite so dutiful in tidying the room, when it suddenly hit me what I'd been humming. "The West, a Nest, and You."

I had thought to take only a brief rest, so I was surprised and disgruntled to wake up some two hours later. Instead of feeling refreshed, my head and body ached and I was in a thoroughly disagreeable mood. When I went downstairs, my frustration was heightened by the news that William had called a half hour before.

"I told him you were sleeping," Jenny informed me as she sat in the recliner, placidly knitting. "Will said to tell you that he and Wade would be meeting with the police chief at three, West Coast time. He'll call you later, but he wasn't sure exactly when."

I sank down on the sofa, trying to hide my disappointment.

"Oh, and William wants you to have my cell phone in case you need to get in touch with him," she added.

"Your cell phone? I–I can't do that."

"Goodness, dear, it's no trouble, if that's what you're thinking. Half the time I forget I even have one. The only people who might be calling would be my daughters, and they've learned to leave messages on our home phone."

"Well, if you're sure . . ."

Jenny glanced up from her knitting. "William was real adamant about it. He said this would be the safest way for you two to keep in touch. And I have to say, it's nice to see my son being so protective."

I just smiled, not knowing how to respond to this last comment.

Jenny's nimble fingers went back to work, and I marveled as single strands of yarn took form and shape.

"Do you knit, dear?"

"No, I'm afraid it's totally beyond me."

As I watched her, a small sigh escaped my lips, but even a small sigh didn't escape her notice.

"Are you feeling all right?" she asked, her brown eyes warm with concern.

I shrugged and shook my head, struggling to find the words. "I know I should be—feeling all right, that is—but I can't help feeling completely useless, and such an imposition."

"You're certainly not an imposition," Jenny responded in a tone that brooked no argument. "But I can understand your frustration. Will told us a little about your job with the magazine. I imagine it must keep you pretty busy."

"Yes, and that's part of the problem. I've gotten used to having too much to do, with a hundred things on my list, and now—well, I guess I'm feeling a little lost as well as frustrated."

Jenny was silent for a moment, a small frown creasing her forehead as she continued knitting. "Maybe this frustration you're feeling is trying to tell you something. Having so much to do isn't always a good thing. There's nothing wrong with slowing down a little, taking time to enjoy the simple things. Sometimes I think all this rushing around is a disease of our modern age. Time goes by fast enough without our trying to hurry it along."

She set the knitting aside to give me a close look. "What you've been through this past week is . . . well, it's terrible—the accident and the death of your friend, and who knows what else. You've suffered a lot more than a few scrapes and bruises on the outside. You've been frightened and hurt on the inside as well."

I glanced down, trying to blink away the tears that threatened.

"I think you need to give yourself permission to slow down for a while," she went on. "Let yourself heal. Healing doesn't happen in a hurry. It takes as long as it takes." Reaching out, she put a gentle hand over one of mine. "Maybe while you're here with us, what you need to do is just rest and be thankful."

Despite my efforts, the tears were flowing freely now. Jenny got up from the recliner, helped me to my feet, and put her arms around me. "You're a brave, wonderful girl, and I'm not the only one who thinks so."

I returned her embrace, my throat still too tight with emotion to allow any words.

"Now then," she said briskly, taking some tissues from her pocket and handing them to me. "You know I'm perfectly happy to have you sit here and keep me company, but if you're bound and determined to find something to do, there is something that comes to mind."

I wiped my eyes and managed a smile. "What's that?"

"Peaches."

"Peaches?"

Jenny nodded. "There're a couple of peach trees near the far end of the orchard that William's sadly neglected, I'm sorry to say. Probably, most of the fruit has fallen by now, but I'll bet you can find enough good ones for a batch of jam, or maybe even a peach cobbler." She paused, then added slyly, "Fresh peach cobbler is just about William's favorite dessert."

My smile broadened and I gave her a quick hug. "Thank you."

"You're welcome," she said, sounding thoroughly pleased with herself. "There's a bucket on the back porch. Take a right past the clotheslines and follow the path around the woodshed out to the orchard. Oh, and don't forget to take my cell phone along, in case William calls back."

Fifteen

Picking peaches in the fading hours of a golden afternoon, I made a unique discovery. Orchards are wonderful places to heal. Everything around me was like a blessed balm. The trees with their bounty of ripe abundance, the lazy drone of insects, air that was dry and crisp, and overhead, the hard blue sky of autumn. The soft azure of summer was long past, giving way to fall's brilliance with a blue that sharpened in intensity and gloried in the change of seasons. Such a sky held thoughts of winter at bay, reveling instead in the mellow joys of the harvest.

My own thoughts were pleasantly idle, content with the task at hand and the sensory pleasures it afforded. True, many of the peaches had fallen to become a feast for worms and other insects. Nature, ever wise and frugal, had a way of providing for all her creatures. But the trees still yielded a goodly amount of fruit—fragrant, fuzzy, and golden. Had I ever picked peaches before? A brief search of my memory brought the realization that this was my first experience, and I gloried in it.

That said, by the time I had a bucket brimming with fruit, my hands and arms were itching from the close contact with peach fuzz. Glancing around, I discovered a small irrigation ditch a short distance away. The water was numbingly cold, and I relished its sting on my wrists and hands. I spotted a wooden stool lying beside one of the trees, sat down with a contented sigh, and gave myself permission to do absolutely nothing.

My thoughts, however, refused to remain idle, and I found myself thinking of my family. Did my parents know I was missing and the subject of an all-state search? They might not if they hadn't returned from Mother's yearly buying trip to Europe. It's possible my brother could have heard by now. The police might even have contacted him. If so, surely Jeremy would contact my parents with the news, although they didn't stay in touch very often.

When was the last time I'd seen my brother? Six months ago or longer? I wondered suddenly if Jeremy's wife had had her baby. I thought she was due to have their first child sometime around the end of September. Or was it October? Surely they would have called to tell me. But then perhaps not, considering how often our family communicated and got together. I called a halt to my thoughts, irritated with the "poor me" direction they were taking. If my family didn't connect as often as they should, part of the blame was mine. I had a phone. I could just as easily call them, rather than expecting them to keep in touch with me. That is, I could have until all this happened.

Sitting on the hard wooden stool in the quiet orchard, I dished out a few bitter pills to myself. It wasn't fair or right that I should be so quick to lay blame on my parents for their busy lifestyle, when my own was much the same. True, we didn't see each other as often as I would like, but that was my fault as much as theirs. When was the last time I'd called my brother, or my parents, just to say hello? The guilty twinge I felt inside was answer enough. Being busy was no excuse. It only made it easier for one's priorities get out of balance. And just what were my priorities? Turning in a brilliant article for the magazine? Being promoted from contributing editor to assistant editor? Suddenly, it all seemed so trivial, so shallow.

What was it the poet had so wisely said? *The world is too much with us; late and soon, getting and spending, we lay waste our powers* . . . If Wordsworth felt that way over two hundred years ago, what would he have to say about the world's current state of affairs, and the computerized rat race we humans compete in so willingly?

Glancing around the peaceful orchard, I thought Wordsworth would probably agree with Jenny Evans' simple advice. How had she put it? Sometimes what we need to do is just rest and be thankful. I smiled, quietly acknowledging that complex, earth-shaking solutions were not always what was needed when confronting a problem. Sometimes the simplest truths were the most profound.

Having reached that conclusion, I looked down at the bucket brimming with ripe fruit and made the brilliant decision that carrying it back to the house would be a much lighter task if I ate one of the peaches right now. My first bite into the fruit's sweet, juicy flesh was ample proof that Costco's finest could never compare with the real thing. By the time the peach was gone, I was in need of another quick wash in the nearby ditch to rid my face and hands of the sticky juice. That accomplished, I bent down to retrieve the bucket when a sudden vibration from my pants pocket took me by surprise. I must have jumped nearly half a foot. I quickly wiped my hands on my pants, then grabbed the cell phone.

"Hello?"

"Hi, it's William. I've been thinking about you."

His words and voice sent a bright arrow of happiness shooting straight through me, and I almost sat down on the bucket of peaches rather than the nearby stool. Realizing my mistake, I changed course halfway down, missed the stool by inches, and landed flat on the ground with a startled *oof.*

"Mackenzie, are you okay?"

I began to laugh, as much from sheer happiness as my own foolishness. "I'm more than okay. Oh, William, I've had the most wonderful time. I've been picking peaches!"

"Peaches," he repeated, his delighted chuckle resonating across the distance. Then, with sudden concern, "I hope you didn't try to climb one of the trees. It sounded like you just fell down."

"I didn't fall down. I sat down. A little too hard actually, but at least I missed the bucket of peaches."

His laughter joined mine, and there was a pause before he said, "It's good to hear your voice."

I smiled and cradled the phone. "It's good to hear you, too."

"Are you really okay?" he asked.

"Yes, much better."

"Hmm, I sense some hesitation in that answer. Is something bothering you?"

"Nothing's bothering me. Not really. Your parents are wonderful and so kind. It's just—I think I'd feel better if I had something to do."

"What? You're tired of picking peaches already?" he teased. Then his voice grew serious. "I'm sorry, Mac. I know all the waiting and uncertainty has to be pretty hard."

"I don't mean to complain. Honestly. But I can't help feeling rather useless."

He was silent a moment before saying quietly, "Maybe there is something you could do—something that would mean a lot to me, and my folks."

I waited for him to go on, and when he didn't reply right away, I burst out with "William, whatever it is, just tell me."

"Okay, but it's totally up to you. For years, I've been trying to get Dad to write a history of his life, along with some of the stories of his parents' and grandparents' lives, but he's always balked at the idea. Said he was too busy and didn't know how or where to begin. When he had the heart attack, we came pretty close to losing him, and it hit me that if Dad had died, a lot of our family history would die, too. He wouldn't do it for me, but if you ask him, I think he might be willing to tell you about his life, and you could write down some of the stories. Just get him to talk. I have a feeling Dad'll open up to you."

"William, I'd love to do it."

"I've got notebooks, pens, paper, and whatever else you need in my office. Help yourself."

I felt a rush of excitement just thinking about the prospect. "Thank you. This will be wonderful. I can hardly wait to get started."

He laughed, sounding pleased. "Maybe you ought to finish the peaches first. Have you got any special plans for those peaches you've been picking?"

"Your mother said we could do a batch of jam or maybe a peach cobbler."

"I vote for the cobbler."

I hesitated a moment, then asked, "Does that mean you'll be coming home soon?"

"Not for a few days. Wade and I really have our work cut out for us."

I drew a tight breath. "The meeting with Chief McIntire . . ."

"Wasn't nearly as productive as I would have liked. But then, we've put the chief in a difficult position. He knows it and we know it."

The sudden tension inside me tightened around my rib cage like a vice. "What was his reaction to the pictures and the recording we made?"

"Mixed," William said. "I'm not saying that he didn't believe us. The chief's a good man and he runs a good department. Seeing those pictures of Lieutenant Dicola with Sarcassian and Judge Wolcott hit him pretty hard. I don't blame him for being on the defensive when it comes to Dicola."

"How defensive was he?"

"Well, at first, McIntire tried to come up with a legitimate reason why Dicola was at Judge Wolcott's place. Undercover work even. Like I said, Dicola's one of his own and the man's had a pretty decent record. But after listening to your recording, the chief backed off from the undercover idea. The break-ins, you being followed, and the shooting incident pretty much shot that down, and he knew it. McIntire might not like it, but he knows Dicola had no business meeting with a circuit court judge on the sly."

I blew out a frustrated breath. "So what happens now? What is Chief McIntire going to do?"

"Officially, McIntire should turn the pictures and Lieutenant Dicola over to Internal Affairs and let that department determine what steps should be taken."

"Internal Affairs? What exactly is that?"

"If a police officer shoots someone in the line of duty or is suspected of improper or illegal actions, it's turned over to Internal Affairs," William explained. "The officer is put on paid leave until the incident can be looked into and a decision made."

"I see. And is that what's going to happen?"

"Not yet. I told McIntire the minute he turned Dicola over to Internal Affairs, we might as well forget about finding out what was going on at that meeting between Sarcassian and Wolcott. And when, not if, Sarcassian gets wind that Dicola's under investigation, the lieutenant's pretty much a dead man. McIntire didn't say a word to that, but his silence and the look on his face was enough to tell me I'd made my point."

"Oh, William, it's just what you said—a real can of worms."

"Yes, it is, but don't be too discouraged, Mac. A can of worms comes in real handy when you're going fishing. And Wade and I are determined to catch a big one. It took a bit of hard talking, but I finally convinced Chief McIntire to give us some time to do a little investigating on our own."

"What kind of investigating?"

"Basically, what we talked about this morning. I told McIntire that I wanted to look into Judge Wolcott's upcoming court docket— that there had to be some connection between him and Sarcassian— and McIntire agreed. He wants to get to the bottom of all this as much as we do, but where police procedure's concerned, his hands are pretty much tied. McIntire told us flat out that he was going out on a limb, but he'd give Wade and me forty-eight hours and not a minute more. Then he'll turn everything over to Internal Affairs."

"Two days. That's not very long."

"No, but let's look on the bright side. If Sarcassian was trying to buy Judge Wolcott's favor, then it stands to reason it must be for a hearing or trial that's due to be heard fairly soon. Something he was willing to pay Wolcott a hefty bribe in order to keep quiet. First thing tomorrow, I'll start going over the court records."

"William, you really are amazing."

"We'll see how amazing I am after the next forty-eight hours," he said. "Oh, and I thought you'd like to know that Chief McIntire's going to keep a very close watch on Dicola. He has some valid concerns about the lieutenant's near-obsessive investigation into your disappearance, rather than putting more effort into solving the actual shooting. Apparently, Dicola's been back to the hospital, and he's asking a lot of questions about your mysterious fiancé."

I felt a sudden stab of worry, thinking over William's arrival in the emergency room. "I'm not sure, but I may have mentioned your name to the nurse," I told him. "I was feeling so fuzzy at the time, I can't really remember."

"You were pretty loopy. But don't worry about it. Wade's done some follow-up checking of his own. The nurse gave Dicola a pretty good description of me, but she couldn't remember a name."

I bit my lip and remained silent.

"You're worrying again," William said.

"I know, but I can't help it."

"Then here's a little good news. Instead of being reprimanded, the chief gave Wade some backhanded praise about the 'unorthodox' way we got you out of the hospital."

"I'm glad about that."

"Well, I probably ought to let you get back to your peaches. I'll give you a call sometime tomorrow afternoon."

There was a moment of silence as I felt an aching reluctance to bring our conversation to an end. "Good luck with the court records."

"Thanks. Let's hope your advice produces the necessary results."

"My advice?"

"You know, positive energy produces positive energy. I'm counting on you to send me some of your centrifugal sparkle."

I smiled as my heart performed a centrifugal somersault. "I will."

"You take care now," he said softly.

"You too."

"And save me some of that peach cobbler, okay?"

The warmth in his voice eased away the worries as well as my defenses. "It'll be waiting for you when you get back," I told him. "And so will I."

Sixteen

The pleasant afternoon waned, and with the coming of evening there was a definite chill in the air. "There'll be plenty of warm days yet," Jenny assured me after dinner was over and we were putting the kitchen to rights. "October's always such a lovely month, but the nights can turn cold. Tom, I think it might be nice to have a fire in the fireplace tonight."

"I'll get some logs from the woodshed," he said, then took his jacket from a hook near the back door and left the kitchen. Before Jenny and I had finished loading the dishwasher, he was back with a bucket of kindling, and some cut logs in his arms.

Soon, the living room was aglow with firelight and the lively crackle and hiss of pine logs. William's parents were sitting on the sofa, and I was settled comfortably in the recliner, content for the moment to enjoy the percussive voice of the fire and the hypnotic dance of the flames. Over dinner, conversation had ebbed and flowed with the import of the day's events—in particular, the results of William and Wade's meeting with Chief McIntire. Jenny's brow had creased with worry when I told her and Tom about the chief's forty-eight-hour deadline and William's proposed investigation, but Tom simply nodded, his firm mouth and steady expression showing nothing but confidence in his eldest son. Discussion had been open and frank, with William's parents acknowledging the seriousness of the situation with an unflinching calm that amazed me.

Now, sitting in contented silence in the fire-lit room, I found my thoughts moving away from the troubles and trauma of the past week, to William's simple request this afternoon.

As I looked at Tom's profile in the flickering light, the man seemed younger somehow, and the past very close. I've never understood the how or why of it; I only know firelight has a magical way of diminishing the distance between the present and the long ago. Years fade away and memories half forgotten return with amazing clarity in the soft light of flame and shadow. Seen in firelight, the past becomes a living thing, no longer blurred and distant.

Tom Evans got up to add another log to the fire and give the burning wood a few jabs with an old iron poker. I waited until he sat back down, then said, "I love the name of your ranch—Hearth Fires. William told me there was a story behind the name. If you wouldn't mind sharing, I'd love to hear it."

"Well, I don't know," he said with a shake of his head.

Jenny put a hand on her husband's knee and gave him a little smile of encouragement.

Tom's gaze left his wife's face to meet mine for an unspoken moment.

"Please," I said softly.

A ghost of a smile touched his lips and he gave an assenting nod. "The story's over a hundred years old now," he began, "but the tellin' of it still tugs at my heart. My grandparents, Amos and Ellie Evans, had a good-sized spread a few miles outside of Kemmerer, Wyoming." He paused, then asked, "Have you ever been to Wyoming?"

"No. I've seen pictures of Yellowstone and Jackson Hole, but I really don't know much about the state."

"Wyoming's tough, rugged country for man and beast alike," Tom told me, "with cold winters and a wind that never stops blowin', summer or winter. My granddad used to say the snow never melted in Wyoming—it just wore out from being blown from one side of the road to the other. Anyway, my dad was next to the youngest in a family of eight, so there were plenty of older brothers and sisters to share the work. And in those days, everyone did his part. Grandpa Amos mostly raised sheep, but he had a few head of cattle and some hogs."

"What were they like—your grandparents?" I prompted.

Tom leaned back and thought a bit before answering. "Grandpa died when I was but nine or ten, so my memories of him are few. But I can still remember sittin' on his lap when I was just a little tyke, and havin' him take out his pocket watch so I could listen to it tick. And I remember the stories he told. About bank robbers, and wolves, and such. Grandpa had a way of tellin' a tale that made it more than real. Something in his words and his voice put pictures in your mind." Tom sent a smile in my direction, but I don't think it was me that he was seeing.

"Grandma Ellie was a small, sturdy woman with strong hands, a sharp tongue, and the softest heart God ever gave to a woman. Eleanor was her Sunday-go-to-meetin' name, but we never knew her as anything but Ellie. She always wore an apron, and her hair was pulled back in a bun as tight as that little mouth of hers. But when that lady laughed, it was like the sun comin' out in the dead of winter. I remember Grandma Ellie's kitchen was always neat as a pin and full of good smells.

"Well, like I was sayin', my Dad was the youngest in the family until little Johnny came along. His birth weakened Grandma some, and with times as hard as they were, you might think havin' one more mouth to feed wouldn't give my grandparents much cause for rejoicing. But it was just the opposite. Everyone in the family just doted on that baby, and no one more than my grandmother. Johnny was a beautiful child, with a curly mop of honey-brown hair, eyes bluer than a sky in summer, and the happiest disposition."

Tom paused, and in the stillness I felt his sunny memories shift and darken into something somber.

"It was autumn, one of the busiest times on a farm or ranch. Johnny was a toddler of two and a bit, and curious as a cat. Always into something or other . . ." Tom paused as the fragmented threads of his story tightened into pain. "Granddad and the older boys had a big iron kettle at the back of the yard. A fire was built and burning hot underneath, and the kettle was filled with boiling water to scald the hogs."

"Scald the hogs?" A shudder went through me. "Is that how they killed pigs?"

"No. No, the hogs were good and dead before they ever went into the kettle. But before a pig could be smoked or cooked, you had to get rid of the hair. Scalding hogs was what you did in those days."

Tom drew a deep breath and stared into the fire for a long moment. Then all he said was "No one really knows how it happened, but little Johnny fell into that kettle of scalding water. His screams brought Granddad and the older boys runnin' from the barn."

I bit my lip, trying to rid my mind of the horrible images his words conjured up. Jenny's hands were clasped tightly in her lap.

Tom Evans cleared his throat and slowly shook his head. "There wasn't much anyone could do. The nearest town and doctor were miles away. And when the doctor did come, there was precious little he could do. Johnny died some ten days later, and Grandma Ellie was never the same. She was always a strong woman, but that little one's death nearly put her down.

"It was worse when winter came, with the wind moanin' and howlin' outside, almost as if it were grievin' that babe's death along with the rest of the family. Dad told me that the winter after Johnny died was one of the worst he'd ever known. They lost several head of sheep and cattle before it was over, and they nearly lost Ellie as well. She took sick with pneumonia. Between that and the grief, times were pretty bad.

"When spring came, Grandpa Amos decided he had to take her away from the place and the constant reminders of little Johnny's death. And he was still worried about Ellie's health and what might happen to her in another one of those wicked Wyoming winters.

Grandpa had some cousins who told him about Utah's 'Dixie' and the mild winters around St. George and other southern Utah towns. When they saw this place, with the Virgin River nearby and good land for pasture, not to mention those towering cliffs of Zion Canyon, well, it was unlike anything they'd ever seen. Grandpa Amos bought the land real cheap, but there wasn't a house or any outbuildings on the property. So Ellie picked out some house plans to her liking from a catalog, and they had the whole kit and caboodle shipped to St. George by rail. Grandpa and his sons worked all that summer, puttin' the house together. They even gathered smooth rocks from the riverbed for the fireplace. They didn't have much, but Grandma Ellie took pride in hanging her favorite pictures on the walls and putting colorful rag rugs on the floors. Before autumn's end, the house was finished and the barn was pretty near built. Grandpa even made a woodshed out back with enough logs cut and stacked to last them the whole winter."

Tom got up to stir the near-blackened wood and glowing embers, then added one last log to the fire. When he turned to face me, a gentle smile touched the corners of his mouth. "Dad was pretty young at the time, but he told me he'd never forget the first night of cold and frost after the family was settled. Grandpa built a big hearty blaze in the fireplace with logs of pinion pine. The whole family gathered round, and Grandma Ellie brought in mugs of hot spiced cider and a plate piled high with homemade doughnuts for everyone. You need to understand that my grandparents were never the kind for public shows of affection, even though we knew they loved each other. With them, it was something understood, rather than talked about.

"But on this night, Grandpa Amos sat down in his favorite old chair, as pleased and happy as any king on a throne, pulled Ellie onto his lap, and wrapped his big arms around her little frame. 'Ellie, my dear,' he said, 'as long as I live and breathe, I promise that you'll never be cold again. That this hearth and my love will keep you warm for all the rest of your days.'"

Tom cleared his throat, and his eyes were suspiciously bright. "Naturally, my dad and his brothers were properly embarrassed by such a display, and his sisters were all pretty nigh blubbering. Aunt Mary, Dad's oldest sister, was always a fanciful sort, and she piped up with the idea that their new home needed a name. The boys pretty much thought this was nothin' but romantic nonsense. In their minds, havin' names and brands for cattle and horses made perfect sense, but why name a house?

"Grandma Ellie just smiled and ran her worn fingers through Grandpa's hair. 'Hearth Fires,' she said, and kissed him full on the mouth. 'We'll call our home Hearth Fires.'"

───❦───

Later that night, as I prepared for bed, it suddenly occurred to me that I had been so engrossed during the telling, I hadn't taken a single note or written down one word of Tom Evans' story. I hauled myself out of William's very comfortable bed and tiptoed downstairs to his office. As familiar as I was with using a laptop for my magazine articles, tonight I opted for a legal-sized notebook of lined paper and some pens. All thoughts of sleep fled as I arranged the bed pillows for a backrest and settled myself with notebook and pen in hand.

I sat for a long moment, thinking about the lives of William's family—about Amos and Ellie Evans, the death of their little boy, and the history of Hearth Fires. Little wonder that William felt so connected to this place, that he loved it so. I stared at the blank pages of the notebook, suddenly plagued with doubts about my ability to record the story I'd heard tonight—to give it the life and meaning it deserved.

I was strongly tempted to put the notebook aside and forget about writing anything until morning. But my mind was filled with the sound of Tom Evans' voice and images of his grandmother, a woman I'd never seen or known, yet whose face burned in my mind.

My heart twisted as I thought of Ellie's grief and helplessness as she watched her young son suffer and die. How could I ever find words to record that kind of pain and loss?

Shivering, I put down the pen. There were no words. Not for something like this. As I thought over all the articles I'd researched and written during the past five years, they suddenly seemed so shallow, so superficial. I was good at finding clever ways to describe a room and its furnishings, tucking in a few interesting nuggets of history, with an occasional vignette. But comparing that to the story I'd heard tonight in all its heart-wrenching simplicity, I'd never felt more inadequate. And yet I'd promised William. Something inside me couldn't bear the thought of letting him down.

I picked up the pen once more. There was no way I could tell the story from Amos' or Ellie's point of view, or even William's father's. But I could at least make a rough outline of the events, get something on paper. If I began with tonight, with the feeling of firelight and closeness, sitting around the same hearth that the Evans family had shared and built stone by stone so many years ago, perhaps the words would come.

Seventeen

Tom Evans glanced up from his morning paper with puzzled interest when I joined him and Jenny at the breakfast table, notebook and pen in hand. Jenny's expression was equally curious as she set a plate of bacon and scrambled eggs in front of me.

"You've got dark shadows under your eyes," she said, fixing me with a look of concern. "Didn't you sleep well?"

"I slept fine—once I finally got to sleep—but, well, I was up quite late . . . writing."

"Writing?" Tom's expression bordered on incredulous. "What in tarnation would you want to be writing about in the middle of the night?"

"You, and your family, and the story of Hearth Fires." I met his eyes with a smile and frank honesty. "You see, I have a confession to make, and I hope you won't be offended."

Tom straightened and set the paper aside. "What sort of confession?"

"Yesterday, when I was talking to William, I told him how frustrated I felt, not having anything to do, and imposing on your kindness—"

"Now Mackenzie," Jenny broke in, "I thought I made it clear when we talked that you're not an imposition—far from it."

"I know you did, and I'm grateful, but I still need something halfway useful to do, to give back a little. William had a suggestion—a wonderful idea. At least, I think it is, and I hope you will too."

Tom's puzzled look shifted to one bordering on obstinate caution. "Well now, I guess that all depends on what this so-called wonderful idea is all about."

"What it's about is writing down the stories and experiences of you and your family." I met his look with one just as direct. "Like the story of Hearth Fires you told me last night. It deserves to be remembered and passed down to your grandchildren, and their children. But that won't happen unless it's written down."

"And William asked you to do this?" Tom looked a bit stunned.

"Yes, and I told him I'd love to—that is, if you'll let me." I gave Tom an encouraging smile.

"Well now, I don't know," Tom said with a shake of his head. "A few years back, Will tried to get me to tell a few family stories on one of those fancy recorders, and I've never felt so awkward. It just didn't feel natural, trying to talk into some fool machine. Nothin' came out right. And as much as I love tellin' a good tale, I've never been good at findin' the right words on paper. I don't have the gift, or the inclination."

"What if you were to just share some of the stories with me, and I wrote them down?" I said. "I'd love to hear more about the lives of your grandparents, and their parents, and . . . and your whole family. It wouldn't have to be anything formal. I'd be perfectly happy to just follow you around with my notebook and pen while you do chores or whatever."

"Now why would you want to do a thing like that?" Tom looked a little embarrassed, but a smile lurked in the corners of his mouth.

I hesitated a moment, feeling a little embarrassed myself. "Partly because I think you have a wonderful family, and writing down some of the history—well, it's a small way for me to say thank you. But it's more than that. I–I promised William. And I know how much this means to him."

Tom Evans glanced down and took an inordinately long time folding his newspaper. "There's a line of fence that's down in the north pasture where Earl Thacker keeps his bulls," he said in an offhand way. "If you'd care to ride out with me this morning and take that notebook of yours along—well, we'll see what we can do."

I beamed at him. "Thank you! I'd love to." I took a forkful of scrambled egg and paused with it halfway to my mouth. "Exactly how will we be riding out? On a horse or in a car?"

Tom's mouth split into a grin. "Neither one. I figured on takin' the truck, if that suits you."

I nodded in relief. "It suits me fine."

Some thirty minutes later found me perched on a weathered gray stump near a straggling line of Russian olive trees, watching while William's father repaired the sagging wire and broken rail of fencing. The morning was warm, but there was still a breath of coolness in the breeze. On the other side of the fence, no more than ten yards away, a dozen or more huge bulls were grazing the pasture's short, tough grass, or lolling in hollows of brown dust. Considering the close proximity of the animals, my initial questions had nothing whatsoever to do with the Evans family or their history.

"William told me these are rodeo bulls," I said, avoiding the unflinching stare of a big black beast with a lethal spread of horns.

"That's right."

After an unnerving moment, the bull turned his back on me and wandered a few yards away to stand beside a brown bull with a missing horn. The black bull placidly nudged the other animal's backside, then proceeded to give him a few licks in a sensitive area.

Tom Evans' tanned cheeks turned a shade ruddier as he observed this. "You'll have to pardon them, Mackenzie," he told me with a lopsided grin. "That's just a bit of male bonding goin' on."

I laughed. "Right now, they don't look very dangerous."

Tom nodded. "Lookin' at 'em here in the field, they do seem right docile, but I wouldn't trust a one of 'em to stay that way. Rodeo bulls are bred to be tough and mean, and most have more than earned their nasty reputations. Have you ever been to a rodeo and seen the bull riding?"

I shook my head. "No, and I don't think I'll ever understand why a man would want to get on the back of one of those brutes."

William's father gave me his slow smile. "Men do lots of things that women'll never understand. And I guess bull riding is one of them."

He went back to stringing a tough strand of barbed wire, and after a moment I had to ask, "Has William ever ridden a bull?"

"Nope. Bronc ridin' is more his style."

I stared at Tom, wide-eyed. "Really?"

He let go a hearty laugh. "Nah, I was just teasin' you a bit. But Will's won more than one prize for calf roping and steer wrestling." Tom smiled and went back to work, deftly stringing new wire and replacing the broken post with a sturdy new one.

I drew a few lazy doodles on the notebook's blank page and shifted position on the stump, wishing I'd thought to bring a pillow along. My lower back and right side were aching, but I hadn't taken anything stronger than ibuprofen with breakfast, wanting to be clearheaded for my task. Now, even though my mind and thoughts were very clear, I had to admit they weren't focused on the past. William's father glanced at my idle hands with a little smile, but said nothing.

"I was wondering," I said at last, "why William chose to go into property law rather than some other field."

"I don't know as there was any one reason," Tom answered, "but living in the West, especially on a farm or ranch, you become more aware of things like water and mineral rights—things that folks in the city take for granted. Land ownership can bring out the best or worst in a man, and if there's anything that gets Will's dander up, it's the way some folks with power and money try to take advantage of someone else's misfortune." He tested the sturdiness of the post he'd repaired, then glanced up at me and tilted his head. "Now that I think about it, there was an incident some years back that happened to Jenny's grandparents. Of course, this was long before Will was even born, but when he heard the story, he got pretty fired up. "

"What was the incident? How long ago was it?" I prompted, sensing another story brimming just beneath the surface.

Tom tipped his cowboy hat back, then glanced at me with a thoughtful frown. "I don't recall the exact year, but it was sometime during the Depression. Jenny's grandparents, George and Mabel Jensen, had a real nice home up in Salt Lake City. The home was all paid for, which was good because George was retired and they were both gettin' on in years. Well, the city levied a tax to build a sidewalk alongside their street, and the Jensens were handed a bill for over a thousand dollars. Can you imagine that? A thousand dollars during the Depression was a huge amount for anyone to come up with, let alone poor older folks. Most families were grateful just to put food on the table. Anyhow, the long and short of it was, George didn't have the money, and he had no way of gettin' it. There were no such things as credit cards, or easy loans—not in those days. And most of the banks were in nearly as much trouble as the rest of the folks. So George and Mabel ended up having to sell their home at a loss. And all because of that blasted tax for a sidewalk."

"But that's so unfair!"

Tom nodded. "That's exactly how Will felt when he heard about it. It rankled that boy something fierce that there was no one to help and nothin' to be done."

"What happened to the Jensens? Where did they go?"

"Oh, George's folks had an old place some seventy miles south in Spanish Fork that he and Mabel were able to move into. Wasn't much. It didn't have indoor plumbing or running water, but they were grateful to have a roof over their heads." Tom shook his head and gave a piece of fencing a particularly vicious snap with his wire cutters. "Will never forgot what happened to his great-grandparents," he went on. "And when he was in college, it seemed like there was always some sort of ruckus goin' on around St. George with land developers and ranchers. Sounds like something out of an old western movie, and I guess it was. Folks don't change much.

"Anyhow, Will got a scholarship to Stanford University and went on after law school to pass the California Bar exam with flyin' colors. Some big law firm snatched him up, and he was doing real well. He'd probably still be practicing law in California if I hadn't had that fool heart attack."

"I can't imagine William blaming you for that," I said gently.

"No, but I can't help blaming myself. Will gave up everything to come back here and help with the ranch."

I said nothing, wondering of the "everything" referred only to William's practice or something more—his marriage perhaps.

More information was not forthcoming as William's father gathered his tools and headed for the truck parked beside the road. I got up from the stump, suppressing a groan, and walked stiffly to the truck. My actions didn't escape Tom's notice.

"If you're feeling up to it, I've been thinkin' of a couple of stories I could toss your way," he said. "That is, if you don't mind following me around for a while longer with that notebook of yours."

"I'm feeling just fine," I told him, determined to set my aches and stiffness aside. "My notebook and I are ready when you are."

The morning passed all too quickly. I felt no need to prompt him with leading questions, or even to try to steer the course of his thoughts and reminiscing. It was a joy just to listen and write and let the memories flow. There was no way I could capture all the charm of Tom's words and delivery; in fact, I was hard pressed to get down the main facts and feelings of a given experience. More than once, I found myself so caught up in what he was saying that I completely forgot to take notes.

By the time we headed back to the ranch house for lunch, the pages of my notebook were brimming over with colorful tales from Tom's life, and I was completely enamored with this soft-spoken man, his wit and wisdom, and the subtle threads of love and loyalty woven through every story.

"Well, it's about time you two came back," Jenny said with mock severity when Tom and I entered the kitchen. "I was about ready to send out a search party."

Tom grinned and stopped her words with a hearty kiss. "It's all Mackenzie's doing," he said. "If she wasn't such a good listener, we would've been back ages ago." He winked at me, and we shared a conspiratorial smile.

"Mackenzie's doing, my foot," she huffed, but there was a pleased twinkle in her eyes. Pulling out a kitchen chair, she motioned for me to sit down. "Lunch is all set, but I think you could do with a cold glass of lemonade. You're looking a bit flushed. I should have given you a hat."

"I'm fine," I told her, accepting the glass. I took a long, cool drink, then asked, "Have you heard from William?"

"Not yet, but I'm sure he'll call as soon as he learns anything."

I nodded, quietly acknowledging to myself that I was almost more eager to hear the sound of his voice than any news he might have.

Tom was ready to start another story session as soon as lunch was over, but Jenny wouldn't hear of it. "Mackenzie's had enough sun and tall tales for today," she pronounced, and Tom didn't argue the point. Turning to me, she added, "William said the doctor wanted you to take it real easy for a few days. And I'm here to make sure you do just that."

Like her husband, I acquiesced without argument.

"While you take a little rest, Tom and I need to make a trip into town for a few things," she went on. "Is there anything you need that we can get for you?"

I hesitated a moment, then gave Jenny a sheepish smile. "I don't know that it's really a need, but I'd love some Pepsi, if it's not too much trouble."

Tom Evans chuckled. "The elixir of the gods. I'll buy you a case."

Upstairs in William's room, I sat down on the edge of the bed with a sigh. Jenny was right. It wouldn't hurt to take a short rest before writing out a more complete version of Tom's stories from my sketchy notes. My injured side was protesting loudly, and the pain medication was taking its own sweet time to ease my discomfort.

It's amazing the kinds of things we take for granted when we're healthy and whole. Like taking off a pair of shoes. Slipping my feet out of sandals was a relatively easy task, but trying to untie and remove a pair of Nikes without bending over was next to impossible. Several groans later, I finally had the shoes off and was sweating and wincing with pain. To add to my discomfort, the new jeans and denim shirt that had seemed such a pleasant choice in the cool of morning were far too warm and heavy for the heat of midday. I wriggled out of the jeans and unbuttoned the shirt. Even the light pressure of my bra against my ribs was too much. I eased myself out of its constraints, then stood in front of the dresser's large oval mirror to survey the bruises on my right side and rib cage. Definitely not a pretty sight. But at least there was some improvement. In the days since my arrival at Hearth Fires, the black and purple hues had faded to bilious shades of green and yellow.

I picked up the jeans and shirt and took them to the closet, where William's mother had made a little space among her son's clothes for my limited wardrobe. The sight of a handsome three-piece suit sharing space with western shirts made me smile. The attorney and the cowboy. Who would have thought . . .

I draped my jeans over a hanger, then hung my denim shirt next to one of his, feeling a strange little pang of longing. William had been gone barely two days. It was impossible, ridiculous even, that I should miss him—that I should feel this queer ache inside just thinking about him. An ache that had nothing to do with injuries or bruises.

I went to his bureau and opened one drawer, then another, until I found what I was seeking. With a sigh that was part pleasure, part pain, I slipped my arms into the sleeves of his pajama top and wrapped it around me, then crawled into bed.

As I burrowed into the softness of his pillow, my mind sent him messages across the miles—messages he would never hear. *Be safe, William. Think of me . . . and come home soon.*

Eighteen

When I awoke, the brightness of midday had passed and the light coming in the window was a mellow gold. I lay still, watching the dusty dance of amber ribbons on the wall, my mind pleasantly idle as it moved lazily out of sleep. Glancing at the digital clock on the bedside table, I was shocked to find it was nearly six. William. Surely, he must have news of some kind by now.

The thought had me out of bed and shedding the pajama top, all drowsiness gone. I dressed quickly, then ran a comb through the tangles of my hair. After snatching the cell phone from the bedside table, I stuffed it in my jeans pocket and left the room.

The delicious aroma of warm peaches wafting from the kitchen told me where William's mother was even before I reached the bottom of the stairs.

"Mmm, something smells absolutely divine," I said as I entered the kitchen.

"Peach cobbler," Jenny announced with a smile. Hot pads in hand, she took a peek in the oven. "Needs just a minute or two more."

"Could we save some for William?"

"Of course, dear. I made a double batch. By the way, your face is looking so much better. Those nasty scrapes and bruises are nearly healed."

"No doubt thanks to your wonder salve." I sat down at the table. "I just wish it didn't make me smell like a cow."

Jenny laughed. "I've always been right fond of cows. They make real good neighbors."

I stared at her with interest, realizing that her words, although lightly spoken, were truly meant. I thought of the years she'd spent living at the ranch, miles from the nearest neighbor or town, and had to ask, "Didn't you ever get lonely, living here at the ranch?"

Jenny took another look in the oven, then lifted out the baking dish of bubbling peach cobbler and set it on top of the stove before answering. "If you mean did I ever miss or want to live in the city—I can't say I ever did. Ranch life isn't easy, but it suits me. Oh, I admit it's nice to drive into St. George now and then for some shopping or a movie, but I'd never want to live there." She gave an adamant shake of her head. "There's just too much noise and confusion. Besides, everything I love is here."

I watched William's mother take a damp dishcloth and wipe some spilled cobbler juice from the stove's surface, as the shades of meaning in her simple statement found a thoughtful place in my mind.

"You and Tom seem very happy," I said after a moment.

Jenny's tender expression answered my comment even before her affirming words. "We've had a good life together. Oh, there are times when we both get good and frustrated with each other, but it never lasts long. After all these years, I still look forward to him coming home each night. And I never get tired of looking at that man's face."

My lips parted as her words touched a sensitive chord deep inside. Had I ever felt that way about Todd? His was certainly a handsome face, and yet, when I tried to fix the image of his face in my mind, it was William's rugged features that readily appeared, William's gray-green eyes that I saw.

"Oh, I nearly forgot," Jenny went on. "Tom bought a whole case of Pepsi for you while we were in town. I've got some cold cans in the fridge if you'd like one."

"Thanks, I'd love one." Not bothering to get a glass from the cupboard, I took a can from the fridge and popped the metal lid. "Bliss. Utter bliss," I said after a long, satisfying drink. Please thank Tom for me."

"You can thank him yourself if you like. He's out to the woodshed gettin' a few more logs cut for tonight." Putting one hand on an ample hip, Jenny gave me a twinkling-eyed glance. "I don't know how you did it, but you sure have put a nickel in that man for telling stories."

"I'm glad." Taking another can of Pepsi from the fridge, I asked her, "Do you think Tom would like some 'elixir of the gods'?"

She chuckled. "If it's coming from you, I'm sure he would."

Walking across the back lawn, a can of Pepsi in each hand, I felt thankfulness welling up inside me. Yesterday's restlessness was gone, replaced by a calm that was altogether strange and unlikely, considering the tenuous circumstances of my stay. Fear and uncertainty felt far away.

I paused to gaze up at the sandstone cliffs to the east, marveling at the way the late-afternoon sun burned light and color into Mount Kinesava's stony surface, when a sudden vibration from my pants pocket made my heart leap. I dumped the cans of Pepsi unceremoniously on the grass and grabbed the cell phone, barely taking time to check the caller ID.

"William!"

"Hi. How are you doing?"

"I'm fine, especially since I've made it a point to follow your mother's advice."

"What advice is that?"

"To rest and be thankful."

"Good girl," he said with a smile in his voice. "Besides, there's no point in arguing with my mother."

"So I'm learning."

Before I could ask about his day, he went on with "What about Dad? Have you dared broach the subject of writing down a few of the family stories?"

"Yes, and you were right. He was more than a little reluctant at first. But last night your father told me the story of your great-grandparents and how Hearth Fires got its name. I stayed up half the night trying to write it all down. And today, I spent the entire morning following him around, notebook in hand. It was awesome."

"You're the one who's awesome," William said softly.

His words sent happy warmth swirling around inside me. "Thanks, but I . . . it was your idea—your suggestion. I was feeling so frustrated, and you gave me exactly what I needed."

I heard his low chuckle, followed by "Now that's what a man likes to hear."

"William!"

He laughed. "I mean it. This is the best news I've had all day."

"Has it been that kind of day? What happened with the court dockets?"

"Nothing! That's the problem," he said with a disgruntled sigh. "I've gone over and over those records, starting with Wolcott's current cases for the next three months. I even looked through his hearings and trials from the past month, but there wasn't anything that jumped out at me."

"I'm so sorry."

"So am I. I never expected to find a case with the name Sarcassian spelled out in bold letters, but I honestly thought I'd come up with some hint or clue."

"There's got to be something."

"I know, but I'm not seeing it. To make matters worse, while I've been coming up with nothing but dead ends, Dicola's been plenty busy. And I don't like where things are headed."

"Why? What's happened?"

"Wade called a little while ago to tell me that Dicola's been talking to people on your magazine staff. In particular, a guy named Corbin Corelli."

"Corbin? What on earth could Lieutenant Dicola learn from him?"

"For one thing, he found out that you have no fiancé. Corelli said you made it very clear that you weren't involved with anyone when the two of you went out together."

"I didn't really go out with him," I said, irritated that Corbin would imply something more. "It was just a business dinner."

"Well, whatever it was, Corelli's got the lieutenant rethinking the whole scenario about who helped you leave the hospital. Besides questioning the magazine staff, Dicola's spent a lot of time going over the hospital's security films."

"But what could he find there? You were wearing scrubs and I had the surgical cap over my hair—"

William interrupted my breathless words. "Dicola didn't recognize us. What he saw was Wade entering the hospital, and that set off some alarm bells."

"Why? I don't understand—"

"Wade told Dicola the last time he saw you was when he dropped you off at your boss's house, remember? It's in his report. There's nothing about him seeing you at the hospital."

Silence stretched on the line between us as I struggled to calm the fears and worries that William's news sent racing through me. I drew a steadying breath. "Has Lieutenant Dicola accused Wade of withholding information?"

"Not openly. He can't do that without giving away the fact that Wade's not the only one who knows more than he's telling. Those two are doing a dangerous dance of deception, each one watching the other to see who misses a step and stumbles. This afternoon Dicola called Wade into his office and asked some pretty pointed questions. He confronted Wade with the fact that he saw him on the hospital's security films and wanted to know why it wasn't included in his report."

I swallowed and put a hand to my throat. "What did Wade tell him?"

"Pieces of the truth—that he heard about the accident on the scanner and dropped by the hospital to check things out. Then he fudged a bit and told Dicola he wasn't able to question you because the doctors were busy treating you and your boss. And while he was waiting, he got an important call on another investigation and had to leave, which is basically the truth. Dicola couldn't argue with that, but he kept badgering Wade, wanting to know why this information wasn't included in his report. Wade said he'd planned to go back and question you about the accident, but before that could happen, you'd left the hospital." William sounded relieved as he added, "I really have to hand it to my little brother. He knows how to think on his feet."

"Thank goodness for that. Do you think Dicola believes what Wade told him?"

"I don't know. I hope so. Like I said, Dicola can't risk asking Wade too many leading questions without incriminating himself. Instead, he did a lot of huffing and puffing and told Wade he'd expect complete reports from him in the future or he'd have to write up a complaint."

"So, is Wade going to be all right? Do you think he's in any danger from Dicola or Sarcassian?"

"I don't think so—at least not yet. But I'm afraid it's only a matter of time before Dicola starts putting two and two together. If there's no fiancé, he's bound to make a list of the people you've had contact with since you've been in California. And Wade will be high on that list." William released a tense breath. "To keep you safe and get Dicola off Wade's back, I've got to find that connection between Wolcott and Sarcassian."

"You will," I told him. "I know you will."

"Thanks for the trust, Mac. I only wish I felt as confident."

"You sound tired. Can't you take a break?"

"I don't want to, but I will. Wade's stopping by the law office after his shift and we'll go somewhere and grab a burger. Then we'll both head back to the office and tackle those court dockets again. There's got to be something I'm not seeing."

"William, please be careful. If Lieutenant Dicola sees you and Wade together, it would be disastrous."

"I know. I seriously doubt Dicola would put a tail on Wade, but I've told him not to take any chances. And if it makes you feel any better, the chief has someone watching Dicola's every move."

"That helps a little, but I'd feel even better if you'd call me in a few hours. It's so hard being far away and hearing everything secondhand, as it were. I need . . . I need to know that you're all right."

"I'll give you a call after dinner—say eight o'clock your time."

"Thank you."

There was a pause, followed by William's tentative "Can I ask you something?"

"Of course."

"When you were out with Corelli, did he come on to you?"

Suddenly I found myself smiling, when only moments before, fear was doing its best to convince me I'd never smile again. "He was a perfect gentleman. Especially when he realized I wasn't at all interested in what he had to offer."

I heard William's chuckle, followed by a husky "Now *I* feel better. Bye, Mac. I'll call you in a couple of hours."

When his father came out of the woodshed minutes later, carrying a bucket of kindling, I was still sitting on the back lawn, staring dreamily at the western sky. Streaks of coral and hot pink emblazoned the thin line of clouds that hovered above the horizon where the sun had set only moments before.

Tom paused and gave a nod in the general direction of the sunset. "Nice evening, isn't it?"

"Yes. Beautiful." I brushed some grass off my pants and got to my feet. Then, seeing the Pepsi cans, I bent to pick them up. "I'm sorry. I was bringing you a drink when William called, and I . . . well . . ."

"And you sorta got distracted," Tom finished with a knowing smile. I answered his smile with one of my own, as we walked in comfortable silence toward the ranch house.

Giving me a sly glance, Tom said, "I take it William's doing okay."

I just nodded and linked my arm through his.

Nineteen

I told myself I was not going to watch the clock, that it would be at least two hours before William called back and I just needed to keep busy. After dinner I excused myself to go up to his room and work on my notes while the details of his father's stories were still fresh in my mind. I probably would have been more comfortable working in William's office at his desk, but Tom and Jenny were watching the latest episode of *Doc Martin* in the living room, and the blare of the TV made concentration more than a little difficult.

It was challenging enough just trying to concentrate on my notes and write anything halfway intelligent. My ribs and injured side were complaining loudly that the day's activities had taken their toll. Determined to ignore my discomfort, I arranged a backrest of pillows on the bed and sat, with the notebook in my lap and the cell phone within easy reach on the bed beside me. It was sheer discipline rather than inspiration that kept me at my task. The words came slowly, almost reluctantly, and the sentences felt stiff and mechanical, but I went doggedly on.

I was reworking the account of Tom Evans' meeting and courtship with his wife when the cell phone's musical chimes set my heart pounding double time. A quick glance at the caller ID showed the number and caller wasn't William. Ignoring the insistent someone, I went back to work.

Not ten minutes later, my writing was interrupted by the same caller—someone by the name of LeAnn. I frowned at the phone, my emotions escalating from mild irritation to a suspicious snit, as I wondered who the persistent LeAnn might be. I was imagining everything from William's ex-wife to a sloe-eyed blond or a sultry brunette when it suddenly hit me that the phone belonged to Jenny Evans, not her son.

My suspicions collapsed in a laughable heap as I adjusted the caller's age and appearance to someone of Jenny's generation. When the cell phone rang yet again, I was halfway tempted to forego William's instructions not to answer, and ask poor LeAnn if I could take a message.

But this time, the caller was William.

"Mac, you're not going to believe this—I can hardly believe it myself," he began with an urgency in his voice that set my pulse racing.

"Believe what? William, are you all right?"

"Honey, I'm more than all right. But Judge Wolcott won't be for much longer."

"Why? What's happened?"

"Something I never expected, but it all fits."

"What fits? Is this going to be good news or bad news?"

"Very good news. I don't have all the pieces to the puzzle yet, but I know where to look to find them."

"What puzzle pieces are you talking about? William, I am literally dying by inches."

"Sorry, Mac," he said, not sounding the least repentant. "I was waiting for Wade and giving the court dockets another go round, when one of the attorneys in the practice stopped by and wanted to know why I was working so late. I've known Chris Newell for years, ever since law school at Stanford, so I felt pretty safe in telling him that I was working on a case involving Judge Wolcott and a possible bribe. Before I could say anything else, Chris shook his head and said if the case had anything to do with drugs, I might as well do myself a favor and go home. Apparently, Chris has had several courtroom experiences with Wolcott and doesn't have a high opinion of the man. Just the opposite."

"Really. Did he say why?"

"Oh, yeah. It seems Wolcott has the reputation of being pretty soft when it comes to trying drug cases. Chris gave me a classic example where he and the police officers involved had a cut-and-dried case of drug dealing and possession. To quote Chris, all their 'i's were dotted and their t's crossed' when it came to their report and presenting the evidence in court. Wolcott's final ruling amounted to a small slap on the wrist and a minimum fine. According to Chris, this wasn't an isolated incident—it's happened several times in Wolcott's court, and the word gets around. There's even a rumor the judge is a user, but no one's been able to get any solid evidence to back it up.

"Anyway, I told Chris that I thought Nick Sarcassian might be bribing Judge Wolcott to throw a case, but couldn't find anything in the court dockets to connect the two. Chris didn't bat an eye. He just nodded and said, 'Then concentrate on the drug cases. Forget the DUIs and domestic disputes. Concentrate on the drugs.' So that's what I'm going to do." Determination was strong in William's voice, all traces of discouragement gone. "Wade and I took time to grab a burger, and we're on our way back to the office now. Between the two of us, we'll find the connection. Focusing on drug cases really narrows the field."

As he spoke, I felt the inner nudging of an idea, a prompting so small I was almost hesitant to share it.

"Mackenzie, are you there?"

"Yes . . . yes. I was just thinking of something that might help you narrow the field even more."

"What's that?"

"Well, it's only a feeling, but I think you should look for a woman."

"Your feelings rate pretty high with me," William said. "I'm intrigued. Why do you think it could be a woman?"

"Partly because of the risk involved. Wade told me that Sarcassian was ultracautious—that he had others do his dirty work. For him to go to Judge Wolcott's home and offer him a bribe was a huge risk. Whoever he's doing it for, and whatever the reason, it seems to me that it might be something personal, as well as business."

"I like your thinking," William said, approval warming his voice. "Well, we're nearly back to the office, so I'd better let you go. I'm not sure how long it's going to take. How late will you be up? Wade and I could be working half the night."

"I don't care how late it is. Just call me."

"I will. Wish us luck, Mac."

"You know I do."

"Oh, and tell Mom and Dad that we're okay and not to worry."

"I'll be glad to."

In the background, I heard a man's voice call out, "Hey, Mackenzie! Don't let my big brother boss you around."

"I guess you heard that," William said dryly.

"Yes, I did. And would you give Wade a message for me?"

There was a long-suffering sigh, then a crisp "Sure. What's the message?"

"Tell Wade I think his brother's wonderful," I said softly and ended the call.

Leaning back against the bed pillows, I felt a happy tide of emotion spill through me. William and Wade were safe. And there was hope—real hope that they would uncover the connection between Sarcassian and Judge Wolcott. The information from William's attorney friend opened up all kinds of possibilities as well as providing an underlying motive for the judge's actions.

Thinking over the conversation with William, a sudden realization brought a soft smile to my lips. He called me *honey.*

Waiting for his phone call was sweet torture. I prepared for bed but didn't dare take any pain medication, wanting to be awake and alert when the call came. Trying to write or even do some simple editing of Tom's stories was an exercise in futility. I switched off the lamp, hoping Tom and Jenny would assume I was tired and had gone to bed early. A little after ten, I heard them come up the stairs, Jenny's voice a whisper. A half hour later, all was quiet.

I waited another ten minutes, then got carefully out of bed and opened the door a crack. There was no sliver of light under the door of their bedroom, and listening for a long moment, I detected the faint rhythm of Tom's snores, nothing more.

After slipping a cotton robe over William's pajama top, I grabbed the cell phone and crept silently down the hall to the stairs. The darkness in the house was thick and enveloping, without so much as a shadow or relieving shade of gray. I literally felt my way along the walls and into the kitchen, stubbing my toe on a kitchen chair as I groped, arms outstretched, toward the general vicinity of the refrigerator.

I took a can of Pepsi from the fridge, then made my way to the table and sat down, waiting for my eyes to become accustomed to the darkness. This was a different kind of darkness altogether from what I was accustomed to, living in the city. My apartment was in a lovely old brownstone just north of Chicago's "Miracle Mile," and even on the blackest night, there was always light and sound of some kind.

I set the cell phone on the table and sipped the Pepsi, my thoughts a strange mixture of tense anticipation and a new, heady kind of happiness I was almost afraid to put a name to. As I sat there, I became aware that the dense texture of the room's darkness had thinned and diluted to a softer shade of black. And from the east window, there was a faint, milky glow.

I crossed to the window, pushed the curtains inside, and watched in wonder as a huge harvest moon rose serenely above the skyline of jagged cliffs and rocky pinnacles. My heart fairly ached with the beauty and splendor of it.

From the table, a rumbling vibration had me making an awkward dash for the cell phone. Heart pounding, I grabbed the phone, my voice breathless and unsteady. "William?"

"We found it," he said without preamble. "And you were right, Mac. It's a woman—Sarcassian's daughter."

My legs went weak and I sank onto a kitchen chair. "Tell me. Tell me everything."

"Wade and I had the judge's case load narrowed down to four hearings and two trials involving drugs during the next two weeks. Thinking about what you said, I kept going back to a hearing where the plaintiff was Arsine, aka Nina Castella. The woman was pulled over for a minor traffic offense, driving on expired plates. Wade happened to be familiar with the case because a buddy of his, Dave Russell, was the arresting officer. Instead of just taking the ticket, this Arsine created a huge scene. At first, she was all sweetness and light, and insisted she had the current registration at home somewhere. When this didn't work, she offered Russell a hefty bribe to forget the whole thing. Having the woman flash several hundred dollars his way made him suspicious and he decided to search the car—which by the way, was a red Porsche Carrera. By that time, Arsine was screaming obscenities at him and threatening lawsuits."

"Did the officer find anything incriminating."

"Oh, yeah. There was a nice stash of cocaine under the seat, and several packets of prescription painkillers, mostly watered-down Mexican oxycontin. This sheds new light on why Sarcassian was so anxious to get Judge Wolcott to throw the case."

"I'm not sure I understand."

"Wade told me the police have suspected for some time that Sarcassian's been involved in illicit trade, and watered-down oxycontin is one of his specialties. If his daughter went to trial, there was always the chance it could blow the lid off Daddy's operation."

"But not if Sarcassian could buy Judge Wolcott's favor before the case went to trial," I filled in breathlessly.

"Exactly."

"I knew you'd find it," I told William with a relieved sigh. "But there's one thing that puzzles me about all this."

"What's that?"

"How did you know that Arsine Castella was Sarcassian's daughter?"

"I didn't. At least, not at first. If you hadn't told me to look for a woman, Arsine's unusual first name never would have caught my eye. That plus the circumstances of the case, the fact that it involved drugs, sent up some red flags. As it turns out, the name Arsine is Armenian. And so's Sarcassian. When I mentioned this to Wade, he remembered pulling someone over for a DUI several months ago by the name of Arsine, but the woman's last name was Woodbury, not Castella. He did a quick background check on the police computer and voilà—up comes a fascinating profile on Arsine Woodbury Castella, maiden name Sarcassian. It seems the current case isn't the first time Sarcassian's had to bail out his little girl. But this time, the repercussions could have a disastrous effect on his shady business dealings."

"Sarcassian knew bribing Wolcott was risky," William went on, "but he probably knew about the judge's cocaine habit and figured his favor could be bought for the right price. But Sarcassian had to move fast."

I drew a shaky breath, my mind fairly spinning with all William had told me. "When is Arsine's case due to be heard?"

"Three days from now."

"That soon?"

"I'm afraid so. Which explains Sarcassian's and Dicola's desperate attempts to get hold of those pictures."

"Oh, William, it all makes sense now—horrible, horrible sense," I said, feeling a cold shiver of nerves.

"Yes, I'm afraid it does."

"But what can we do? Even with all this information, the forty-eight hours Chief McIntire gave you is up tomorrow afternoon, and Arsine's hearing is only two days after that."

"I know," William said calmly, "so I think it's time to shake things up, let Nicolas Sarcassian know he's not the one holding all the aces."

"But how can we do that?"

"By releasing those pictures."

"What?"

"I know a guy, a former client actually, who writes a political column for the *San Francisco Tribune*. Joel Blackhurst also has connections with CNN and some local TV stations. I'm thinking if he posted those pictures on his website and e-mailed them to his media contacts, along with some leading questions—say, something like 'What was behind Nicolas Sarcassian's secret meeting with Judge Peter Wolcott, only days before his daughter's case was due to be heard in Wolcott's court?'—it would really shake things up. At the very least, it'll put a halt to Arsine's hearing until the matter can be looked into. And that's the last thing Sarcassian and Wolcott want. Dicola, too, for that matter." William paused and said in a tight voice, "But it's not my call to make. It's up to you, Mac. If releasing those pictures puts you in more danger, I'll never forgive myself. You have the final say in this. If you want to get rid of those damn pictures and let the whole thing die, I'll back you a hundred percent. It's up to you."

"Allison's the one who died," I said evenly. "Let's release the pictures."

Twenty

"Are you sure about this?" William asked, his voice tentative. "Releasing the pictures could be risky."

"I'm very sure," I replied. "How soon can you get hold of this Joel Blackhurst?"

"Tonight—right away. I don't care how late it is, and neither will Joel when he learns what's at stake. I wouldn't be at all surprised if he managed to have those pictures plastered all over the internet and several TV stations before the morning news. Sarcassian and Judge Wolcott are going to have a very rude awakening come morning."

"What about Chief McIntire? Do you think there'll be any negative fallout for Wade when the chief learns what we've done?"

"I doubt it. The fact that it was your decision to release the pictures pretty much lets Wade off the hook. McIntire might not be too happy that he's been left out of the loop, but we can't afford to wait around for his approval. Assuming, of course, that he'd give it. Then too, Blackhurst is my contact, not Wade's. McIntire can't accuse Wade of doing anything underhanded. It's all been strictly aboveboard."

"That's good to know. What about Lieutenant Dicola?"

"Good old Sloppy Joe?" William said with relish. "Believe me, once those pictures come out, my brother will be the last thing on Dicola's mind. He'll be too worried about saving his own skin. Oh, and I don't want you to worry that your name will be released along with the photos. Blackhurst knows how to keep his sources confidential."

"I'm not worried. Just incredibly relieved that we finally have some answers."

"Me too. Well, if I'm going to get hold of Joel before it gets any later, we'd better say good night. It must be close to midnight where you are."

"Almost. Oh, William, I was just wondering. What do you want me to tell your parents?"

"Don't worry about that, honey. I'll give them a call tomorrow."

A place in my midsection that had been aching only minutes before suddenly went soft and warm. *Honey.* Again.

"By the way, where are you right now?" William asked. "My mother is a notoriously light sleeper, and I'm surprised the phone didn't wake her."

"I'm downstairs in the kitchen. And there is the most glorious harvest moon shining outside the window. I was watching the moonrise just before you called."

"I'm sorry I'm not there to share it," he said softly. "But I will be soon. Good night, Mac."

I tiptoed up the stairs and climbed into bed, aching, tired, and unbearably happy. My mind couldn't stop going over the day's discoveries and all that William had told me, while my foolish heart was making some surprising discoveries of its own. Even after the pain medication took effect, sleep was a long time coming.

An insistent buzzing brought me out of the depths of sleep. I groaned and gave the air a clumsy swat, trying to avoid the annoying insect. By the time my groggy brain realized the sound was not an insect, but Jenny's cell phone, the caller had hung up. Frustrated, I quickly checked the missed calls and discovered the caller was not William, but the persistent LeAnn from yesterday. I set the phone aside with a sigh, ready to turn over and go back to sleep when I caught a glimpse of the time. My eyes widened and I sat up with a start. It was nearly ten thirty!

If William's contact, Joel Blackhurst, had done his job, the pictures should be causing quite a stir by now. I smiled and tossed back the bedcovers, imagining the resulting furor with great satisfaction. Seeing those incriminating photos, whether on the internet or the morning news, definitely ought to weaken the bite of the pit bull Sarcassian. And it would wipe that smug look right off Judge Wolcott's face.

By the time I showered and dressed, it was close to eleven. Already the temperature outside was climbing from comfortably warm to hot. I abandoned the thought of jeans in favor of cotton capris and the apple green blouse. Applying a little makeup and lip gloss, I was relieved to see the pale-faced witch woman was nearly gone. The bruises around my right eye were fading fast, and with the added help of a little makeup, barely noticeable. I brushed some wavy strands of hair away from my face and fastened them with a metal clip, then left the room.

By now, William should have called his parents with the news of his discovery and the release of the pictures. He and Wade had their meeting with Chief McIntire this afternoon, but after that . . . if he could get a flight, William might even be home by tonight. The thought of seeing him again made me catch my breath, and I entered the kitchen with a smile as bright as my hopes. If I'd been blessed with a voice for singing, I could have outwarbled any meadowlark.

"Good morning!"

William's mother glanced over her shoulder from her perch on a kitchen chair where she was scrubbing the inside of a cupboard. Plates, dishes, and bowls were stacked on the counter on either side of her, and the pungent smell of Pine-Sol filled the air.

"There you are," she said cheerfully. "I hope you slept well. When Tom and I came down for breakfast you were sleeping so soundly, I didn't have the heart to disturb you."

"I had no idea it was so late. I never meant to sleep away half the morning."

"Well, it must have been what you needed." Jenny gave me a nod of approval as she got down from the chair. "You look so lovely today—positively glowing."

I felt a warm flush creep up my neck. "Where's Tom?"

"He drove into town a couple of hours ago. He promised to drive one of our neighbors into St. George for a doctor's appointment. He asked me to make his apologies to you. I know he was looking forward to sharing some more family stories. As it is, he probably won't be back until this afternoon."

"That's all right." I said, thinking William must not have called his parents, or Jenny surely would have mentioned it. What if something had gone wrong? Maybe his contact had refused to release the photos. I felt a sudden tightness inside just thinking about the possibility.

"I thought I'd use the morning to clean out a few cupboards," Jenny was saying. "William's been so busy with his practice in St. George, plus taking care of the ranch, the house cleaning has suffered some." She gave me a womanly look. "Even if he was around more often, I doubt cleaning cupboards would rank very high on his list of things to do."

"Probably not," I agreed, hoping that the worry growing inside didn't show on my face.

"Is there anything special you'd like me to cook for your breakfast?"

I shook my head. "Seeing as how it's practically lunch time, just some toast and juice will be fine. But please, go on with what you were doing. I'll be glad to fix something for myself."

"There's some fresh cinnamon rolls in the breadbox, if you'd prefer one of those to toast," she said.

"You talked me into it."

I opted for a tall glass of milk rather than juice, put one of the soft, sticky rolls on a plate, and took it to the table, all the while debating whether or not I should ask Jenny about William. If something had gone wrong, he'd certainly call and let us know. Perhaps there was just a delay in releasing the pictures. And if this were the case, there was no point in burdening Jenny with unfounded worries.

She was back on the chair, putting a stack of dinner plates on a newly washed shelf, when we heard the back door slam. Seconds later, an attractive young woman wearing jeans, and a T-shirt that emphasized her pregnant belly, burst into the kitchen.

"Mom, are you all right? I've been trying to get hold of you for two days, and no one's answered your home phone or the cell. I finally stopped by the house, and one of your neighbors said—" She stopped midsentence when she saw me sitting at the table, and curiosity wiped the worry off her face.

"I'm sorry, LeAnn. Dad and I have been—well, we've been sort of busy here at the ranch and . . ." Jenny's explanation came to a stumbling halt as she got down off the chair, her nervous gaze shifting from the young woman to me. "Mackenzie, this is my daughter LeAnn. Mackenzie is—well, she and William—"

"I'm Mackenzie Jones, William's fiancé," I filled in, giving his sister a quick smile.

LeAnn's eyes widened, but no more so than her mother's. A moment of stunned silence followed my announcement, as William's sister gaped at me in astonishment. I didn't dare look at Jenny.

"His fiancé," LeAnn repeated. "Well, this is a surprise—a very good surprise," she added with a dazed shake of her head. "I had no idea Will was seeing someone."

"I— we— it was sort of sudden," I told her, not knowing what else to say now that the damage was done.

LeAnn recovered enough to send me a warm smile that was part apology. With her honey-blond hair tied back in a ponytail and her light-blue eyes, she resembled her brother Wade much more than

William. "I'm sorry if I sounded shocked," she said. "But along with my congratulations, I'm going to have to give my brother a bad time about this. Where is Will, by the way?"

"He had some business in California," Jenny put in quickly, "but we expect him back soon."

LeAnn gave me an incredulous look. "And he left you here at the ranch?"

I moistened my lips and said with a little shrug, "I've loved being here. It's, uh, given me some time to get to know your parents."

"Mackenzie's been writing down some of your father's experiences and family stories," Jenny put in.

LeAnn pulled out a kitchen chair and sat down. "Holy Hannah," she said fervently, a hand on her rounded tummy. "How on earth did you get Dad to do that?"

Before I could answer, Jenny snatched the pan of sweet rolls from the breadbox and offered one to her daughter.

"No thanks, Mom. I really can't stay. I only came by because you offered to help with the twins' birthday party, and—" She stopped as Jenny put a sweet roll on a napkin and set it in front of her. "Well, maybe just a half," LeAnn relented. "I never could refuse your cinnamon rolls."

"You have twins?" I said, hoping to avoid further questions.

She nodded, licking some frosting off her fingers. "Gavin and Quinn are turning four, and believe me, that's reason enough to celebrate! We're having a dinosaur party this evening, and the boys have put in a request for one of Grandma Evans' homemade chocolate cakes."

Jenny clapped a hand to her head as she faced her daughter. "I'm sorry, LeAnn. There's been so much happening, I completely forgot."

"Obviously." LeAnn's smile was teasing. "Don't worry about it, Mom. If you don't have time, I can always buy one at the store."

"And disappoint those darling boys? I wouldn't dream of it. There's plenty of time to bake a cake before tonight. The problem is, your father's gone to St. George and won't be back until this afternoon."

LeAnn gave her mother a puzzled look. "Why is that a problem?"

"Well, I hate to leave Mackenzie here alone . . ."

"Mackenzie's welcome to come along," LeAnn said easily. "It'll give us a chance to get acquainted," she added with a smile.

"Thanks, I'd love to, but I planned on reworking some of Tom's stories this afternoon," I told her. "Jenny, why don't you go with LeAnn? I'd hate to be the cause of your grandsons not having their birthday cake."

Jenny bit her lip and sent me a worried look. "But William said—"

"I know." I cut her off before she could divulge anything more. "But I promised him I'd have some stories ready when he gets back."

"When is Will coming home?" LeAnn asked me.

"I'm not exactly sure, but when we talked last night, he thought it wouldn't be too long."

LeAnn shook her blond head, her expression slightly dazed. "I'm sorry, but I'm still blown away by the news. I talked with Will barely a week ago and he never said a word about being engaged."

"Well, we haven't told many people . . ."

LeAnn gave her mother an accusing look. "I had no idea you were so good at keeping a secret. How long have you known about this?"

"Not long," her mother answered faintly.

"How did you and William meet?" LeAnn took another bite of sweet roll. "I want to hear all the details."

I finished the last of my own sweet roll, needing some time to come up with an answer. "Wade introduced us," I said finally.

"Oh, so you're from California?"

"Not originally. I've just been . . . working there for a while."

"I don't know which is more amazing—that Wade has been playing matchmaker, or that Will is actually engaged," LeAnn said.

"To tell you the truth, none of us thought he would ever marry again after the nightmare that Melanie put him through."

"Now, LeAnn," Jenny put in tactfully.

"Mom, I know how kind you are, but there's no way you can sugarcoat what that woman did." LeAnn fixed me with a savvy, woman-to-woman look. "Knowing my brother, I'll bet he hasn't told you much about what he fondly calls his 'unfortunate incarceration.'"

"Well, no, he hasn't."

Jenny tried once again to curb her daughter's candid tongue. "LeAnn, it really isn't our place."

"Sorry, Mom," LeAnn said, not in the least contrite. "But since Mackenzie's going to be my new sister, I think she should know how glad I am that she's not another Melanie."

Jenny gave a helpless shake of her head as LeAnn went on with a mischievous grin and a sparkle in her blue eyes. "Unlike my mother, I have a terrible time keeping secrets—especially happy ones. And this has got to be the ultimate secret! But I will try to keep the news to myself until Will gets back."

"I'm sure William would like to tell you himself" was all I could say.

"Oh, dear, and now I've spoiled the surprise. Well, I'll just have to act terribly surprised and pleased when he breaks the news. Which I am—surprised and pleased," she said warmly, then gave a little gasp. "Oh, this one's a real kicker." LeAnn smiled and put a fond hand to her pregnant belly, then got up from the table. "Mom, are you ready? If we're going to get that cake made in time for the party, we'd better go."

"I just need to get my purse," Jenny told her, sending me another concerned look. "Are you sure you wouldn't like to come with us?"

I shook my head, trying to convey the silent message that leaving the ranch would not be a good idea. "I'll be fine. I've got plenty to keep me busy."

Jenny sighed and picked up her purse from the counter. "If Tom should get back sooner than we expected, just tell him I'm at LeAnn's."

"I will." I stood up and gave William's sister a smile. "I'm glad to meet you, LeAnn."

"Same here." She gave me a quick hug. "And I really hope you'll come to the birthday party this evening. The whole family will be there, and I know my children will be eager to meet their new aunt."

Just the thought was staggering, but somehow I managed to thank her for the invitation without committing myself one way or the other.

"Now, I don't want you worrying about the mess." Jenny waved a hand toward the clutter of dishes and bowls on the counter. "I can always finish doing the cupboards tomorrow."

I kept my smile firmly in place until they had gone and I was standing alone in the kitchen. Then my control crumpled and I sank down on a chair, staring at nothing. What possessed me to tell William's sister that I was his fiancé—to just blurt it out without giving a single thought to the consequences? What was I thinking? It was one thing for William to introduce himself as my fiancé to a physician and nurse we'd never see again. Quite another for me to announce the news of our fictitious engagement to his sister. Considering LeAnn's gregarious nature, I seriously doubted the word would stop with her. In fact, I wouldn't be surprised if the entire Evans family was buzzing with the news before the day was out.

I leaned my chin in my hand with a little groan. In one careless moment of sheer idiocy, I'd managed to undermine all William's efforts to keep my whereabouts and identity unknown. I tried to rationalize away my foolishness with the fact that now the pictures had been released, my stay at the ranch would most likely be coming to an end, but that thought only added to my depression.

Had the photos been released? I wondered. And if so, why hadn't William called his parents? I gathered my runaway thoughts into a worrisome bundle and left the kitchen, determined not to let fear take control of my thinking. Working on some of Tom Evans' stories would at least keep my mind occupied, and I went upstairs to collect my notes from yesterday.

The house seemed even more silent than usual now that Tom and Jenny were both gone. I hadn't fully realized until now how much comfort and assurance their company had given me. Picking up my notebook and pens, I decided that writing at the kitchen table would be more comfortable, and a lot cooler than the upstairs bedroom, which was stuffy and airless from the noonday heat. But inside, I knew it was nerves more than comfort that prompted the change.

I kept the cell phone on the table within arm's reach, hoping to hear from William, but no call came. Thirty long minutes dragged by while I wrestled with words that refused to cooperate and made revisions that were as unsatisfactory as the original version.

I tensed, suddenly aware of the sound of a car coming down the road to the house. This was followed moments later by the sharp slam of a car door. I got stiffly to my feet, grateful Tom had returned earlier than expected from St. George, and turning, saw William standing in the doorway. His hair was mussed and blown, and his face showed lines of weariness, but the light in those gray-green eyes started my heart pounding double time.

I swallowed and managed the brilliant statement "William . . . you're back."

He nodded and stepped toward me, a half smile lifting the corners of his bearded mouth. He took off the sport coat worn over his T-shirt and jeans and tossed it on one of the kitchen chairs, his eyes never leaving my face.

A sudden weakness in my legs had me gripping the edge of the table for support. "I didn't expect—that is, I didn't think . . ."

"I caught an early flight to Las Vegas and managed to get on board a puddle jumper to St. George."

I drew a shaky breath. "What about the meeting with Chief McIntire?"

"I told Wade to take care of that. I have more important things to do."

"And the pictures?" I asked faintly.

"Everything's out there," William told me. "I wouldn't be surprised if they've gone viral by now. But we can talk about that later."

I smiled, and there was a moment of sweet silence between us.

"I hope that look means you're glad to see me," he said.

"You know I am."

"Then how about a kiss for your fiancé?"

Twenty-one

My lips parted, but I was suddenly incapable of uttering a single word.

William grinned and answered my stricken look with "LeAnn called me around twenty minutes ago to offer her congratulations on our engagement. And Mom called five minutes after that. I understand the conversation got kind of personal."

Warmth crept up my face as I struggled for something to say. "William, I–I'm so sorry. I just wasn't thinking. LeAnn sort of surprised us, and your poor mother was trying to make introductions, not sure how much, or what to say . . ." I broke off and shook my head. "I know this really complicates things and I— well, I'm sorry."

"Are you?" He moved closer. "I'm not."

"You're not?"

"I'm the one who started the rumor, remember?" Putting both hands on my shoulders, he drew me to him, his head bending toward mine.

My eyes closed as my own hands found the firmness of his chest, my breath coming more quickly as I anticipated the touch of his lips on mine. It didn't come. Instead he began kissing my face—a tender exploration of my cheeks, my eyes, and my chin that had me leaning weakly against him.

"I missed you," he breathed, his beard rough against my cheek.

"I missed you too." My hands left his chest to touch his face, eagerly guiding his mouth to mine.

His kiss filled every aching, lonely part of me, breathing new life into dreams I had foolishly abandoned, believing they were possible only for others, never for me. When our lips finally parted, William and I stood, smiling into each other's eyes. I put a hand to his face, letting the wonder spill over and through me like a rainbow of light. Then his mouth was on mine again, and all that mattered was the giving, taking, and tasting of joy.

From the kitchen table, a buzzing vibration startled us out of the netherworld of pleasure, back into now.

"Ignore it," William said as I reached for the phone.

"But it might be important."

He groaned an acknowledgement, and I left his arms long enough to check the caller ID. I smiled. "It's LeAnn."

"All the more reason to ignore it," he said and reached for me once more.

Not two minutes later, the cell phone buzzed again.

I picked up the phone. "This time it's your mother."

William groaned again and raised his eyes.

"She's probably calling to see how I am," I told him. "And I'm sure she'd like to know that you're back."

He sighed, nodded, and took the phone from me. "Hi, Mom. It's William. Yeah, I'm back and everything's fine. No, we won't be coming to the birthday party. Mackenzie and I are going to spend the day together, so tell LeAnn to stop bugging me. My fiancé and I will be busy. Bye, Mom."

I laughed and went into his waiting arms. "Are we really going to spend the day together?"

He nodded, then kissed me. "I thought you might like a change of scenery other than these four walls. It's probably too soon for that horseback ride, but if you're feeling up to it, there are some places around here that I'd like to show you."

"I'm definitely up to it."

"How are the bruises?" He put a gentle hand on my side.

"Colorful, but improving."

"Mind if I take a look?"

I hesitated briefly, then lifted the right side of my blouse, realizing he'd seen a lot more of me than a few inches of bare midriff when I was wearing the hospital gown.

William made a frowning inspection and shook his head. "I thought you said they were improving."

"It looks worse than it is," I told him, straightening the blouse.

"Are you sure you're up to it? We'll be driving on dirt roads most of the time, and it could get pretty bumpy."

I reached up to give him a kiss. "I'll be fine. Having you home is better than any pain pill."

This brought a smile to his face. "I just need to grab a quick shower and change, then we can go."

"There's no rush," I said. "Have you had anything to eat?"

He shook his head. "Only coffee and peanuts on the plane."

"Then why don't I cook you some breakfast. I'll have it ready by the time you're showered and dressed."

His lips parted, and there was a flicker of surprise in his eyes. "You don't mind?"

"Of course I don't mind." I put a hand on the side of his face. "You've taken such good care of me, I'd like to return the favor."

"It was my pleasure—taking care of you." He took my hand and planted a warm kiss on my palm. "Be back in a few."

I floated over to the refrigerator after he had gone and made a quick survey of the possibilities—eggs, cheese, onions, and fresh tomatoes. Even a few mushrooms. A Spanish omelet would be quick and easy to prepare. And there were some leftover boiled potatoes that I could cut up and fry into hash browns. Smiling, I went to work, feeling delightfully domestic and utterly happy.

When I heard the distinctive sound of William's cowboy boots coming down the hall some twelve minutes later, the table was set, toast made, juice poured, and the omelet was fluffy and steaming in the pan.

"Something smells mighty good." He came toward me with an appreciative smile, tucking a blue-gray Henley into tight-fitting jeans.

"Spanish omelet." I glanced away from the wonderfully disturbing sight of him to give the hash browns a quick stir.

"Is there anything I can do?" he offered, planting a kiss on my cheek.

"Not a thing. Everything's ready."

William sat down at the table, watching me as I dished the omelet onto his plate. "Whoa there, that'll do," he said with a laugh. "Save some for yourself."

We shared a smile, and suddenly I felt a little awkward as well as very much aware of the new intimacy between us. Removing the elements of danger and urgency that had brought us together, this morning it was just William and me.

"Are you okay?" he asked softly.

I nodded, not meeting his eyes as I dished the remaining omelet onto my plate. I took the pan back to the stove, then sat down across from him, trying to smile away the awkwardness.

William said nothing for a long moment, just watched me with a patient, knowing look. "Talk to me, Mac."

"It'll keep. You need to eat your omelet while it's hot."

"The omelet can wait. Talk to me."

I drew a long breath and met his eyes. "It's hard to explain, but . . . being together like this, after all that's happened, it's just— well, it feels different."

William acknowledged my attempt with a nod and gentle smile, then leaned over to give me a lingering, thoroughly enjoyable kiss. "Different in a good way," he said with satisfaction.

I sighed and agreed, "A very good way."

He gave me a look that made global warming seem positively frigid by comparison, then took a forkful of steaming omelet.

We ate in comfortable silence for a few moments, and the way William was wolfing his food was a good indication he wasn't indifferent to my cooking.

He glanced up at me. "Mac, this is incredible. Where'd you learn to be such a good cook?"

"From my parents' cooks and domestics."

He paused, a forkful of omelet halfway to his mouth. "Your parents' maids taught you how to cook?"

I nodded. "My mother was never home in time to cook dinner. Even if she had been, cooking wasn't something she enjoyed. Dinner parties, yes. Cooking, no."

William acknowledged this with a crooked smile and the wry comment "Your mother and my ex-wife have a lot in common."

I stared at him and had to ask, "Didn't she ever cook breakfast for you?"

"She didn't cook, period. Or do housework. Melanie's career took precedence over both those things."

"Are you serious?"

He nodded and took another bite of omelet.

"Well, for goodness sake, what did she do?" I burst out. Then, seeing his look and raised eyebrows, I added quickly, "Never mind. You don't have to answer that."

William just chuckled and said in a low tone, "There wasn't much of *that* either."

I waited a moment, then said, "Do you mind if I ask you what went wrong?"

He leaned back in his chair, clearly in thought, but his face was untroubled and I couldn't detect the slightest hint of pain in his eyes.

"We didn't want the same things," he said, his words an echo of my own response to Corbin Corelli's similar question. "Sometimes it takes a while to find that out," he added easily.

"Yes, it does."

We shared a smile, and there was no need for either of us to explain or say anything further.

"So tell me more about your morning with Dad," William said as we were taking our dishes to the sink. "Frankly, I'm amazed that you've been able to get him to open up as much as you have."

"Your father is a wonderful man. Besides being a natural-born storyteller, he's really very modest. In fact, I think modesty is the main reason for his reluctance to write things down."

William's gaze was warm with affection. "I agree. Dad's always been quick to give someone else the praise or credit, rather than himself."

Like his son, I thought.

"So what kind of stories did he share?" William asked. "Did any family skeletons come out of the closet?"

I laughed. "Not a one. But I did find out that your father is quite the romantic. When he was telling me about his and Jenny's courtship—the things he did to 'win her favor' was how he put it—I was, well, very touched."

William put an empty bowl on the counter, then removed a carved wooden spoon from its place on the wall beside the stove. "Speaking of courtship, did Dad tell you anything about Welsh love spoons?"

"No, he didn't."

"The legend of the love spoon goes back hundreds of years," William said, fingering the wooden spoon in his hand. "Wales was a poor society, and young men couldn't afford to give their sweethearts expensive gifts or jewelry. Instead, they put a great deal of time and thought into carving a special spoon for the one they loved. There are a lot of different designs, and each one has its own symbolism and meaning. A message of love, so to speak. My great-grandfather carved this spoon and gave it to my great-grandmother when they were courting."

"Amos and Ellie," I said softly.

William nodded, then took my right hand in his and placed the wooden spoon in my palm. "The bowl of the spoon was always carved first, a symbol of the man's promise to provide for his sweetheart—to feed and clothe her and take care of her needs. The two hearts carved above that represent the lovers' hearts joined together."

I glanced up to find William's eyes on my face. "Their hearts are joined by more than just physical passion," he said, his voice softly serious. "He promises to love and understand her, that they'll share a harmony of thought as well as affection. These sharp little points carved near the hearts are tears. Besides sharing the trials of life along with its joys, the tears mean the man is willing to bear his soul to his sweetheart, to let her see all that he is and feels."

William was silent for a long moment as his eyes spoke to mine. Then he glanced down at the spoon in my hand. "The dragon at the top of the spoon is the symbol of Wales, but it also signifies the man's promise to protect and care for the woman he loves throughout their lives." He paused and covered my hand with both of his. "When the woman accepts the spoon, she accepts the man, and acknowledges that their souls as well as their lives are now connected."

I couldn't speak. Standing together in the old ranch kitchen, with clasped hands and solemn eyes, it was as if William and I had just exchanged sacred vows. Without a word, he bent his head, and I lifted my lips to his.

Twenty-two

As we drove away from Hearth Fires, the sky was a defiant blue and there were mountains of billowing white clouds teasing the jagged cliff tops of Mount Kinesava. Our course was not east, however, but a winding dirt road that hugged the sandstone ridges to the southwest. The road was every bit as bumpy as William had said, with the occasional pothole that required some deft maneuvering on his part to avoid. I didn't mind. In fact, I scarcely noticed. A slight twinge now and then was a small price to pay for the pleasure of seeing this rugged land with him by my side.

There was an austere beauty to the landscape with its colorful cliffs and sparse fauna, as if the land was determined to hold on to its wildness, defying man's attempts to tame it. Sandstone ridges and pinnacles had been carved by centuries of wind and weather into fantastical shapes, with sun-baked hues ranging from tawny yellow, saffron, and sulfur, to burnt orange and vivid coral. Plant life away from the life-giving river was meager but determined to survive, with tough, spiny plants growing in the fissures of the rocks. Weeds and some parched grasses struggled near the roadside, and in the open spaces there was the ever-present sagebrush, along with a similar shrub that flaunted its brilliant fall color of mustard yellow.

"What are those gorgeous yellow bushes?" I asked William.

"Rabbit brush." He gave me an amused look. "It's pretty common throughout the West. Most folks consider it a weed."

"Well, there's nothing common about that color. Especially seen against the sky and those amazing cliffs."

I gave a little cry of delight as we drove past some rock formations that looked for all the world like medieval goblins turned to stone.

Following my glance, William smiled and told me, "They're called hoodoos."

"Hoodoos," I repeated. "The name fits."

The place was a far cry from storybook cottages and rose-covered arbors, but suddenly those lovely fairy-tale elements of romance ceased to matter. Sitting next to William as his truck jostled along the dusty road was all the romance my heart needed.

He reached over to take my hand, saying nothing, but I saw happiness shining in his eyes, felt it in the warm clasp of his fingers enfolding mine. His thumb gently explored the inside of my wrist, his touch sure, yet featherlight.

"Where are we going?" I asked a few moments later, needing to calm things down into words.

"The old ghost town of Grafton isn't far from here. There are several homes and buildings still standing that I thought you'd enjoy seeing. And there's a pioneer cemetery close by."

"You're right. I'd love to see it."

I don't know what I had expected, but Grafton's pioneer graveyard bore no resemblance to any of the cemeteries I'd visited in my travels back East. Set on a barren shelf of land with the stark backdrop of sandstone cliffs, there were perhaps three dozen or so marked graves; others were just oblong mounds of dry, cracked earth.

Some of the tombstones, carved from native rock, dated back to the 1860s. There was a hushed stillness about the place, a solemnity that made me want to speak in whispers. The sound of the desert wind moaning around the cliffs was like a mother's mournful keening over the loss of her little ones. And perhaps it was, as many of the graves belonged to infants and young children. Childhood diseases must have taken a heavy toll on the town's young.

Others met more violent deaths. A fenced enclosure protected one of the larger headstones, where the deaths of two brothers, Robert and Joseph Berry, along with Robert's young wife Isabella, were recorded in bleak terms: *Died 2 April 1862. Killed by Indians.*

"The Berry brothers were killed during the Blackhawk War," William explained. "Between the floods and Indian attacks, life back then was pretty harsh."

"Indian attacks and floods weren't the only problems." I said, looking at a group of graves for the Ballard family. "Five children, and not one lived to be older than nine. How terrible for that poor mother."

"And father," William added quietly.

I nodded and met his eyes, touched by the gentle compassion in his voice.

Names and dates spoke to us from the silent stones as we wandered on.

"This place reminds me of a poem," I said softly. *"After a hundred years nobody knows the place. Agony, that enacted there, motionless as peace."*

"Dickinson," William said with a nod.

"Yes."

I paused to look down at one of the unmarked mounds, where a small yellow wildflower bloomed in a crack of hard-baked earth, my thoughts shifting from the deaths of long ago to one more recent. It hurt to think of Allison—the vibrant, living Allison I had known for such a short time, now buried in some cemetery in Palo Alto. I blinked back tears and tried to swallow the tightness in my throat. At least she wasn't lying in a forgotten grave on this barren hillside. And there would be flowers. Allison should have lots of flowers—roses, like those in her garden and the hatbox guest room.

William wrapped his arm around my shoulders, pulling me close to his side. "I'm sorry. Maybe coming to the cemetery wasn't such a good idea. I didn't mean to be insensitive."

Lifting my gaze from the mound of earth, I saw concern as well as sympathy in his eyes. "I know you didn't. It's just sometimes the guilt and the sadness—" I shook my head, unable to speak past the ache.

He gathered me into his arms and pressed my head close against the warmth of his neck and chest. "Do you remember what you said to me, that first night, after the nightmare?" he asked softly.

All I could do was shake my head and cling to his strength.

"You said it should have been you, that it wouldn't matter if you had died." His arms tightened around me, and I felt the warmth of his lips against my face. "Well, it matters to me," he said thickly. "And I thank God it wasn't you—that you're here, now, safe in my arms."

Before I could say more than his name, his mouth took mine in a kiss that pushed away all the sadness and any lingering ghosts from the past, leaving me weak with the wonder of this man, and breathlessly, fiercely alive.

When my emotions, not to mention my feet, touched solid ground once more, William gave me a wink and a smile. "That's my girl. Come on, Mac. The town isn't far from here—just down the hill and around the corner."

If I had been on assignment for the magazine, the old ghost town of Grafton would have had me filling a notebook and my camera with written and digital impressions of the place—the old sandstone church and meeting hall that stood in solitary splendor against the autumn sky, with the stunning backdrop of Zion's colorful cliffs. And the homes, some looking more asleep than deserted, as if the owners were merely away for the afternoon. Others were derelict and decaying. Happily, I wasn't on assignment, nor did I have the slightest desire to let go of William's hand long enough to take even one picture. Assuming of course, that I had my camera with me, which I didn't.

As we explored the remains of the town, I tried to picture Grafton the way it had been over a hundred years ago—a thriving community of hardy pioneer families, with children running along the dusty pathways, and crops planted in the now-barren fields.

"Why did they leave?" I asked William as we wandered away from the ruined timbers of what had once been a family's home. "What happened to the town?"

"It wasn't just one thing, or some cataclysmic event like a flood, although the town had more than its share of those. People stayed and struggled and did the best they could. But after a while, folks got tired of fighting against the elements and disease, and began moving into larger towns, where there were more amenities—like electricity and indoor plumbing. You can't blame them for wanting something better. Like I said, life back then was pretty harsh. Grafton didn't die a sudden death like some of the mining towns. It just sort of faded away."

I looked up at William's rugged profile, my mind turning the page from the past to the immediate present. "Do you think you'll stay at Hearth Fires?"

He gave me a sideways glance, his dark brows lifting at my question.

"For now," he answered, and there was a tentative note in his voice. "I've had some offers from law firms in California, but it hasn't felt right. What about you? Are you eager to get back to Chicago and your job with the magazine?"

I hesitated, glancing away from the searching look in his eyes. "Not eager, exactly." I took a little breath, my heart suddenly beating hard and fast. "But it's something I have to do."

"Is it?" he asked softly.

I stared at him, not knowing what to say. My heart was pounding out one message that was utterly terrifying and completely wonderful, while my mind was staunchly dictating another.

The silence stretched out between us, aching with unexpressed words and emotions. Then William gave a short nod and said, "I guess what you're not telling me is—we're going to have to wait awhile before taking that horseback ride. Am I right?"

"We might have to—the way things are . . ."

"It's okay, Mac" was all he said, but the understanding in his voice and eyes eased what could have been an awkward moment.

I put a hand to the side of his face, and his kiss was gentle, making no demands.

"How are you feeling?" he asked. "Any complaints from those colorful ribs of yours?"

"No complaints, but I wouldn't mind some shade. "

"I know just the place. And there's some bottled water in the truck if you're thirsty. It might not be very cold, but at least it's wet."

"I'd love some."

We returned to the truck for the bottled water, then William led me away from the main area of the ghost town, toward an old orchard where there was grass instead of baked earth and where the cool sound of water quenched the parched air. Following the sound, I saw a small brook, scarcely two feet across, winding a cheerful path through the trees on its way to meet the parent river. Under the shade of the ancient orchard, the air was markedly cooler and sweetened with the fragrance of wild roses still blooming in an unrestrained tangle along the remains of an old wire fence.

William found a tree whose girth would provide a comfortable backrest, and I eased myself down by degrees before leaning gratefully against the trunk. He handed me the bottled water, then sat beside me, his eyes sending an unspoken message that warmed my heart, even as the water cooled my throat.

The leaves above us were a pale yellow, and every now and then one or two drifted down on a quiet breath of air. I didn't want to think of anything beyond this moment, but the shadow of weariness marking William's features was a visual reminder of recent events and the revelatory discoveries made only the night before. Had Lieutenant Dicola seen the photos yet? Or Judge Wolcott?

"Are you worried about what's happening with the pictures?" William asked.

I gave him an amazed smile. "Are you a mind reader as well as an attorney?"

"If I were, it might give me a real advantage in the courtroom," he said with a low chuckle.

I plucked a few blades of grass and crushed them in my hand. "I don't really want to think about it, but knowing the pictures are out there, I can't help wondering about Judge Wolcott's reaction . . ."

"Not to mention Sarcassian's," William added. "Wade said he'd call and give us an update later this afternoon."

I nodded. "Did you get any sleep at all last night?"

"Not much," William admitted. "By the time I got the pictures to Joel and everything squared away on his end, there was barely enough time to pack and get to the airport."

"Maybe we should go back to the ranch so you can get some rest."

"No need." William finished the last of his water and set the bottle aside. "If it's okay with you, I can get a little shut-eye right now." Shifting position, he stretched out beside me with his head in my lap.

"It's more than okay," I told him, caressing the side of his face.

Covering my hand with one of his, he brought it to his lips. "We've both done more than our share of thinking and worrying the past few days," he said. "Right now, this is all I need."

He let go a sigh that was part weariness, part sheer contentment, then kissed my fingers and closed his eyes. It wasn't long before the hand holding mine eased its grip.

I watched his face as sleep eased the weariness and softened the lines of worry. "Darling William," I whispered, then leaned back against the broad trunk and closed my eyes.

Sometime later, a low rumbling moved into my drowsy consciousness, and a gust of wind shook the branches above us. William stirred, then sat up, his eyes alert, all traces of sleep gone.

"Storm's coming," he said. "The wind's changed."

He got to his feet and offered me his hand as the rumbling came again, growing in volume to a threatening grumble that echoed along the cliffs.

Hurrying back to the truck, I saw lightning cut a jagged path across the darkening sky. Seconds later, thunder answered with a loud crack and hearty boom.

A grin split William's handsome features as he glanced skyward. "Looks like it's going to be a good one."

Nature added her agreement to his words as the sky above us shuddered with light, and thunder followed soon after as a resounding amen.

I jumped from the suddenness as well as the ear-splitting volume and got quickly into the truck. William ran around to the driver's side, climbed in, and shoved the key into the ignition. After backing the truck off the shoulder, he pulled onto the road, then gave me a rakish look.

"What are you doin' way over there, when I need you next to me?"

Laughing, I unfastened my seat belt and erased the scant few inches between us.

"That's better," he said, with a kiss to prove the point.

A fireworks display on the Fourth of July couldn't have given us a better show as we drove back to the ranch. Lightning was doing a white-hot tango across the sky, with thunder adding its percussive voice to nature's stormy dance. There was no rain as yet, but William assured me it would come when the storm was good and ready.

As we turned down the long lane leading to the ranch house, I saw horses racing about in one of the pastures, manes and tails flying in the wind.

"Are they frightened by the storm?" I asked William.

"No, they're excited. I don't know why, but a thunderstorm really stirs them up. How about you, Mac? Are you afraid of storms?"

I shook my head. "No, storms stir me up, too." I leaned closer to plant some warm kisses on his neck. "But not as much as you do."

William's sudden intake of breath and surprised jerk on the steering wheel had us heading toward the roadside ditch before he recovered enough to right our course. Braking to a stop, he turned to me with a gleam of devilry in his eyes.

"Now that calls for some retaliation," he said and took my face between his strong brown hands.

Needless to say, the lightning and thunder of the approaching storm was nothing compared to the storm of emotion he unleashed inside me.

Lightning hit the ground somewhere nearby, and the ear-splitting crack that followed effectively jerked us apart.

"We'd better get out of the open." William said. He kissed me once more for good measure, then continued down the road.

We hadn't gone far when he gave a nod and pointed to the holding pen straight ahead. The corral, which had been empty when we drove by earlier in the day, was now crowded with the massive bodies of some eight or ten bulls. I scooted across the seat to lower the window on the truck's passenger side, awed and a little unnerved by the sight and sound of the animals, their throaty grunts and bellows competing with the thunder overhead.

"Earl must be taking this bunch to a rodeo," William said. "He'll probably be by this evening to load them into his rig. If you're interested in watching, I could give him a call, find out when he's coming."

One of the bulls, a huge black beast with a lethal spread of horns, turned his head to stare straight at me. I gave a nervous laugh and quickly raised the window. "No thanks, maybe another time."

As we continued down the road, an unwanted question slipped into my thoughts, disturbing the happiness that surrounded them. Would there be another time? I moved closer to William's side and pushed the thought away.

He had just parked the truck beside the house when his cell phone sounded. "This better not be LeAnn wondering why we're not coming to the birthday party," he began, then frowned when he saw the caller ID. "Hey, Wade, what's up? I wasn't expecting your call until later." As William listened, his expression stiffened into shock, and the look in his eyes sent a cold shudder through me.

"What is it?" I asked in a dry whisper.

He blew out a long breath and reached for my hand. "This is bad. Judge Wolcott's committed suicide—and Lieutenant Dicola's missing."

Twenty-three

My stunned mind could scarcely take it in. Judge Wolcott dead, and Dicola missing. The news, delivered in such blunt terms, was like a sudden blow to the stomach. I sat in silence as William talked with his brother, while outside the truck, the wind increased from a whine to a gusty roar and the sky darkened.

Then, overhead there was a blinding flash followed by a deafening crack and boom. I gave a startled jump, more unnerved than I cared to admit.

"That one hit somewhere pretty close by," William said. "Wade? Wade, are you there?" He pocketed the phone then reached for my hand. "I've lost him. Too much interference from the storm. Let's go inside. Hopefully, we'll be able to get more details on the internet."

The details were sparse and grim. Dana Wolcott had returned home from shopping to find her husband slumped over his desk in their study. Paramedics pronounced the judge dead at the scene from a self-inflicted gunshot to the head. Police had no answers or comments for the media, who were clamoring to know all the whys and wherefores about Peter Wolcott's "alleged" involvement with Nicholas Sarcassian and the incriminating pictures published on the internet only hours before the judge's suicide. The information on Vince Dicola's whereabouts was even sketchier. According to Chief

McIntire, Lieutenant Dicola had failed to appear at a meeting with the Department of Internal Affairs and hadn't been seen since the previous day. Nicholas Sarcassian was not available for comment on either situation.

"What do you think's happened to Dicola?" I asked William as we sat side by side in his office.

"I don't know, and if Sarcassian's involved in his disappearance, we may never know—at least, not until his body is found."

The thought made me shiver. "What do we do now?"

"There's not a lot we can do. Things are pretty much out of our hands. I'm sure Wade will be in touch as soon as he can get through. Reception is always iffy around here during a storm. I'm hoping he'll call back on the land line."

When the phone in the kitchen rang not five minutes later, William got up and gave me an encouraging smile. "That's probably Wade now."

I followed him into the kitchen and turned on the lights to alleviate the gloom. It was even darker in the house than outside, where the storm had turned late afternoon into an early dusk.

William grabbed the receiver on the wall phone, and after listening for a few moments gave me a quick shake of his head, indicating the caller was not Wade. "It's okay, Alice, I'll be glad to help." He listened a moment more, then gave calm instructions. "Don't go outside, and don't touch a thing. There's nothing you can do for the horse. I'll be right over and get the propane turned off. Just stay inside, okay? I'll see you in a few minutes."

He hung up and explained hurriedly, "Lightning's hit the ground at the Washburn's place a few miles from here. It electrified an iron fence and killed at least one of their horses."

"Oh, no, that's terrible."

He nodded. "Alice is pretty much in a panic. She's home alone and doesn't expect her husband back for at least an hour. I've got to get that propane tank turned off before she has an even bigger problem on her hands."

"William, that sounds dangerous."

"Not as dangerous as it would be if that tank blows. They could lose everything." He grabbed his keys and gave me a quick kiss.

"I'll come with you—"

He shook his head. "Better not, honey. If Wade calls back, someone needs to be here. I won't be gone long—fifteen, twenty minutes at most."

"Please be careful."

My plea was cut short by another hard kiss. Then William grabbed his cowboy hat and jacket from a peg on the back porch and hurried out of the house.

I watched from the porch as he got quickly into his truck, backed around, and drove away. The storm that had seemed so exhilarating when I was with him put on a more ominous face now that I was alone. The temperature had dropped considerably, and it was beginning to rain. As yet, the rain was far from a downpour—more like small, stinging pellets driven sideways by the wind.

Shivering, I went back inside. I had no idea what was involved in turning off a propane tank, but worry for William's safety effectively blotted out everything else, even the startling news from California.

I tried to fill the anxious minutes of waiting by tidying up the kitchen and washing our dishes from this morning, but my efforts were clumsy and halfhearted. The sudden ringing of the kitchen phone jerked me out of my thoughts, and I nearly dropped the bowl I was putting away.

The sound of Wade's voice, taut, with a clipped urgency, did nothing to calm the sudden pounding of my heart.

"Hey, Mackenzie, can I speak to Will? I tried reaching him on his cell, but couldn't get through."

"He's not here. He left a few minutes ago to help one of the neighbors."

"When do you think he'll be back?"

"He said fifteen or twenty minutes."

Wade swore and blew out a frustrated sigh. "Okay. I'll keep trying, but if I can't get through on his cell, have him call me as soon as he gets back."

"You sound worried," I said, trying to keep my own feelings of disquiet at bay. "What's happened?"

"I'm not sure, but there's something going on with Sarcassian. I just got word that two of his men—Brock Symonds and Martin Covill—caught a flight early this afternoon to Las Vegas, and that bothers me. It bothers me a lot."

"What are you saying? Do you think Sarcassian's found out where I am?"

"I don't know. I don't see how he could, but be careful, Mackenzie. I hope I'm wrong, but I have a feeling the trouble's far from over. Have Will call me ASAP."

Wade's call left me feeling more unsettled than ever, with the dark stirrings of fear gnawing at my already precarious calm. I didn't want to believe Sarcassian had somehow ferreted out where I was, but once Wade's warning planted the seeds of that possibility, my mind refused to leave it alone, creating all kinds of terrifying scenarios. When the lights flickered then died only minutes later, the near darkness and angry sounds of the storm had me pacing about the room. Rather than look for candles or a flashlight, I ran upstairs to get my hoodie, thinking it would be easier on my nerves if I waited for William's return on the front porch, where I'd have a clear view of the road.

I grabbed the hoodie from the closet and pulled it on, hating the fact that my hands were trembling as I tried to zip it up. Lightning flashed, illuminating the room's shadowy grayness with white-hot brilliance. In those brief seconds, my gaze caught sight of Jenny's cell phone on the bedside table, and I snatched it up. If William were delayed or tried to call, it wouldn't hurt to have it handy.

Thunder rumbled overhead as I made my way downstairs to the living room. I tried to calm the nagging fear inside me with the sensible rationale that Wade was just being cautious, and William would be back soon. He'd been gone at least ten minutes already, probably closer to fifteen. I was opening the front door when the strident ring of the kitchen phone stopped me in my tracks.

"William . . ." Just saying his name lit a lantern of hope inside me, and I ran through the shadowy house to the kitchen. I lifted the receiver, my hello breathless and eager.

There was no answering voice, only the raspy sound of a man's breathing.

"William?"

Again silence, followed by the dial tone as the caller hung up.

The rapid pulse beating in my throat refused to be calmed as I put the receiver back. I wasted no time trying to find a plausible reason for the call, but left the house by the back door and ran around the side yard to the shelter of the porch. My eyes peered through the grayness, down the long stretch of road leading to the ranch house, but there was no sign of William's truck. I grabbed the afghan from the porch swing, wrapped it around my shoulders, and stood beside one of the pillars, my nerves too edgy to allow me to sit down. Frightened pleas thrummed through my mind in a jumbled prayer for William's safety and quick return. Above the wind, I could hear the throaty bellows of the bulls and the occasional high whinny of a horse.

Then, far down the road I glimpsed a dark shape moving slowly through the false dusk. I squinted and leaned forward, trying to mold the shape into the outline of William's truck. Seconds later, the sky shuddered as lightning cut a white-hot path across the murky gray. In that brief instant, the dark shape became a long black car driven with deliberate slowness, and no headlights.

My blood began to pound as every instinct told me this was no ordinary car—that danger was moving slowly, steadily toward me. Dropping the afghan, I stumbled off the porch, knowing only that I had to get away from the house, that if I attempted to hide inside, I would be trapped.

Hunched over, I half ran, half crawled across the yard and gravel drive to the border of trees and weedy ditch that lined one side of the road. I glanced frantically around, looking for possible escape routes. The choices were few. Either the path leading to the river, or the road. The thick belt of trees bordering the river would provide more cover, but they were some distance away, with a worrisome stretch of open field between them and the house. There was every chance I would be seen before I reached the trees, and the surrounding pastures were all fenced.

Cold pellets of spotty rain stung my face as I glanced down the road once more. William would be returning soon. He might be on his way even now. Thoughts of him driving straight into trouble was the deciding factor. I had to warn him. So it had to be the road.

I made a frantic dive for the ditch, praying the scruffy clumps of Russian olive trees and patchy weeds growing along the bank would provide enough cover. Bent low on hands and knees, I inched my way along the ditch, mindless of the sharp thistles that pricked my hands, and the thorny branches of the Russian olives snatching at my clothes. Above the sound of the wind, the throaty growl of the car's engine grew steadily louder. I flattened myself in the weedy hollow just as the black car drove past the holding pen with the bulls. I didn't dare move or look up after that, but I could hear the crunch of the vehicle's tires on the road as it passed by me, coming to a stop somewhere near the ranch house.

I made myself count to thirty, then, turning on my side, lifted my head just enough to see past the weeds and dry grasses. Two men dressed in dark clothes stood next to the car. My breath caught in a strangled gasp as the big man near the passenger side pulled the collar of his jacket closer to his face and glanced around. Brock. Was that a gun in his right hand? Wind and rain blurred the distance between us, and I couldn't be sure.

I watched, hardly daring to breathe, as Brock gave a nod to the other man and waved him toward the corrals and barn, while he moved stealthily toward the house. I waited a few seconds more, then continued my crawl along the ditch, desperate to put as much distance between myself and the house as possible. Something hard bumped against my hipbone, and I suddenly remembered the cell phone in my pants pocket. I lay flat and quickly drew it out, praying there would be enough reception to make a call. Covering the light of the phone with my body, I retrieved William's number, then listened, praying for an answer. Nothing. And I didn't dare try again.

I tried to think how long it would take Brock to search the house. Probably no more than a few minutes before he realized no one was there. Then what? Would he and his cohort leave or wait for my return? As much as I wanted to get to my feet and start running, caution insisted I had to be far enough away from the house so the men wouldn't see my flight down the road.

I tossed a quick glance behind me. Neither man was in sight. Looking ahead, I realized I was only a few yards from the holding pen with the bulls. Once I reached that, the concealing cover of the ditch with its weeds and low lying trees would be gone. The corral was practically flush with the road, and past that there was only a long stretch of open road with fenced pastures on either side.

My heart sank, and the smothering feeling of being caught and trapped rose like bile in my throat. I swallowed hard, trying to choke down the fear. William would come. He had to. I flung another hurried look over my shoulder. Still no movement near the house. Was that Brock's companion near the barn and corrals? Objects and shapes were indistinct, ghostly gray blurs in the growing dusk. Hopefully, that same deceiving dusk would conceal me as well. I bit my lip and drew a ragged breath. I had to risk it.

I clambered out of the ditch and started to run. It felt as if I were running in a nightmare. The wind was against me, and my ribs and chest burned with pain. Gasping and holding my side, I pushed against the wind and ran on. Somewhere behind me I heard a man's angry shout. The sound sent a burst of adrenalin rushing through me, and I surged forward, only to stumble and trip in the road's loose gravel. Almost the same instant I heard a soft whine as a bullet sang over my head, only scant inches from its mark.

Struggling to my feet, I saw Brock no more than twenty yards down the road, arms outstretched, a revolver in his hands. Not far behind him, the second man came running from the direction of the barn.

Crouching low, I stumbled on. The bull pen was only a few feet away when two more shots ripped the stormy air. One must have hit an iron bar of the corral, because there was a loud ringing as metal sang against metal, then ricocheted with a whine. The second bullet found a softer target as one of the bulls gave a bellow of rage and pain. The others responded with nervous snorts, pawing the ground and milling around the wounded animal.

I reached the holding pen, and the next instant my fear turned to blind fury when I saw blood seeping bright red from the black hide of the injured beast's shoulder. I didn't think at all after that. I only knew the all-encompassing need for flight left me as quickly as it had come. Grabbing hold of the corral's iron gate, I found the bolt holding it in place and yanked it up, releasing the catch. I pulled the gate wide open, yelling at the top of my lungs. The bulls didn't need further encouragement to surge through the opening in a powerful mass of muscled bodies, the wounded beast blazing mad and shoving his way ahead of the rest.

I climbed onto the gate's bottom rung as the bulls went tearing past me, their bellows carrying on the wind like demons from hell.

Not ten yards behind me, Brock's running approach came to a startled halt. I saw his head jerk to the right, then the left, searching for a way to escape the animals charging straight for him. There wasn't one. Still standing his ground, Brock fired a shot into the herd, but that didn't stop them. By the time the man turned to run, the injured bull was close on his heels. Head lowered, the bull tossed Brock into the air as if he were nothing more than a rag doll. Before he could get to his feet, the animal was on him, sharp hooves pounding and horns lowered. Once more, Brock was airborne, landing on his back with a sickening cry. Even if he'd been able to rise, the angry mass of fleeing bulls ended his struggle to get away. Their massive bodies pounded over him, trampling the helpless man.

Shuddering, I shut my eyes to the bloody sight and clung to the gate for dear life. When I dared open them again, I saw Brock's body lying off the side of the road in a crumpled heap, the black bull nearby, still pawing the ground. A few of the bulls were headed toward the ranch house in a nervous gait; others had calmed enough to graze some roadside grasses, no longer interested in the action or the man's lifeless body.

Thunder clapped an angry finish to the deadly drama, and the rain began in earnest, carried by the wind in driving sheets. In the midst of this, there was another sound, the throaty roar of an engine.

My heart gave a frightened lurch as I saw the black car moving toward me up the road. Brock's cohort must have run back to the safety of the car, but there was no way the man could make a fast escape with nearly a dozen bulls either blocking or meandering down the rain-pelted road. But then, neither could I. My hands felt as if they were frozen to the gate's metal bars, and fear had an even colder grip on me. I couldn't move and I couldn't cry out. All I could do was cling to the gate in the pouring rain as the black car drew closer.

Twenty-four

The driver was nothing if not determined. Laying on the horn, he plowed a steady path through the massive animals, heading straight for me. I glanced around wildly, but there was nowhere to go. Between the advancing car and the nearness of half a dozen angry bulls, my chances for escape were nonexistent. My heart choking me, I could only watch with a frozen kind of fear as the sedan drew alongside the holding pen. The window on the driver's side slid down. I shivered and huddled closer to the gate's metal bars, instantly recognizing the sharp features and straggly hair of the man behind the wheel. The same man who had followed me in the mall with such cold-eyed determination.

Now, I saw that same determination in his face as he raised a revolver and leveled it in my direction. The moment of my impending death hung suspended in the stormy air between us. My mind had gone beyond fear. All I could do was stare into the man's unfeeling eyes, willing him with my whole soul not to pull the trigger. There was a moment when I felt his sudden indecision, a brief, wavering second of doubt. Then purpose hardened his expression once more. Before he could shoot, one of the bulls, a huge, brindled beast, moved between the black car and me, spoiling the man's aim. Brock's cohort laid on the horn again and waved his revolver at the bull, which accomplished nothing at all, except to anger the animal. With a frustrated snort, the bull butted the side of the black car, and the man's shot went wild. Then, above the grunting and bellowing and the wind's stormy roar, there came another sound—the strident, steady blast of a horn, growing louder and closer with every second. Brock's cohort gave a startled glance down the road, and I saw him stiffen.

The next moment he was revving the engine and gunning the black car through a narrow gap between two of the bulls. Tires squealed and loose gravel sprayed the road as the sedan shot forward.

Looking ahead, I realized the man's escape was blocked by more than the bulls. William's truck was racing straight down the road's center, not thirty yards away. My breath caught in my throat as the black car charged forward, not slowing at all. The next instant, William slammed on the brakes and turned his truck sideways, neatly blocking the entire width of the road.

The vehicles were scant seconds apart when Brock's cohort decided to avoid a collision and swerved off the road, plowing through a wire fence, which wrapped itself across the car's windshield and sent the vehicle crashing into a thorny barrier of Russian olive trees.

The man staggered out of the car and was turning to run when William reached him, grabbing hold of the man's shoulder. In a desperate frenzy, the man twisted out of his jacket and made a frantic grab for the revolver at his waist. William was too fast for him. Seizing the man's gun arm, he wrestled him to the ground.

Between the rain and the grayness, I could no longer distinguish between the two men, or see what was happening. The rain was blinding and the wind had whipped sodden strands of hair across my face, but I couldn't let go of the gate. It was as if my clenched hands were forever locked on those cold metal bars. I could only listen to the sounds of the struggle. Then one of the men got to his feet, gun in hand. The other lay motionless on the ground.

"William—!"

His name came out in a choking sob that was carried away by a wet gust of wind. Then lightning flashed above us and dread released its hold all in the same moment as I recognized William's tall form. Leaving the inert form of Brock's cohort, William ran to his truck and retrieved a coil of rope from the back. In seconds, he had the man's hands and feet bound as neatly as if he were roping a runaway calf at a rodeo. William hauled the man over to the black car and shoved him into the back seat before retrieving the car keys and slamming the door.

Moments later William was at my side, wiping the hair out of my eyes, his own stark with worry.

"Mackenzie—are you hurt? Did they touch you?"

"No . . . no, but I— I can't let go of the gate."

One finger at a time, he pried my hands loose, then gathered me in his arms and carried me to his truck.

Safe inside the cab, all I could do was cling to him, as shock and terror left me in a series of hard shudders. "Sarcassian," I choked. "He found out— he sent them—"

"It's okay, it's okay. I've got you—you're safe now."

The soft voice and hard strength in the arms that held me gradually calmed the fear, leaving me weak and spent. I was still shivering, but it was more from the cold and the fact that we were both soaking wet. William took off his jacket and wrapped it around my shoulders, then started the truck.

The bulls that had blocked the path of the black car gave way to William's truck without protest and with only passing interest. Three of the beasts were huddled head to tail off the roadside in the pouring rain.

William slowed the truck, his mouth tightening in a grim line when he took in Brock's lifeless body lying beside the road. Nearby, the wounded bull had dropped down on his forelegs, its rage spent and the massive head drooping.

"Oh, the poor thing," I murmured, realizing with painful clarity that the bull's fury toward Brock had very likely saved my life.

William shook his head, his expression grim. "I'll give Earl a call. Let him know about the bull."

When we reached the house, he parked the truck, then came around to the passenger side and took me in his arms. My hands that had clung so fiercely to the iron bars of the gate now fastened themselves around William's neck as he carried me into the house.

"It's all right. I can walk," I told him, but my legs were even shakier than my voice as I made my way to a kitchen chair and sat down in a trembling heap.

He knelt beside me, wrapped his arms around my back, and held me close against him. We were both soaked to the skin, but where our bodies met there was warmth. Wonderful warmth. And safety.

"Mackenzie, honey, are you all right?"

I nodded, shivering, and pressed my face against the roughness of his bearded jaw. "Yes, I–I'm sorry. It's just re–reaction . . ."

William pulled me closer still and said, "I'm the one who's sorry. I should have been here."

"You're here now," I told him, not wanting to think what might have happened if he and I had been caught unaware when Brock and his cohort arrived, armed and ready to kill. "Thank God you're here," I murmured against William's neck.

There was no further need for words, only the strength and safety of his arms and the feel of his lips on mine.

He helped me to my feet then touched my damp hair. "I'd better call the sheriff and get the authorities out here. And you need to get out of those wet clothes before you catch pneumonia." William went to a cupboard under the sink, took out a flashlight, and handed it to me. "As soon as I've talked with the sheriff, I'll get some wood for a fire. Can you manage okay?"

I gave him a shaky nod and smile.

"Good girl." His lips found my cheek, then moved to the corners of my mouth. "You'd better go, or we'll be building our own fire right here," he told me, his voice as unsteady as my legs.

Rather than change clothes upstairs, I grabbed a pair of pajama pants, some thick stockings, and one of William's flannel shirts, then made my way downstairs to the bathroom. I propped the flashlight on the sink, then peeled off my sodden clothes. Thankfully, there was enough hot water for a quick shower. It was heaven to be warm and dry, although now that my body had shed the numbing effects of shock, pain was eager to take its place. My injured side was complaining loudly, and the palms of my hands were scratched and sore. Still, compared to what could have happened, a little pain and discomfort mattered not at all.

By the time I entered the living room, William had a fire blazing bright in the fireplace, and candles burning on top of the old piano as well as the mantle. I took in the candles' flickering glow, the crackling sputter of pine logs, and knew Hearth Fires was itself again, a warm refuge from darkness and fear.

William sent a smile my way, gave the wood another stir with the poker, and got to his feet. Fingering the collar of the flannel shirt, he gave me an approving nod. "Nice."

"Nice yourself," I said, noting his own change into dry clothes, a pair of snug-fitting jeans, and a black Henley, open at the throat.

"The sheriff and a deputy are on their way. Can I get you anything before they come?"

I smiled and shook my head as his arms came around me. "Just you."

"Honey, you've got me," he muttered in a low tone that left no doubts whatsoever.

Not ten minutes later, a patrol car pulled alongside the house, with an ambulance following close behind, their blue and red lights swirling spirals of color in the growing darkness.

Two men exited the car, hurrying out of the rain and onto the porch, where William made introductions. The handshakes and greeting exchanged told me they were long-time friends, as well as officers responding to a call. After conferring with William for a moment, the sheriff directed his deputy to assist the EMTs, who had parked the ambulance a few yards down the road, nearer Brock's body.

Broad-shouldered and burly, Sheriff John Fuller was in his late forties or early fifties, with a thick shock of sandy hair, and craggy features that had seen their share of wind and weather. The tight fit of his uniform revealed some bulges around the middle, but he still had the neck and shoulders of a boxer in his prime.

Shaking the rain off his hat and jacket, Sheriff Fuller settled himself in the recliner and took out a notebook and pen. "Judging from the dispatcher's call and what we saw on the road coming in, I'd say you've had a bit more excitement around here than usual."

William's response to this dry understatement was a tight-lipped "You might say that."

Sheriff Fuller frowned at his notes. "So, it looks like what we've got is one man dead at the scene, with another hogtied in the back of that Cadillac, and eight of Earl Thacker's best bulls runnin' loose." The sheriff's voice was as easygoing as if he were merely checking off items on a grocery list. "And from the looks of it, that black bull will have to be put down," he added with a shake of his head.

"Has someone let Earl know about the bulls?" William asked. "I meant to give him a call, but with all that's happened I—" He shook his head.

"No need," Fuller answered shortly. "He's out there now with his rig and a couple of his boys, trying to round 'em up. I don't need to tell you that Earl was madder than hell when he saw that big Spanish black on its knees. That animal was worth plenty. Any idea how they got out?"

"I let them out," I said quietly.

Sheriff Fuller gaped at me, and there was a potent moment when the only sound was the snap and hiss of burning logs. "You let them out?" he repeated.

"There's a lot more at stake here than a few of Earl Thacker's bulls," William said, anger heating his voice. "Those two men came here to kill Mackenzie. She's already had one attempt on her life last week in California. You can get the details from Wade or his police chief in Palo Alto."

"I'll do that. But first, I'd like to know exactly what's been goin' on around here," Fuller said mildly. "How do you know those men were sent to harm Miss Graham? And who sent them?" He fixed William with a sharp-eyed glance. "I'm assuming you witnessed whatever took place."

William gave a frustrated shake of his head. "I wasn't here. I was over at the Washburns, turning off their propane tank."

"In that case, I think it'd be best if Miss Graham told me what happened."

William leaned forward, his face and voice taut with concern. "Look, John, I know you have to make a report, but can't some of this wait until morning? Mackenzie's already been through enough—"

"Settle down, Will. You know as well as I do that I can't arrest someone without knowin' what the Sam Hill I'm arresting him for."

I put a hand on William's arm. "It's all right. I'm fine."

The warm fire, flickering candles, and William's solid presence beside me provided a comfortable distance between me and the terror that had taken place earlier. Giving Sheriff Fuller an account of the afternoon's events and those preceding it, I felt amazingly calm, almost as if I were describing what had happened to someone else.

The sheriff's questions were few but pertinent as he made notes. Other than telling him about the discovery in Judge Wolcott's court dockets and the subsequent release of the pictures, William said very little.

When I'd finished, John Fuller looked up from his notebook to give me a nod and an approving glance, then reached for the two-way radio attached to his belt.

"Callahan? You there?"

When an affirming answer came, Sheriff Fuller asked in the same mild tone, "How's the guy in the Cadillac?"

"A bit shocky, but swearing a blue streak and demanding to be let loose," Callahan said.

"Read the guy his rights and cuff him," Fuller instructed. "I'll be out in a few minutes."

"Anything else?"

Sheriff Fuller paused, giving me a glance that softened his craggy features. "Yeah. You can tell Thacker for me that his bull did some good work tonight."

"So what happens next?" William asked as the sheriff reached for his jacket.

"I'll give Wade and Chief McIntire a call as soon as I get back to the station," Fuller said, stuffing beefy arms into the sleeves of his jacket. "Fill them in on tonight and see what their plans are. Then Marty Covill and I are going to have a nice long chat. It'll be interesting to see how he reacts to the charge of attempted murder."

William nodded. "You'll keep us informed?"

"I'll be in touch. Give you a call in the morning."

"Sooner, if there's a problem, or anything we should know," William put in.

The sheriff met William's hard-eyed look with one of his own. "If you're worried about having any more unwanted visitors tonight, don't be," he said flatly. "For one thing, that guy Sarcassian isn't likely to stir up any more trouble until he gets a report from Brock and Covill. And since that won't be coming, the man's going to be stewin' in his juices for a while, wondering if something went wrong." Fuller picked up his hat and added with a grim-faced smile, "But just in case, I'll have one of my men posted near the trestle bridge for the rest of the night."

William shook the sheriff's hand. "Thanks for your help, John."

"No problem." Sheriff Fuller tipped his hat to me and said in his easygoing way, "And thanks for all your help, Miss Graham. I know you've had a pretty rough time of it, but I wouldn't worry too much." He turned to go, then gave me a knowing wink. "I think your attorney has everything under control."

Twenty-five

Nature's fireworks were over for the night, and the sky was a soft blanket of darkness. It was still raining, but lightly, and the wind had calmed. The ambulance carrying Brock Symond's body had already left the ranch, and soon the taillights of Sheriff Fuller's patrol car were only small blinks of red diminishing in the blackness.

William and I left the porch to go inside, shutting out the night and all that had happened with the simple closing of a door.

"I don't know about you, but your attorney is pretty near starving to death," he said, putting an arm around my shoulders as we entered the candlelit living room. "And as much as I'd like to wine and dine you in some fancy restaurant, I think we'd better stay put."

I smiled at his use of "pretty near." "Well, there's plenty of peach cobbler. I promised I'd save you some, remember?"

"Mmm, that'll do for starters."

William took two candles off the mantle, then led the way from the living room to the dark kitchen, the candles' flickering light casting wavering shadows on the walls around us. He set the candleholders on the kitchen table and asked, "Do you have anything else in mind?"

"Knowing your mother, I'm sure there'll be some leftovers in the fridge that we can heat up."

I opened the refrigerator door and stared blankly at the dark insides.

"And you were going to heat up these leftovers how?" William asked.

"I suppose all my positive energy won't make the microwave work, will it?"

He laughed and moved close behind me. "I'm afraid not."

"Oh well. There's still peach cobbler. And I agree with what you said. I couldn't be happier to stay put."

William was silent for a moment then turned me to face him, both hands on my shoulders. "Do you mean that?" His voice was a warm whisper in the darkness. "When all this is over, would you be happy to stay put? Here, with me . . . because I love you."

"You love me?"

He drew me close against his chest. "I love you. And I don't care if it's too soon. It's not too soon for me. I couldn't let you go without telling you how I feel."

I sighed and kissed him. "I'm not going anywhere—not yet."

"But you will. We both know that."

I shook my head, not wanting to face the idea of leaving, let alone speak of it. Arms around his neck, I held him closer, hoping my kisses would tell him all the words my heart was too full to speak.

His mouth answered mine, giving, taking, and soon our hunger for each other drove away everything else—conscious thought, words, and definitely all thoughts of supper. In the midst of this sweet madness the power came on, with the kitchen lights near blinding after the darkness, and the refrigerator's hum sounding like a swarm of angry bees. Then there was the slam of the back door, the scuff of footsteps, and voices intruded into our timeless world.

Thankfully, by the time Tom and Jenny entered the room, William and I were at least two feet apart and I was reaching for the pan of peach cobbler instead of him.

Jenny was openly relieved when she saw us, and Tom wore a tight frown of concern.

"We passed an ambulance and Sheriff Fuller on the way in," Tom said.

"And Wade's been trying to reach you all evening," Jenny put in. "He called twice while we were at LeAnn's."

"We had a bit of trouble with two of Sarcassian's men," William said. "One of them won't be causing anybody any more trouble. His body's in the ambulance. The other guy's in custody. Sheriff Fuller will deal with him."

"God help us," Tom muttered.

"Thankfully, He already has," I said quietly.

William took the pan of peach cobbler out of my hands and set it on the counter, then slipped an arm around my waist, pulling me close to his side.

Jenny's eyebrows went up a notch, but all she said was "Well, I take it you two haven't had time for supper. Sit down, both of you, and I'll fix something while you tell your father and me what happened."

"You might want to give your brother a call first," Tom said to William. "Let him know you're all right."

"I'll do that right now."

William went to the phone, while I made my way to the table, suddenly needing to sit down. Jenny was already taking a bowl of this and a container of that out of the refrigerator. I briefly considered offering to help, then silently acknowledged that I was far too spent to be of any use to her.

William's father joined me at the table, his eyes gentle as he placed a rough, calloused hand over one of mine. "You look as if you could use a little elixir of the gods," he said. "I'm pretty sure there's a can of Pepsi in the fridge, if you'd care for one."

"Thanks. I'd love one."

Tom patted my hand and got up from the table. I glanced over at William, who was deep in conversation with his brother. He caught my look and sent me a smile so tender it made my heart ache. Sitting there in Hearth Fires' homey kitchen, I couldn't remember a time ever in my life when I'd felt such love and caring.

The meal was simple and the talk plain. William must have sensed my weariness, because he took the lead and spared me most of the retelling, including the latest developments from Wade. Apparently, Sarcassian had called in a high-power attorney who was responding with arrogant indignation to any and all questions regarding his client. And there was still no word as to Lieutenant Dicola's whereabouts.

Jenny's mouth was tight and her brown eyes horrified when she learned how I'd run away from the house and released the bulls, but all she said was "Well, we'd better put some of my salve on your hands. Those scratches could get infected."

"I'm glad Sheriff Fuller had the sense to put one of his men on the bridge," Tom commented gruffly, turning a worried gaze on William. "But I'd feel a lot better if you and I kept watch on the house tonight, just to make sure."

"Thanks, Dad. I was going to suggest that."

"Surely there's no need for that now," I said, thinking how little sleep William had had the night before.

"Maybe not, but I'd rather not take any chances," he told me.

"I'll take the first watch, if you like," his father offered.

"It's okay, Dad. I'm too wired to sleep now anyway."

"Well then, I'd better get a pot of coffee brewing," Jenny said matter-of-factly. "And I know someone who's half asleep already." She gave me a smile.

"I'm all right, really," I protested, stifling a yawn.

"You're not all right. You're completely worn out. I'll get some of my salve for your hands and then it's straight to bed for you. When was the last time you had any pain medication?"

I shook my head. "I'm not sure. Last night, I think. But the pain isn't too bad."

"There's no point in arguing with my mother when she gets into her Nurse Evans mode," William said with a grin. He helped me up from the table, then kissed me in full view of his parents. "Good night, Mac. Sleep well."

Some two hours later, I was still wide awake, staring out the window of William's room at the huge harvest moon that had risen. The rain had ceased and only a few clouds remained, drifting lazily across a deep mother-of-pearl sky.

Was it only last night I had watched the moon's rising, anxiously waiting for William's call and wondering when he would return? So much had happened since then, it seemed ages instead of hours.

I left the window and climbed back into bed, willing myself to relax. During our late supper it was all I could do to keep my head up and my eyes open, yet now sleep refused to come.

I turned over with a sigh, watching the delicate pattern of moon shadows on the wall. The house was silent. Jenny and Tom had come up to bed well over an hour ago. As I lay there, the moon's glow grew brighter, diluting the darkness with its milky light. Like the moonlit room, the glow in my heart grew warmer and brighter every time I thought of William and his words of love.

I sat up with a sudden start, painfully aware I hadn't answered him—at least, not in words. The unexpected arrival of his parents had seen to that, and we hadn't had a moment alone since. Now my pounding heart dictated exactly what I needed to do. I got quickly out of bed and left the room.

The sound of Tom's snores coming from his and Jenny's room effectively muffled the squeak or two marking my quiet passage down the stairs.

There was no lamp burning in the living room, only the orange-red embers glowing in the fireplace. Sheets and a blanket were made up for William's bed on the couch, but he wasn't there.

I stood for a moment, not sure what to do or where to find him. Then, hearing a faint sound from the front porch, I glanced out the living room window. A wash of moonlight revealed his tall form near one of the pillars, standing with rifle in hand, staring out at the night. Looking at his rugged silhouette, I felt a wave of sheer amazement that this man would go to such lengths to protect me— that he loved me.

I opened the front door and heard his quiet "It's okay, Dad. Go back to bed. I'm wide awake."

"It's not Dad," I said, stepping onto the moon-washed porch. "And I can't sleep either."

He jerked around. "Mackenzie?"

"The moon's up and I wanted to share it with you. And— and there's something I didn't have the chance to say . . ."

He set the rifle down and came toward me. We were in each other's arms before I could speak. Held close against him, I felt the pent-up river of emotion inside me overflow in a flood of sweet certainty.

"I love you, William. I do love you."

He bent his head to kiss me, and words came easily after that. Words that might never be spoken in daylight hours found eager expression in the moonlight, tumbling out in joyful whispers between us. Love, so new, received and returned, made us both a little crazy. But even love couldn't prevent me from starting to shiver. My pajama pants were thin cotton, and though William's flannel shirt was a bit warmer, it couldn't keep out the penetrating chill of the night breeze.

"Good grief, girl, you'll catch your death," William scolded between our laughter and kisses. "No jacket and your feet are bare. What were you thinking?"

"I wasn't thinking—only that I needed to tell you how much I love you."

The next moment I was lifted in his arms and planted firmly down on the porch swing. "Don't go anywhere," he said, then went inside the house, returning seconds later with a blanket. After shaking out the folds, he wrapped the blanket around me, then sat down and lifted my legs across his lap.

"Your feet are like ice," he said, massaging them with warm, strong fingers.

I smiled at him in the moonlight. "Cold feet, warm heart."

William chuckled low and leaned over to plant a path of kisses down my neck and throat. "Mmm. Very warm heart."

Sometime later, he straightened with a groan. "I hope you realize what a lovely distraction you are. The entire Chinese army could invade the ranch and I'd never know it."

I laughed softly. "I think I'd be more worried about waking your mother."

"You have a point there."

I sat up and disentangled myself from the blanket. "I guess I'd better go back to bed."

"I guess you'd better before my resolve weakens."

"I do love you, William."

"And I love you," he said, cradling my face in his hands. "Sweet dreams, Mac."

I don't remember dreaming at all, but when I finally drifted off to sleep, it was with the taste of his kisses still warm on my lips, and the soft smile of a woman who knows she is truly cherished.

Twenty-six

The sun was up and shining long before I awakened, spilling its gold on the cliff tops of Mount Kinesava and warming rain-wet fields and pastures. Standing next to the open window in William's room, I breathed in the freshness of the morning, knowing with quiet sureness that the golden light outside couldn't begin to compare with the warmth and happiness rising inside me. I lifted my arms above my head, ignoring the few aches and pains that persisted as reminders of yesterday's dark fears and danger. This was now. A sun-bright autumn morning. The very first morning of knowing that William Evans loved me and I loved him. My heart and mind patently refused to dwell on anything beyond that amazing fact.

I left the window to dress. Unbuttoning William's flannel shirt, I considered my limited choices. Wardrobe A: green blouse and capris, or wardrobe B: denim shirt and jeans. The gray sweats and hoodie were totally out of the question. On closer examination, so were the green blouse and capris. Both were dirt-stained from last night's crawl through the ditch, and the blouse had a jagged tear in one of the sleeves.

I pulled on the jeans, then went to William's dresser. I found a sage-green T-shirt in one of the drawers and held it up to me. The color went well with my eyes and hair, but the shirt was yards too big. No matter. Wearing William's clothes was getting to be a very pleasant habit. I pulled the shirt over my head, twisted one side into a narrow roll, then tied it close to my waist and rolled up the sleeves. I brushed my hair until it gleamed like burnished copper and left it loose to fall around my shoulders. A little green eye shadow, some mascara and lip gloss, and I was ready to face the day.

William's arms and the hearty aromas of eggs and bacon greeted me the moment I entered the kitchen. He gave the T-shirt an approving once-over and said huskily in my ear, "Dang, I'm jealous of my shirt."

His mother, busy at the stove stirring scrambled eggs in one pan and turning slices of bacon in another, pretended not to notice the kiss he gave me, but her own lips kept twitching into a smile.

"Sleep well?" William asked softly.

I nodded. "How about you?"

"Dad relieved me around four, so I had a few hours."

Looking into his eyes, I was amazed to see no weariness there, only the warmth of his love. William smiled at me and we proceeded to have a wordless conversation that rivaled the temperature of the bacon sizzling in the frying pan.

Then Jenny's matter-of-fact announcement broke into our world. "Your Dad's out feeding the horses. Would you let him know that breakfast is about ready? We're getting such a late start on the day, I don't know whether to call it breakfast or brunch, but whatever it is, he needs to come and eat while it's hot."

William grinned and left the kitchen to do his mother's bidding, while I floated over to the stove to ask, "Is there anything I can do to help?"

Jenny didn't answer right away, just stared at the contents of the frying pan as if something there was commanding all her attention. When she finally glanced up, I saw the unmistakable shine of tears in her brown eyes.

"You have helped. In more ways than you know." She put down the spatula and took me in her arms for a brief, hard hug. "Thank you for making my son so happy," she said. This was followed by brisk instructions to finish setting the table and butter the toast.

Halfway through breakfast, a harsh reminder of yesterday's trauma forced its way into my sunny world with the simple ringing of the phone. William got up to answer it as I tried to calm the rapid beating of my heart. In a moment's breath, I found myself reliving that ominous phone call from the day before. I shook myself free of the memory as William returned to the table with the news that Sheriff Fuller was on his way to the ranch.

William must have seen the remnants of fear in my eyes, because he reached for my hand and told me, "It's all right. Apparently, John has some good news that he wants to share in person."

Some twenty minutes later, Sheriff John Fuller was sitting at the kitchen table accepting a fresh cup of coffee and one of Jenny's cinnamon rolls. Lines of weariness from a sleepless night were pronounced in the man's craggy features, but there was a satisfied gleam in his eyes.

"Marty Covill wasn't very talkative at first," he told us after downing half the cinnamon roll in a few bites. "But after we'd had a nice discussion about him being an accessory to murder, among other things, he started opening up some. I have Marty's signed statement that Sarcassian hired him and Brock Symonds to follow Miss Graham and get her camera." Sheriff Fuller glanced my way. "According to Covill, you were trying to blackmail Sarcassian by threatening to use some incriminating pictures against him."

My jaw dropped as I heard the manipulative lie, and Jenny burst out with "That's ridiculous! Mackenzie doesn't even know that snake Sarcassian."

John Fuller's craggy face eased into a smile at her indignant defense of me. "It's okay, Jenny. I figured it wouldn't hurt to let him run on a bit. Sooner or later, he was bound to trip over his lies and we'd get around to the truth. Marty was adamant that all he did was drive the car, that he had nothing to do with Allison Meyers' death, that it was Brock Symonds who fired the shot. And I'm inclined to believe him on that point."

"What about last night?" William inserted. "Were he and Symonds supposed to be paying us a friendly visit? The pictures had already been released, so there was little substance in his excuse about trying to get Mackenzie's camera."

Sheriff Fuller nodded his agreement with a disgusted snort. "I made a point of telling him just that, but Marty kept to his story, insisting that he was only hired to be the driver and didn't know anything about Sarcassian's plans to harm Miss Graham. By that time, I was gettin' pretty tired of listening to all his BS—pardon the language. So I asked him, if he was so all-fired innocent, why was he carrying a gun, and what reason did he have for firing at an unarmed woman.

"Covill sputtered a bit, but couldn't come up with any clever lies to answer that. So I asked him if he'd like to change his story and help us out, or I'd make good and sure he faced charges of attempted murder." Fuller took a gulp of coffee and added, "Our conversation was a lot more productive after that."

"Were you able to find out how Sarcassian learned where Mackenzie was?" William asked him.

Fuller nodded. "That was Dicola's doing. Apparently, he had some suspicions about the extent of Wade's involvement with Miss Graham. He started nosing around, asking a lot of questions, and one way or another, found out that Wade had a brother who was an attorney and lived on a ranch in southern Utah. That by itself didn't prove anything, but Dicola was determined and desperate." John Fuller put down his coffee cup and fixed William with a shrewd-eyed look. "According to Covill, Dicola managed to get a picture of you and Wade. With what's available on the internet, that wouldn't be difficult. All he had to do then was show the photo to the nurse at the hospital. She confirmed that you were the fiancé, and after that, it was easy. Dicola went straight to Sarcassian, thinking this information would save his own neck."

"It probably did just the opposite," William said. "Dicola had outlived his usefulness."

"Unfortunately for the lieutenant, that's pretty much what happened," Fuller replied. "Covill told me that Sarcassian was furious when he saw those pictures on the internet. In his mind, the only way out of the situation was to remove Miss Graham as a possible witness."

William said nothing, just reached for my hand, his fingers enclosing mine in a protective grip.

"Both Covill and Symonds were at Sarcassian's place when Dicola showed up with the news that he'd found out where you were," the sheriff went on, giving me a nod. "Dicola thought he was giving Sarcassian a real ace in the hole and demanded protection as well as some cash in exchange for the information. Instead, Sarcassian blew up and accused the lieutenant of double-crossing him. Said it was all Dicola's fault he was under investigation."

"Sarcassian blamed Dicola?" I asked. "Why would he think it was the lieutenant's fault?"

"Guys like Sarcassian always need someone else to blame for their own mistakes," Fuller said bluntly.

"If you think about it, in a twisted way it makes sense," William said. "Dicola was being paid to look the other way and protect Sarcassian and his interests. I can see where the fact that it was Wade—one of Dicola's own, so to speak—who got Mackenzie out of Sarcassian's reach would not sit well with the man."

"Wade and you," I inserted, putting a hand on William's thigh.

"You've got a point there," Sheriff Fuller said. "At any rate, according to Covill, the two men got into a heated argument. Dicola was stupid enough to threaten Sarcassian and told him he was through doing his dirty work." Fuller shook his head, adding with a grimace, "He was through all right. Dicola was leaving the house when Sarcassian shot him in the back. Symonds and Covill were given the job of disposing of the body."

I shuddered and leaned back against the chair, stunned and sickened by the news. William's parents sat as still and silent as I.

"Does Wade know all this?" William asked. "And Chief McIntire?"

Fuller nodded. "I called McIntire early this morning. He's already sent a team of officers to get Dicola's body. And before the day's out, Nicolas Sarcassian will be served with a warrant for his arrest."

"What about Wade?" Jenny asked. "Is he all right?"

"He's fine," Fuller assured her, then turned to me. "I hope knowing all this'll put your mind at ease. Sarcassian and his crew are definitely out of commission, so there's no need for you to be lookin' over your shoulder. You can rest easy now."

"Even with Sarcassian's high-power attorney doing his best to get him off?" I couldn't help asking.

"No judge or jury can dispute the fact that it was a bullet from Sarcassian's gun that killed Vince Dicola," William told me.

"Or the fact that Marty Covill witnessed the shooting," Fuller put in. "I have his signed statement that he's willing to testify to that fact. Like I said, you can rest easy now. Besides, it looks to me like you've got your own high-power attorney."

William's tight expression eased into a smile. "She does at that."

Not half an hour after Sheriff Fuller had left, William got a call from Wade with the latest updates on his end. I sat beside William on the porch swing, listening while he talked with his brother and alternately shared the news with me.

Wade confirmed that a team of officers had found Lieutenant Dicola's body dumped in a wooded ravine off Highway 1. He also had a surprising development relating to Judge Wolcott's suicide. Apparently, before taking his life, Peter Wolcott had an attack of conscience and wrote a letter that was found by his wife. In addition to apologizing to his family, the judge admitted he had accepted a bribe of fifty thousand dollars to get Nicholas Sarcassian's daughter out of her legal difficulties.

By the time William hung up with Wade, the last bit of strain and worry had left his face. He blew out a long sigh and uttered, "Thank the Lord, I really believe the worst is over. Sarcassian's no longer a threat, and you're safe." Taking my face in his hands, William kissed me long and hard.

When I could breathe and speak again, I said, "I keep thinking of your mother's advice to me, that I should rest and be thankful. Oh, William, I'm so thankful—especially for you!"

Loud honking and the unmistakable sound of a car's approach interrupted our kiss. William released me and glanced toward the road, where a tan SUV was stirring up the dust.

"Hell's bells," he muttered. "It's my sister and the twins."

Moments later, a smiling LeAnn and two dark-haired munchkins were headed up the front walk.

The twins broke away from their mother and made a beeline for William with delighted cries of "Uncle Will!" He met them halfway and scooped up both little boys, one in each arm.

Watching the boys hug and kiss their uncle and seeing his smiling return of their affection, I felt a warm, happy ache inside.

"We brought you some birthday cake," one of the twins told him.

"We had a dinosaur party," the other announced with bright eyes.

"You did?" William said with appropriate amazement. "How many dinosaurs did you invite?"

One of the twins laughed and pulled a face. "Dinosaurs can't come to a party," he told his uncle. "They're 'stinct!"

"Then it's a good thing they didn't come," William said. "Who wants a bunch of stinky dinosaurs coming to their birthday party?"

"Now you've done it," LeAnn told her brother as the twins giggled and started naming off their favorite "stinky" dinosaurs. "Go give Grandma and Grandpa a hug," she instructed, shooing them towards the house. "Go on now."

William just laughed and took my hand as the little boys ran off with giggles and shouts about who was a "poo-poo dinosaur."

"So much for good first impressions," LeAnn said with a shake of her blond ponytail. "Potty humor is their latest thing—and Will's no help at all."

He gave her an unrepentant grin. "I believe you met Mackenzie yesterday."

"Yes, I did." Curiosity sparkled in LeAnn's blue eyes.

"They're such handsome little boys," I said before she could ask any leading questions about her brother and me. "Do you ever have trouble telling them apart?"

"All the time. That's why Gavin's in the blue shirt and Quinn's wearing green."

There was a pregnant pause in the conversation that had nothing to do with LeAnn's condition, and I wondered if William or I should try to explain that we weren't really engaged—at least not yet. The problem was, telling her that much would also entail giving other, more difficult explanations, and I wasn't sure how much she knew about the previous day's dangerous events.

William managed to postpone any immediate questions by giving his sister's ponytail an affectionate tug and saying, "You're looking good, Sis. Sorry we had to miss the party. Where's that birthday cake?"

Between the birthday cake and the twins' antics, conversation stayed fairly general. Thankfully, LeAnn's surprise visit wouldn't be a long one as she had to leave by midafternoon to pick up her eldest child from school, seven-year-old Jenny. I took a quick glance at the kitchen clock as we finished eating the birthday cake, thinking we still had nearly two hours to fill without discussing wedding plans.

The twins helped solve the dilemma by begging their uncle to take them for a horseback ride.

William turned to me. "How about it, Mac? Are you feeling up to it?"

Either option had its downside. Climbing on the back of a huge animal that would instantly know how inexperienced I was, or staying behind to face a barrage of awkward questions for which I had no ready answer. At least the horse couldn't ask questions and I'd be with William.

"If you're up to teaching me," I said.

"Oh, I think we can manage," he answered in that soft-spoken way of his that played havoc with my insides.

LeAnn's pregnancy was advanced enough that she declined to come with us and was more than happy to have someone else in charge of her energetic four-year-olds for an hour or two.

As we walked to the barn and corrals, the sun was high in the sky and the day pleasantly warm. In their eagerness, Gavin and Quinn ran ahead of us and began climbing the lower rungs of the corral fence.

"Are they old enough to ride by themselves?" I asked William.

"They think they are," he said with a chuckle, "but I figured you and I could each take one of the boys with us. Gavin's totally fearless, but Quinn's still a bit unsure around horses."

"And so am I," I said. "Do you really trust me that much?"

"Sure, I trust you." Those attractive creases appeared in his cheeks, along with a teasing smile. "And I trust the horse. Shiloh's a real lady."

The boys and I watched while William saddled Strider and a chestnut mare with white stockings on each foreleg and a spot of white on her forehead.

"She's beautiful," I said as William led both horses to the corral fence. "I love the star on her forehead."

"It's not a star," Gavin informed me. "It's called a blaze."

"Oh, I see. I didn't know that."

"Mackenzie lives in the city where there aren't any horses," William told the boys. "So this is her first horseback ride."

Quinn looked at me in wide-eyed disbelief. "No horses?"

"No horses," I said. "Only cars and trucks."

"Boring," Gavin pronounced with all the wisdom of his age.

"I totally agree," I told him.

"Gavin, I want you to sit in front of Mackenzie and help her get to know Shiloh," William said. "Quinn, you'll be my buddy." After tying Strider's reins to the corral fence, William moved to Shiloh's head and took the bridle. "Come say hello, Mac."

I got down off the fence and approached the mare, hating the fact that my heart was thumping uncomfortably.

William put his face next to the mare's, and she gave him an affectionate nudge with her magnificent head. "This is Mackenzie," he told the horse in soft tones, then took my hand and placed it on the animal's velvety muzzle. "I want you to take real good care of my girl," he said to the mare. "Easy does it, today. Okay, Shiloh?"

Looking into the mare's dark, intelligent eyes, I swear I felt her acceptance of me even before she answered William with a pleasant nicker.

Before I knew it, I was sitting astride the horse, and William was adjusting the stirrups.

He grinned up at me. "How does it feel?"

"Good. It feels good," I answered with some amazement.

William lifted Gavin up, and the little boy immediately settled himself in front of me. Quinn's eyes were round as William swung him up onto Strider's back, but he said not a word, just clung to the saddle horn. The next moment William had mounted the long-legged buckskin and was giving his nephew an encouraging hug.

"Good going, Quinn. Just lean against me, buddy. That's the way."

After giving me a few basic instructions, William turned Strider's head toward the open fields, and Shiloh followed obediently after.

As William said, the mare was a perfect lady, accepting me, as well as her place beside long-legged Strider, with dignity and grace. It wasn't long before my nervousness dissolved and sheer enjoyment took its place. The warm sun, a fresh breeze, and the comfortable smells of leather and horseflesh filled my senses with near-primitive delight.

William kept his horse at an easy walk, taking us through an open field where the grass was long and gleaming with moisture from last night's rain. Here and there, a few wildflowers still bloomed, despite the lateness of the season. At the field's end, a dirt trail, still damp and puddled in places, led us towards the river, where the air was rich with the pungent, musty smell of autumn. The river itself had shrunk to scarcely more than a shallow stream, with smooth rocks and boulders along its bed exposed to the sun. Ancient cottonwoods and box elder trees grew alongside the bank, their leaves shining gold and yellow in the afternoon sun.

I drank in every sight, marveling at the day's gifts to us as the breeze stirred the branches, sending a shower of gold swirling and dancing in the bright air. Seen against the hard blue sky of autumn, the contrast in colors—deepest blue and shimmering yellow—took my breath away.

We followed the river's winding path for a short distance, then William reined in Strider and glanced around. "This'll do," he said.

"Do?"

He nodded. "This looks like a good place to skim a few rocks. What do you say, guys?"

The boys were vocal in their agreement. William dismounted, then lifted the eager twins down. They were off to the river in a flash as William approached Shiloh to help me dismount. I practically fell into his waiting arms, my stiff legs suddenly refusing to cooperate. Laughing, he helped me to a grassy spot near the bank, then tied the horses' reins to some low-growing willows. I eased myself down with a smile that was part grimace, but mostly pure pleasure.

William settled himself beside me, plucked a blade of grass, and put it between his teeth. Leaning back on one elbow, he gave me a warm, slant-eyed look. "Looks like we got our horseback ride after all."

"Looks like we did," I said.

Time drifted by as lazily as the sparkling stream while we watched the twins' tireless delight in throwing rocks into the water. The little boys' laughter and the liquid plopping of rocks seemed to fade into the background as I leaned against William and watched cloud shadows moving across the far cliffs. The peace was profound—almost a presence. And the love that sang between us in sweet, silent melodies needed no words for expression.

When William announced it was time to head back, Gavin and Quinn were equally vocal in their reluctance to bring the afternoon's excursion to a close. But long before we crossed the last field leading back to the ranch, their dark heads and sturdy little bodies were drooping with sleep. I had one arm around Gavin to keep him from toppling over, and the other held the reins.

As Strider and Shiloh ambled homeward side by side, William glanced over at me with a soft smile and an even softer "I love you, Mac."

My heart was so full that "Darling William" was all I could say.

He had a tired twin in each arm and we were walking across the back lawn to the house when I noticed a silver sedan parked beside LeAnn's SUV. I glanced at William, but his face wore a puzzled frown rather than any sign of recognition.

Then two people came out of the house onto the back porch, a man and a woman, followed by William's parents.

I gasped and my heart made a sudden, surprised leap. "I don't believe it . . . it can't be."

William glanced my way. "Can't be what?"

"It's my parents!"

Twenty-seven

For nearly all of my twenty-eight years, I had respectfully referred to my parents as Mother and Father. They expected and preferred nothing less. Now, running toward them across the lawn, I let out a delighted shout. "Mom! Dad!"

They turned at the sound of my voice, and the next moment we were in each other's arms.

"Thank God you're all right," my mother choked. "I've been half out of my mind."

I could feel her trembling as she held me, and found myself offering words of comfort. "It's all right . . . it's all right . . . I'm fine."

My father said not a word as they hugged and kissed me in turn. Then he gave me a broken, crumpled smile and looked into my eyes. Tears were running down his cheeks.

Something I had always known on the deepest level but never truly acknowledged surfaced when I saw those tears and felt my mother's trembling. My parents loved me. And I loved them.

"I wanted to call you, but there was no way I could . . ."

"Considering the circumstances, that's understandable," my father said, regaining some control. "While we were waiting for you, Mr. and Mrs. Evans have been kind enough to tell us some of what's been happening." His chin started to quiver, and he gave me another hard hug. "Maybe it was kinder in the long run that your Mother and I didn't know all the details."

"But how did you get here? How did you know where I was?"

William's mother came forward then, offering with her usual warmth, "Why don't we go inside where it's more comfortable? I'm sure you have a lot to talk about."

I glanced around, suddenly aware that William was nowhere to be seen. "Where's William?"

"He'll be back in a few minutes," Jenny told me. "He's helping LeAnn get the twins buckled into their car seats, and then he has to see to the horses. Oh, and LeAnn wanted me to thank you for watching the boys. She doesn't often get a rest, and she needs it right now."

"I can't imagine how your daughter manages," Mother said politely as we followed Jenny inside.

I had to smile. Having a seven-year-old, plus four-year old twins and expecting a baby, was indeed something my mother could never imagine. Not in a million years.

"I'll be with you as soon as I wash up," I told my parents, leaving them in Jenny's capable hands, and headed for the bathroom.

When I joined them in the living room a few minutes later, the emotional levels had calmed down considerably. Jenny was serving my parents tall glasses of lemonade, along with a plate of chocolate-chip cookies. Mother passed on the cookies as I knew she would, but my father reluctantly accepted one after Jenny's inimitable urging. After one bite, an expression of pleased surprise lightened his features.

It was an extraordinary sight—my stylish parents sitting rather stiffly on the Evans' soft lumpy sofa, the epitome of politeness and charm, but totally out of their element. As Jenny handed me a glass of lemonade, something in her expression struck me as unusual, but I couldn't be sure what it was.

"You were going to tell me how you found out where I was," I began, sitting in the recliner.

"We didn't know until late last night," Mother told me as my father was still enjoying his cookie. "But it was Claire Langley who told us you were missing. She'd received a call from one of her editors in San Francisco with the terrible news of Allison Meyers' death. When she told us you'd been with Allison when she was shot—well, I was stunned and worried sick. Then, later that same day, we got a phone call from some man who claimed he was with the Palo Alto police department."

"Claimed to be?" I said.

Mother nodded. "He asked a lot of questions, wanting to know if we'd heard from you, or had any idea where you were."

"It wasn't until I called Chief McIntire the next day that we found out whoever had called definitely wasn't with their department," my father put in, licking a bit of chocolate from his lower lip. "McIntire filled us in on the accident, along with the fact that you'd disappeared from the hospital, but refused to tell us anything more."

"It was horrible, not knowing," Mother said, and the pain in her eyes cut through me.

"I'm so sorry, Mom."

"We've kept in touch with Chief McIntire or someone from his department ever since," my father continued, "but the response was always the same. They did tell us you were somewhere safe, but refused to give out any more information than that. So I decided it was high time that McIntire and I had a little chat—in person."

I stared at my distinguished father, whose clothes and polished manner could give Ralph Lauren a run for his money.

"Your mother and I flew to San Francisco late yesterday afternoon, determined to get some answers one way or another. We were in McIntire's office when he got word from some sheriff in southern Utah that two of Sarcassian's men had caused some trouble at the ranch where you were in protective custody." My father cleared his throat, then ran a hand through his perfectly groomed hair. "All we got was bits and pieces, but it was enough to make my blood run cold. McIntire left us, and another officer, the

Evanses' son Wade, took over. I'm sure he broke the rules in doing so, but he took pity on your mother and me and assured us you were safe and well—that you'd been staying with his brother and parents on their ranch. It wasn't too difficult after that to find out exactly where the ranch was."

"We didn't know what to expect," Mother put in, "knowing you'd been in that terrible accident and who knows what else. But you look wonderful, Mackenzie." She gave William's T-shirt a scrutinizing glance but refrained from comment. "In fact, I don't know when I've seen you looking better."

I smiled at her. "William and his parents have taken good care of me."

"And we're very grateful for that," Mother said, including Jenny in her smile.

My father gave his Rolex a pointed glance. The second time he had done so since we'd sat down to talk.

Noting this, Mother put her glass of lemonade on the lamp table and turned to me. "Can I help you pack your things?"

"What?"

"Can I help you pack?"

A sudden coldness gripped my heart, and I couldn't answer her.

"It's a good three-hour drive from here to Las Vegas, and our flight's at nine," my father said. "We really need to be on our way."

"You . . . you're leaving," I mumbled, my throat dry.

Mother smiled and shook her head. "Not your father and me. We're all leaving together. We booked a ticket for you as well as ours. We knew how anxious you'd be to get back, and there's no reason to impose on the Evanses' kindness any longer."

My lips parted, but I couldn't move or speak. The time had come for me to leave. And it was now. Not some nebulous far-off moment in the future. Now. I should have realized. I should have known. Mother was right. There was no longer any reason for me to stay. My parents had come all this way just to find me, and I was touched beyond expression that they had. Of course they would expect me to come with them.

Glancing away from my mother's puzzled expression, I saw William standing in the doorway of the living room, his face like stone, except for his eyes. I met his gaze and saw a hard, cold realization that mirrored my own.

I got to my feet and moved to stand beside him, instinctively reaching for his hand. His fingers grasped mine. "Mom, Dad, I'd like you to meet William." My voice sounded strangely hollow and flat.

My father got off the sofa and came forward with a grateful smile. William had to release my hand to accept the one my father extended, quietly accepting his words of thanks. Mother did the same, but not before giving me a speculative, searching look.

"There really are no words to thank you for all you've done," she said with smiling lips and that same puzzled expression.

William just nodded and said, "I'm glad I could help," his movements as stiff and wooden as mine.

I gave him a helpless look, suddenly fighting back tears.

Mother touched my arm. "Mackenzie? I hate to rush you, dear, but we do need to pack if we're going to make that flight."

I felt William's hand on the small of my back. "You're going to need something to put your things in," he said. "I've got a bag upstairs that should work. Will you excuse us, Mrs. Graham? We won't be long."

When we reached his room, William shut the door and wrapped his arms around me, crushing me against his chest. My arms went around his neck, pulling him closer still as his mouth took mine in a bruising kiss.

"Oh, William—"

"It's all right, honey. It's all right. I know you have to go." He pressed my head to his chest as I fought back hot tears.

Beneath my cheek, I felt him draw a long breath. Then he released me and went to the closet to take a canvas bag down from the shelf. "It isn't fancy, but this ought to do." He brought it to the bed and unzipped the top.

I swallowed hard and gathered my things together, dumping them in the bag any which way.

William took his pajama top from one of the dresser drawers. "Better not forget this. It looked a lot better on you than it ever did on me."

I couldn't keep back a smile as he handed me the top.

"That's better," he said, touching a hand to my cheek.

There was a soft tap on the bedroom door, and Jenny stepped inside. "Your folks are ready to go," she said tightly.

I bit my lip and nodded.

"I, uh, wanted you to have a little something to take with you. It's not much, but . . ." Her voice trailed off as she handed me a pint jar of apricot jam.

When I tried to thank her, the words got stuck on the hard lump in my throat. I put my arms around her and we held each other close. Neither of us could say goodbye.

As we came downstairs I saw Tom Evans waiting beside my parents, who were standing near the front door, trying their best not to appear impatient.

I kissed Tom's cheek and whispered, "Thank you for the stories . . . and . . . and everything."

He nodded and gave my shoulder an awkward pat. "There's a lot more stories to tell," he said gruffly, his eyes suspiciously bright. "They'll be here, waitin' for you."

William walked me out to the car, put the canvas bag in the back seat, and then straightened to face me. My parents were already in the front seat with seat belts fastened and the motor running.

William touched a hand to my hair. "Take care, Mac."

"You too." I looked at him a moment longer, then climbed inside.

He shut the car door and stepped away, his gaze holding mine. I lifted my hand in farewell as the vehicle began moving down the road.

"This really is a dreadful road," Mother commented in a low voice, but still loud enough for me to hear. "It'll be so wonderful to have you home," she added over her shoulder.

I said nothing, just stared straight ahead, knowing only that Hearth Fires and William were behind me.

Twenty-eight

I awoke in the bitter hour before dawn, feeling lost and confused. Pulling the bedcovers up around my shoulders, I stared through the bleak half-light that was more darkness than light, at strange surroundings. And yet they weren't really strange. At my parents' urging, I'd agreed to spend a day or two with them before returning to my apartment in the city. Yet even here, surrounded by every comfort and the plush furnishings of my parents' guest room, I felt an aching emptiness inside.

During the long drive to Las Vegas and the endless flight across the country to Chicago, I was dry-eyed and numb, responding to my parents' questions and comments as best I could. Their caring and concern carried me through some of the miles, but it couldn't lessen the painful tearing inside me, or the wrenching loss that had turned my sun-bright world an unrelenting gray.

Now, after getting out of bed, I made my way across the room to the west window, where I raised the blinds and pushed open the double-paned glass. There was no welcoming warble of meadowlarks singing on a fence post, no pungent whiff of dry alfalfa in the fields. Only a cold wind stirring the predawn darkness, sifting the fallen leaves and speaking of storms to come. Shivering, I pulled William's pajama top closer about me and let the tears fall.

By the time I showered and dressed, I fully expected my parents would have left for their respective places of work. Entering the kitchen, I was surprised to find my mother sitting at the table in the pleasant breakfast nook overlooking the patio. She looked quite lovely, dressed in slim pants and a shirt the same shade as her lavender-blue eyes. The morning light was kind as it glanced off the soft waves of her sable hair and touched her porcelain skin.

Mother smiled a good morning at my approach and set her cup of tea on its saucer. "I thought I'd see what plans you might have for today and then go into work a little later on. And I've given Carla instructions to fix you something special for breakfast. I thought strawberry crepes would be nice. Would you prefer tea or coffee? Carla brews the most marvelous cup of orange pekoe."

"Thank you, Mother. I–I'm not very hungry. If you don't mind, I think I'll just have some juice and toast. Jenny gave me a jar of her apricot jam, if you'd care to try some." I set the pint bottle on the table and took the chair beside my mother.

She gave the jam a raised-eyebrow look and said faintly, "Maybe another time." To Carla, a dark-eyed little woman with smooth olive skin, who was hovering in the doorway of the nook, she said in a slightly stilted voice, "Would you bring Mackenzie a chilled glass of juice, please? Apple, I think. And two slices of toast." Then, in that same stilted tone, Mother asked me, "White or wheat?"

"Whatever's handy. It doesn't matter. Thank you, Carla."

Mother picked up her cup and saucer and handed them to the cook. "And could I have a fresh cup, please?" She waited until Carla had left to fetch the tea and toast, then turned those lovely eyes on me. "Did you sleep well?"

I shrugged. "Well enough, I suppose."

She gave me a close look and I knew she couldn't miss my red-rimmed eyes, or the fact that I was still wearing William's T-shirt. After a moment's pause, she asked quietly, "Are you feeling all right?"

"Yes, Mother. Just a little . . . lost and disoriented."

She nodded, then said with an awkward little smile, "Yesterday you called me 'Mom.' And I— well, I think that's something I could get used to."

I smiled and reached over to give her hand a squeeze. "Thanks, Mom."

She glanced down suddenly and took the linen napkin in her lap to dab at her eyes.

Carla returned during the awkward moment that followed and set a tall glass of chilled apple juice in front of me. "The toast will be ready una momento," she told me, flashing a brilliant smile.

I thanked her and sipped the cold juice.

"The Evanses seem like very fine people," Mother said.

"Yes, they are."

"And their son—not the policeman, the other one—" She paused, blue-violet eyes intent on my face.

"William," I filled in, needing to say his name.

"Yes, William. I couldn't help noticing that he seemed—well, very protective of you."

I didn't answer right away, and thankfully Carla chose that moment to reappear with a tray of toast—four slices instead of two—and a fresh pot of tea with two cups and saucers.

"I think Carla's hinting that she'd like me to try some of that orange pekoe you were telling me about." I said. I took one of the cups and poured the hot tea. "I suppose I'd better, rather than hurt her feelings."

"And I suppose I'd better try a little of that apricot jam, rather than hurt your feelings." Mother helped herself to a slice of toast.

I pried the lid off the pint jar and offered her the jam as we shared a smile that was tender with new understanding. Mother took a piece of toast, and to give her due credit, spread a healthy layer of apricot jam on the top rather than the thin dab she usually used.

I spread jam on my own toast, and the first bite transported me back to Hearth Fires' homey kitchen. I smiled and decided this was as good a time as any.

"I'm in love with William," I said. "And he loves me."

Mother's lips parted, but she said not a word. She took a careful sip of her tea, then said without looking up, "And you've known this man how long?"

"I know. I know what you're trying to say. And I know how I feel."

"Do you?" she asked gently. "You've had a terrible shock and been under tremendous pressure. I can't begin to imagine what it must have been like. But it's over now, and you're back in your own world. With a little time, I'm sure you'll see things more clearly."

"My world?" I said slowly.

She nodded. "Everything you know is here. You have a wonderful job, friends, family. I can't imagine that you'd want to throw all that away. Honestly, dear, it might seem romantic right now, but can you really see yourself living on some ranch in the middle of nowhere?"

"Mother, please—"

"I'm sorry if I've spoken too plainly, but I'm only thinking of your happiness. Can you really be sure about a man that you've known for what—a week? Ten days? All I'm asking is that you give it some time. Is that unreasonable?"

"No. No, of course not."

"And it might be wise to give him a little time as well." Mother took another bite of toast, chewed a moment, and nodded. "Lovely jam."

"What do you mean, give him some time?"

"I suppose I mean that now all the drama and danger is past, it's not unreasonable to think William might need a little time to examine his feelings for you. You told us he's an attorney. In my experience, attorneys are very good at picking things apart and examining all the facts. And the facts of the matter are quite plain if you think about it a little less emotionally. It's not difficult to see how the two of you could form an attachment of sorts. But whether there's any permanency to those feelings—well, I think you both need more time to be sure."

End of discussion. Having done her best to plant some small seeds of doubt in my mind, Mother went on brightly, as if the previous conversation had never taken place. "So what are your plans for today?"

I sighed, trying to rid myself of the uncertainty she had introduced. I had no doubts where my own feelings were concerned. Loving William felt as right and natural as breathing. But was I assuming too much about his feelings for me?

"If you wouldn't mind giving me a ride to my apartment, I'd like to take care of a few things," I told her.

"I'll be glad to. And I was thinking it wouldn't hurt to give Claire a call, let her know you're safe and back home."

Claire Langley. Mother's dear friend and the magazine's editor-in-chief. And farther down the ladder of the magazine's hierarchy, I had better touch bases with my immediate boss, feature editor Lisa Golinske.

"Before I can do any calling, I need to get a new cell phone and a laptop," I said.

Mother's smooth brow wrinkled slightly. "Did you lose yours?"

"Not exactly. The laptop was stolen when Sarcassian's men broke into the inn, and my cell is—well, it's no longer functioning." My lips curved into a smile when I thought of William taking a tire iron to the phone and kicking its smashed remains off the roadside.

"Do you feel up to tackling all that so soon?" Mother asked. "Wouldn't it be better to take it easy for a few days?"

I shook my head. "I'd rather keep busy."

"Well then, I was wondering how you'd feel about having a small get-together Friday night? Nothing formal. Just a few friends and maybe some people from the magazine."

"I don't know, Mother. I appreciate the thought, but you really don't need—"

"I know I don't need to, but I'd like to, if you'll let me." She paused, then added with a catch in her voice, "Your safe return is certainly worthy of a celebration."

Put in those terms, there was no way I could refuse.

The day passed. And the next. And the day after that, with no word from William. I tried to squash the niggling doubts that tortured me by reminding myself that he didn't have the number of my new cell phone and I didn't have his. It wouldn't have taken more than a few seconds to get the number of his law office, but every time I thought about it, my mother's words stopped me cold. William's entire life had been put on hold while I was at the ranch. He probably had a mountain of work waiting for him, possibly even court dates that couldn't be postponed. The least I could do was give him some space and time to take care of his normal life. Quite possibly, he might even be thinking the same about me. That is, if he were thinking about me . . .

The meeting with my managing editor, Lisa Golinske, was brief and stress free. Along with the rest of the magazine staff, she was still reeling with the news of Allison's death and what had happened in California. My article on storybook homes was temporarily shelved and I was told, "Take the rest of the week off. Come in Monday morning and we'll discuss options for your next assignment."

By Friday morning, Mother was in the throes of party mania, and I began to have serious doubts about the size of the "small get-together" she had described earlier. Midmorning, she insisted on taking me shopping for something to wear. I hadn't been shopping with my mother since I was ten years old. Admittedly, my wardrobe could use a little help. Even though the luggage left at the Residence Inn had been returned, I didn't own much that would be suitable for one of my mother's soirées. Part of me was touched that she would suggest such an outing, but the larger part knew she wanted to make sure I had something exactly right for the occasion, according to her standards.

There was a time when I would have resisted and resented such a suggestion, labeling it interference on her part because she didn't think I was capable of choosing my own clothes. Even if those motives were still partly true, somehow it didn't matter anymore.

Something in me had softened and changed. And I felt the same softening in her. Why not give her the pleasure of doing something for me?

We did have a lovely time. Mother still had her preferences and distinctive eye for fashion. And I had my own yardstick. Namely, what would William like to see me wearing? What outfit or color would ignite that warm, smoldering look in his gray-green eyes?

Initially, Mother had her eye on a tailored little black dress, but we finally settled on one that reminded me of a painting by Monet. It was short and soft and floaty, with floral swirls of palest lavender, periwinkle blue, and soft sea-green. One shoulder was draped in a cascading ripple of fabric, and the other was bare.

"Oh, yes," Mother pronounced with a satisfied sigh. "This is exquisite. Absolutely exquisite. Turn around, dear, so I can see the back."

I whirled accordingly in front of the dressing room's full-length mirror, loving the soft feel of the fabric against my skin, and the romantic femininity of the style. If only William could see me in this dress. Remembering our first meeting in the ER, I couldn't have looked much worse—my face and body bruised, and wearing a shapeless hospital gown. More memories came flooding back. The look on William's face when I walked out of the bathroom wearing his pajama top. The sound of his voice when he returned from work and saw me waiting on the porch. *Now that's a sight worth coming home to.*

"Oh, yes," Mother said again, bringing me back to the present. "It's perfect."

We found a pair of earrings that cost nearly half a month's salary, and Mother bought them without blinking an eye. I managed to talk her out of a fifteen-hundred-dollar pair of Jimmy Choo stilettos, and we finally settled on some classy Stuart Weisman heels for a mere six hundred.

Mother saw my eye-popping expression when she handed her ever-ready plastic to the sales clerk, who rang up the heart-stopping total. "There's no need to look so shell-shocked, Mackenzie. You're worth every penny, and I'm having a marvelous time."

"I'm glad," I said, giving her a hug. But the thought came drifting by as we left the shopping mall that this was her world, not mine.

My welcome-home party was yet another example of my mother's world. Everything was stylish, elegant, and beautifully presented, from the canapés to the floral arrangements. My suspicions about the "small" gathering proved to be correct. I'd given her the names of some close friends and two or three colleagues from the magazine who might want to come, but that number was surpassed three times over by the thirty-odd people who arrived by seven thirty. Several of my parents' friends were there as well, including my ex-boyfriend's parents, Jim and Brenda Latimer, who gushed on about how wonderful I looked to the point of embarrassment.

In fact, most of the conversation throughout the evening wasn't what I would call natural. After the initial expressions of polite sympathy and shock over what I'd been through, what else does one say?

I watched my parents mingling effortlessly among the guests, ever elegant and gracious, while I made the rounds, feeling strangely displaced. The room was full of smiles and laughter, good food and flowers. The clink of glasses and a dozen different conversations swirled about me, like eddies in a whirlpool of sound. Somehow, I managed to smile and respond appropriately, knowing all the while that I'd never felt so lonely in my life.

Midway through the evening, Mother approached me with a beaming smile and none other than the magazine's editor-in-chief, Claire Langley, at her side.

"Here's someone who wants to say hello." Mother's tone of voice implied I was receiving a visitation from British royalty.

I had been talking with Patti Flynn, one of the magazine's contributing editors, as they approached. Seeing Claire Langley, Patti stared and stiffened into attention, a canapé halfway to her mouth.

"Ms. Langley, how nice of you to come," I said, my voice as stiff as Patti Flynn's body.

Claire seized both my hands in a chummy grip and gave me a frozen smile that was more the fault of Botox than any insincerity on her part. "Mackenzie, you look stunning. Absolutely stunning!"

Claire is a lovely woman around my mother's age, who probably spends at least half her salary in a determined effort to banish every line, wrinkle, and bulge from her slender form and face. Botox and a facelift have given her features a look of perpetual surprise, and collagen has added puffy fullness to her mouth. Tonight she was wearing a short, pencil-thin skirt that emphasized her trim tummy but did nothing for her legs and thick ankles. Bad choice. That said, her low-cut wraparound shirt in hot tangerine definitely accomplished its mission by emphasizing the silicone enhancements to her bust line. Considering the time Claire must spend in spas and clinics, one might wonder how she manages to keep tabs on a magazine with a staff and circulation as large as *Hearth & Home*. But she does, as her next comment aptly indicated.

"Lisa tells me that you've been in to see her, and the article on storybook homes has been temporarily shelved."

"Yes, and I'm sorry about that, but I—"

"There's no need to apologize. It's perfectly understandable," Claire said, waving a hand with enough bling to light a football stadium. "Besides, I have something else in mind for you. Why don't you drop by my office tomorrow morning, and we can discuss it. Say ten thirty?"

I nodded, knowing this was not a suggestion, but an edict from on high. "I'll be there."

"Good. I'll see you then."

She and Mother moved off to visit with other guests, leaving me with a huge knot in my stomach that was part curiosity and part dread.

"I wonder what that's all about," Patti said, coming back to life now that the visiting royalty had passed by. She popped the canapé into her mouth and added, "Good luck tomorrow," then headed back to the buffet table.

My curiosity about Claire Langley's request dwindled and died the next moment when I heard a low male voice speak my name. Turning, I saw Todd Latimer striding toward me with a smile on his handsome face and a warm glimmer lighting his dark eyes.

Twenty-nine

Todd's smile widened as he took in my stunned expression, and taking advantage of the situation, he planted a kiss on my cheek.

"Hi, beautiful. It's been awhile."

"Yes, it has."

"Two years and eight months, if I'm not mistaken."

My brows lifted, not expecting such an admission. "You have a very good memory."

"You're a hard woman to forget," he said softly, looking me up and down with frank appreciation.

There was a time when that certain tone of voice and the look in his eyes would have had a definite effect on my then-vulnerable emotions. Now, his words skipped harmlessly off the surface.

"You're looking good," I said. "How did you find out about the party? Have our two mothers been putting their heads together?"

"Something like that," he admitted with a laugh. "And I can't say I'm sorry. I've been hoping for the chance to see you again."

Todd reached out to caress my shoulder, and I instinctively shied away from his touch, not needing or wanting it. In a way, it was a relief to see him again and know he no longer had the power to hurt me. My heart was forever out of his reach.

"Have you had something to eat?" I asked. "The caterers have really out done themselves."

Todd caught hold of my arm. "I'm not hungry, and it's way too crowded in here. Isn't there someplace we can talk?"

I met his eyes. "I don't know that we have much to talk about."

"Maybe you don't, but I do. Couldn't you at least hear me out, for old times' sake?"

I hesitated and glanced around, not wanting to draw any undue attention. As it was, I caught sight of Todd's mother and mine glancing our way with pleased, hopeful smiles.

I turned my attention back to Todd, whose dark brows were narrowed. "All right. If you like." I led the way out of the living room and down the hall to my father's study, leaving the door open.

Todd shut the door behind him and gave me a long look. "Do you have any idea how much I've missed you?"

"No. I didn't know that you had."

His mouth tightened. "You're not making this easy for me."

"I'm not trying to be difficult, Todd. Just honest."

"You want honesty? Okay. How about, I was a total idiot for ever letting you go? There's never been anyone like you."

I leaned against the front of my father's desk and gave Todd a quizzical look. "Really? What about Leslie? And Jessica. And Fiona—or was it Felicia? I can't quite remember."

"They weren't you," he tossed back, a spark of anger lighting his eyes. "None of them were. That's what I'm trying to tell you, if you'd just listen, dammit."

"I'm listening," I said quietly.

He blew out a long breath and stepped closer. "I'd like to try again." When I said nothing, just stared at him with disbelief more than surprise, he shrugged and said, "You know how I feel about marriage. I guess I made that all too clear three years ago. But if a piece of paper means that much to you—well, I'm willing to give it a try."

My lips parted. "Really?" I couldn't keep the trace of sarcasm from my voice.

He nodded, giving me a crooked grin. "Really. What do you say, baby? I know it's not too late for us, and I think you know that, too." He reached out to take me in his arms, and I quickly backed away.

His surprise at my reaction had to be genuine. "Mackenzie, what's wrong with you? What kind of game are you playing?"

"There's nothing wrong with me, and it's not a game. I'm not in love with you, Todd, that's all. Not anymore. In fact, I'm not sure I ever was."

"You don't mean that." He reached out, taking firm hold of my shoulders, and his dark head bent closer.

I stiffened and pushed him away. "I do mean it. It would never work between us. So you won't have to make the noble sacrifice of marrying me. Now if you'll excuse me, I'd better get back to the party."

Not surprisingly, Todd left soon after.

Later that night, after all the guests had gone, Mother put an arm about me and asked if I'd enjoyed the evening. I knew what she was really asking, but I just smiled and told her, "It was wonderful. Everything was perfect."

"I thought I saw you talking with Todd," she said with just enough reticence to sound convincing. "I hope everything's all right between you two."

"We reached a perfect understanding," I told her. "Todd asked me to marry him—well, not asked exactly. It was more like, if a piece of paper was all that important to me, he was willing to give it a try. But I'm not. Not with him."

Mother stared at me, her expression stricken. "Mackenzie, are you sure? Think what you're throwing away."

"I'm not throwing anything away. I don't love Todd. Besides, marriage isn't something you try on like a pair of shoes, to see if it fits or not, and if it doesn't, you start looking for another pair." I smiled at her dazed expression and kissed her cheek. "It's okay, Mom. He'll recover. Faster than you might think."

"What about you?" she asked slowly. "Are you going to recover?"

"From Todd? I told you, there's nothing to recover from."

She shook her head. "Not Todd. William."

"No," I said softly. "I never want to recover from William.

I arrived at the magazine's offices in downtown Chicago by ten twenty the next morning, curiosity mingling with a fair amount of dread. I couldn't help wondering if the purpose of the meeting was merely a polite way of informing me that my services were no longer needed. Maybe, after the fiasco in California, Claire Langley considered me too much of a liability, despite the fact that I was Vanessa Graham's daughter.

There were very few employees around on a Saturday morning. Patti Flynn was slaving away at her computer, putting the finishing touches on a piece about springtime salads—always a challenge when you had to work at least four to six months ahead. And Amanda Porter was wrestling with some revisions on a celebrity photo shoot. Both Patti and Amanda had come to last night's party and sent me their smiling thanks as I walked by. Other than the receptionist and Claire's personal secretary, Paula Davis, the place was a morgue.

Paula's stolid expression offered no clue whatsoever about what might be awaiting me behind those closed doors, and I knew better than to ask. After eight interminable minutes, Paula opened the door to Claire's inner sanctum and delivered her standard "Ms. Langley will see you now." The secretary's solemn tone and demeanor made me feel as if I were entering a doctor's office to hear a terminal diagnosis.

I thanked her, swallowed hard, and stepped inside the room.

Claire looked up from the layout she was marking with red ink and motioned for me to sit. After the preliminary pleasantries and complimentary comments about the party, she put down the marker and took off her reading glasses.

"I'm sure you've been wondering why I wanted to see you," she said, giving me her best paraffin smile. Before I could reply, she cocked her head and told me, "I've been very impressed with the quality of your work this past year. Very impressed."

"Thank you."

"And your managing editor tells me that the magazine's received a good deal of positive feedback on your articles from our readership."

"That's nice to hear."

Claire leaned across the desk, and I felt the full force of her canny gray eyes. "I don't know if you're aware that Liz Turnbow, our East Coast managing editor, is getting married—again," she said, with heavy inflection on the *again*. "She'll be moving to Canada soon after the wedding. After giving it some thought, I think you're the ideal person to fill that spot. It would mean a considerable raise in salary, and of course, you'd need to move to Boston, but that shouldn't be a problem."

The paraffin smile stretched her full lips as she waited for my response.

My throat was suddenly dry and my pulse was hammering away in my throat. "I–I'm very flattered—very flattered by your offer . . ."

"As you should be," Claire said crisply. "There are several others who have been with the magazine longer than you, who would love to have this position."

"I'm sure there are." I straightened and drew a shaky breath. "But I . . . I was wondering if I could I have a day or two to think about it."

Surprise widened the look of perpetual surprise in her wrinkle-free features, and I knew she had been expecting effusive, grateful acceptance on my part, rather than stammering uncertainty. "You realize, I hope, the significance of this opportunity?" she said evenly.

"I do. Yes, I do—and I'm very grateful. Could I give you my decision around the first of the week?"

"Monday morning," she pronounced.

I nodded. "Monday morning."

I left her office in a complete and total daze. There was a time when I would have been over the moon with such an offer. Now, all I felt was a strange heaviness inside that made it difficult to put one foot in front of the other.

Molly Connolly, the receptionist, was on the phone as I walked by. I gave her a halfhearted wave and dragged my leaden feet toward the gleaming glass doors of the entryway.

"Oh, Mackenzie—Mackenzie, could you wait a minute?"

I glanced over my shoulder as she put down the phone and took a small package from a drawer in her desk.

"This came for you in yesterday's mail, but I wasn't sure when you'd be coming in to the office, so I kept it here." She shoved her harlequin-style glasses back and shrugged an apology. "Sorry. I nearly forgot all about it."

"That's okay. Thanks, Molly." I took the package from her. It was fairly light, wrapped in brown paper, and had no return address.

Rather than go back to my cubicle, I sat on one of the leather chairs in the reception area and tried to pry off the packing tape that sealed the small parcel.

"Here, use these," Molly offered, handing me a pair of scissors.

I cut through the tape and brown paper to see a small, oblong box.

"You don't think it's a bomb or something dangerous, do you?" she asked tentatively.

I answered her nervous look with a smile and lifted the lid of the box. "No. It's not heavy enough to be . . . to be . . ." My heart nearly stopped when I pushed aside some tissue paper and saw the carved wooden spoon inside. Holding it in a trembling hand, I ran my fingers over the two hearts joined together, the roughly carved dragon, and the sharp little points symbolizing tears. My own tears were spilling freely down my cheeks.

"Mackenzie?" Molly stared at me. "I hope it's not bad news."

I smiled at her through my tears, all the heaviness gone, and joy fairly bursting inside me. "No . . . no, it's wonderful news. The most wonderful news in the world!" My happiness couldn't be contained. I had to hug someone. And since William wasn't in range, funny little Molly would have to do. I went over to her desk and hugged her so hard, her glasses fell off.

"Thank you, Molly. Thank you!"

"You're welcome." She stared at me with a confused smile. "I think."

Still clutching the spoon, I hugged her again, then sat back down, suddenly noticing a folded sheet of stationery in the box.

Molly put her glasses back on and handed me a couple of tissues from the box on her desk.

I wiped my eyes and set the love spoon in the box long enough to open the note paper.

Darling Mackenzie,

Please accept this spoon as a symbol of my love. I promise always to care, protect, and provide for you. I can think of no greater happiness than to share my life with you—the tears and the joys.

All that I am or ever hope to be is yours.

Love,

William

I put the letter next to the love spoon and marched straight back to Claire Langley's office. There was no need to wait until Monday morning to give her my answer. I've never had such an easy decision.

Thirty

It was interesting, for want of a better word, to suddenly find myself feeling whole and happy and completely certain of my course in life, and to discover that nearly everyone else of my acquaintance was equally certain I had lost my mind. Mother was appalled, then angry, then hurt when I announced I was going to marry William and would be flying back to Utah as soon as possible. When she realized this entailed turning down Claire Langley's once-in-a-lifetime job offer, her reaction went beyond stunned. In fact, I was afraid she would be ill from the shock. My father was clearly confused and attributed the whole thing to delayed shock combined with some wild romantic fantasy. When I called my brother Jeremy, it didn't take long to realize my parents had gotten to him first and enlisted his aid to help talk me out of such madness. I didn't bother trying to argue or explain, just gave him my love and told him he'd be getting an invitation to the wedding.

Even some of my close friends at the magazine office couldn't believe that I would turn down a promotion and a raise to move out West and "marry some cowboy."

Surprisingly, it was Claire Langley who responded with understanding and approval, neither of which I had expected when I returned to her office.

As she listened to my shining-eyed, happy refusal of what she considered to be the opportunity of a lifetime, I saw her gray eyes narrow and her lips tighten with displeasure. When I told her that I was going to be married, I knew full well the dreaded Langley storm clouds were brewing, but my heart was too happy to mind.

"I would think at the very least you owed me the courtesy of telling me this when we talked earlier," she said icily, then gave her gold wristwatch a pointed glance. "Which was, I believe, roughly seven minutes ago."

"I totally agree," I said. "And I would have, but that was before I got the love spoon. So technically, when I talked with you, I didn't know that William had proposed."

"And am I to believe that this proposal took place sometime in the last seven minutes?" Sarcasm dripped into the iciness of her voice.

"Yes," I said with a happy sigh, unable to stop smiling. "When he sent me this—it's the love spoon his great-grandfather carved for his great-grandmother. William didn't have my address, so he had to send the spoon to the office."

As I took the love spoon out of its box, my clumsy fingers dropped William's letter on Claire's desk. She picked it up and gave the note a scornful glance, then paused, her eyes widening as she scanned the contents.

"I assume this is the man who took care of you after the accident." She handed me the note, and her voice had lost some of its coldness.

"Yes."

"And he loves you," she said slowly.

"Yes."

"And you're going to drop everything, including my offer, to go back to Utah and marry this man."

"Yes."

"May I?" She reached a perfectly manicured hand toward the love spoon.

"Of course." I handed it to her, watching in silent surprise as her slender fingers gently touched the carvings.

"It's very lovely," she said softly. "I'm not familiar with love spoons. Would you like to tell me more about them, and this William that you love—say, over lunch?"

"I'd love to," I said, smiling into her eyes.

Claire took me to her favorite restaurant, and we talked for over an hour as easily as if we'd been friends for years. We talked about Allison and William and Hearth Fires, and as we talked I saw softness in her gray eyes, and a wistful sadness touching the manufactured features of her face. Seeing that softness, I decided that Claire Langley was really a romantic at heart despite her fierce reputation.

"When your life calms down a bit, assuming that it will at some point," she said as we were finishing lunch, "I'd like you to consider doing a feature article about love spoons."

"Then . . . then you'd like me to stay on at the magazine?"

Claire dabbed a napkin to her lips. "Mackenzie, my dear, I told you before that there were several others who would jump at the chance to fill the position in New England. But that doesn't mean I'm about to let go of an excellent writer—even if she is foolish enough to move to some forsaken ranch in Utah." The words sounded stern, but her gray eyes were sparkling. "I hope you'll send me an invitation to the wedding. I'd like to meet this William of yours."

"Of course I will." I smiled at her, then sighed. "Wish me luck in breaking the news to Mother."

Claire just nodded and smiled. "Leave your mother to me. She'll be fine."

———

Skies were overcast and there was a biting wind off the Great Lakes as I boarded a nonstop flight to Salt Lake City at eight forty the next morning. My heart was flying long before the plane left the ground for its journey through the sky. Three and a half hours later, we landed in Salt Lake, and I made the connecting flight to St. George with plenty of time to spare. I had my day's itinerary carefully thought out, and so far, everything was going exactly as planned. After landing in St. George, I would pick up a rental car, then find a place to freshen up and change clothes before driving to the ranch. Blame it on feminine vanity, but I was determined that today William would see me at my best. Wearing my beautiful party dress might not be an option, but he was definitely going to see me in something other than jeans or sweats. I'd packed one of my favorite dresses, a silky sheath in soft sea-green with a matching cardigan. Yes, everything was going exactly as planned.

Then, as the plane started its descent into St. George, a worrisome thought wormed its way into my happy anticipation. What if William wasn't at the ranch when I arrived? How would I find him? I had no phone numbers for him or his parents. Not even his law partner in Silver Reef. The shining certainty that had swept me along for the past twenty-four hours suddenly darkened into doubt. And the thumps and bumps of the small plane as it made its final approach were nothing compared to the turbulence inside me.

Mother had told me from the outset that my idea of surprising William was a foolish one—that surprises very often didn't work out the way one hoped. And I had blithely ignored her. But what if she was right? I put a hand to my stomach as the plane gave another rattling lurch. *Please don't let her be right,* I prayed. *And please let the plane land in one piece. I don't want to die without seeing him again.*

Minutes later, I stepped off the plane into the blazing brilliance of an October afternoon in southern Utah. Red rocks and a clear cobalt sky welcomed me with dramatic clarity, and I felt my doubts dissolving into nervous excitement. In less than half an hour, I'd collected my luggage, changed clothes, and picked up a rental car. After consulting my phone's GPS, I was on my way. Remembering that first drive to William's ranch and my condition at the time, I wasn't about to trust finding the ranch to memory.

Fall colors were at their peak as I took the freeway north out of St. George, and I found myself fairly breathless with all the beauty as well as anticipation. Crimson maples, golden yellow cottonwoods, and burnt-orange Gambel oaks flaunted their autumn finery throughout the miles, dazzling the eye with their brilliance. Soon the towns of Hurricane and La Verkin were behind me and I found myself on the narrow road to Rockville, searching for that small turnoff to the ranch. I needn't have worried. The voice of "Madge," my faithful GPS, blandly instructed me to make a right turn in eight hundred feet, which I did. After crossing the old iron trestle bridge, memory led the way—with fields and the tree-lined river on my right, tawny sandstone ridges and buttes on the left.

Earl Thacker's rodeo bulls were grazing idly in a fenced pasture as I drove by. I slowed the car and smiled a hello to the massive animals. Two or three lifted their heads to look my way, but the rest paid me little mind.

Please be there. Please be there. My thoughts called out the fervent message as I turned down the dirt road to the ranch house.

My rapid heartbeat slowed to a worrisome thud when I pulled up beside the house. William's black truck was parked beside the cottonwoods, but there was no Range Rover. I got out of the car, smoothed my dress with sweaty palms, and glanced around. Scarcely a breeze stirred the warm air, and the lonely song of cicadas in the fields was far from welcoming. The silence hovering around the old ranch house seemed to confirm my fears even before I knocked on the door. William wasn't here.

I slumped down on the porch swing, feeling disappointment's heavy weight. So much for my well-thought-out plans. I leaned back against the swing with a frustrated sigh, wondering what to do. If I could get an internet signal on my phone, I might be able to discover Tom and Jenny's address. If not, I'd have to drive back to La Verkin. Even if it was a sleepy Sunday, there ought to be at least one store or gas station open that had a phone directory. Hopefully, William's parents would know where he was. It might even be that he was there now, enjoying a pleasant Sunday dinner with his family. That would explain why the Range Rover was gone.

In spite of this rationale, I couldn't dismiss the very real possibility that William might not be at his parents' home. For all I knew, he could have flown back to California to take care of some police details with Wade and Captain McIntire. The plain fact of the matter was I didn't have the faintest idea where he was, or how to get hold of him. To make matters worse, it was already past midafternoon, with shadows lengthening across the lawn. The idea of spending the night alone at the ranch was not at all appealing. Assuming of course, that the house was unlocked and I could get inside. Unpleasant as it might be, the most sensible solution to my dilemma would be to drive back to Hurricane or St. George and get a motel for the night, then try to reach William or his parents in the morning.

I got off the swing and left the porch, cursing myself for being every kind of fool, when I heard the distinctive whinny of a horse. I straightened, listening, trying to determine the direction of the sound. Seconds later, it came again, followed by the answering whinny of another horse. My heart began a nervous pounding, and I hurried across the back lawn toward the barn and corrals.

Shiloh was in the main corral, ears pricked, her lovely head turned in the direction of some nearby fields. My gaze followed hers, and the next moment my dashed hopes sprang back to life.

William was no more than ten or twelve yards away, trudging across the field on foot, leading Strider behind him. Both man and horse were a sorry sight. William's jeans and shirt were covered in dust, and his head was down. Although his cowboy hat hid his face from me, there was no mistaking the dispirited bent of his shoulders. Strider's plodding walk matched William's in weariness, and the horse was definitely favoring his left front leg.

Ironically, Strider saw me before William did, nickered a greeting, and came to a sudden stop.

William gave the horse's head an encouraging pat. "It's all right, boy. We're nearly there."

Strider just shook his head and stood his ground.

"Hey, boy, what's got into—"

William glanced up then and saw me hurrying toward him across the lawn. His entire body went as rigid as the horse beside him.

My own steps slowed and came to a shaky halt.

William tipped his hat back, and the raw emotion in his eyes made my heart ache. He shook his head as if he couldn't quite believe what he was seeing, then a slow smile lifted the corners of his mouth.

"Now that's a sight worth coming home to," he said softly. He dropped the reins, and I flew into his waiting arms.

We held each other, not speaking, and it took some time for the rough reality of his arms and mouth to convince me that our time of separation was truly past.

"You came back . . ." William muttered against my neck, one of his hands entwined in the thickness of my hair.

Smiling through my tears, I told him, "I haven't come back— I've come home."

—❧—

The glories of autumn were past; all the color and the brilliance had faded into the last gray days of November. Trees were leafless and bare, fields shorn of their harvest. Yet despite the grayness outside, there was gratitude and thanksgiving all around me—in my heart, most of all.

On this afternoon in late November, members of the Evans family were gathered at the home of LeAnn and her husband David for their traditional Thanksgiving dinner. Extra tables and chairs had been set up in the spacious great room adjoining the kitchen, and not counting LeAnn's two-week-old daughter, Rebecca Ann, there were sixteen places set. I was still hard pressed to remember all the names and ages of the various family members. LeAnn and David and their children accounted for five places; Tom and Jenny's oldest daughter Kathy and her husband Brad, along with four children ranging in age from nine to three, had traveled from their home in Logan, Utah, to be with the family; and Wade had flown in from California.

And then there was my husband and me. Being a bride of not quite one month, I was still a bit weak-kneed just saying the words *my husband*. The past twenty-six days had been a joyous journey of love and sharing. Our discovery of one another and our life together was just beginning, but one thing I was delightfully sure of. Mackenzie Graham was now thoroughly and completely the wife of William T. Evans. The woman I was always meant to be.

By three o'clock that afternoon, the tables were fairly groaning with food: turkey with all the trimmings—including Jenny's famous stuffing, mashed potatoes and gravy, hot rolls, vegetables, relishes, and a variety of Jell-O salads. Tom Evans took his place at the head of the main table and offered a prayer of heartfelt thanks. Then the happy destruction began.

I watched in amazement as hours of work and preparation were devoured in mere minutes. Admittedly, I did my part with much enjoyment. Cleanup and pumpkin pie were postponed as family members sprawled in sated satisfaction around the great room and nearby living room, happily complaining of turkey overload.

Tom vetoed the boy cousins' request to play The Avengers on their PlayStation 4, by announcing that before the killing of any aliens took place, he wanted to watch the DVD recording of our wedding. Jenny and her daughters gave immediate approval to this suggestion, and the little boys gave in with only a few groans.

William gestured for me to join him on the couch and threaded his fingers through mine as images of our wedding day filled the TV screen.

The video began with a classic shot of the main lodge in Zion Canyon, then shifted to a large courtyard outside the lodge where wedding guests were congregating. Moving higher, the videographer captured a panoramic sweep of our surroundings. Towering thousands of feet above the lodge, the Temple of Moroni, the Great White Throne, and the Court of the Patriarchs looked down upon our small mortal gathering. No church could have had a more sacred setting for our union than this magnificent realm of ancient stone.

Returning to the courtyard, the camera moved among the guests seated there. In harmony with the murmur of a nearby stream, there was the timeless music of a classical guitar, played by one of William's close friends.

William gave my hand a squeeze as we watched our parents smiling and talking together. My brother and his wife with their month-old son were comparing notes on parenthood with LeAnn and her husband. Seated nearby, Claire Langley was chatting with Sheriff Fuller, who looked more than a little overwhelmed by her stylish presence and attentions. Rather than seating guests of the bride and groom in rows on either side of a center aisle, chairs had been set up in two wide circles, so William and I would be surrounded by dear friends and family as we made our vows. In another break from tradition, William and I chose not to have him wait alone, while I made a grand entrance on the arm of my father. Instead, we entered the circle together—side by side, and arm in arm, the way we would live out our lives.

There was an excited murmur among the guests, then silence as everyone got to their feet. I felt a pleasant tug of emotion, watching our entrance into the circle. William, looking so tall and distinguished in his dark suit, and me, glowing from the inside out, with gardenias in my hair and a long white gown that even Mother thought was completely lovely.

When the camera moved in for a close-up of William and me, his hand tightened around mine and he whispered in my ear, "I have the most beautiful wife."

Glancing away from the TV for a moment, I smiled at him and snuggled closer to his side.

A series of candid shots followed the ceremony, as family and friends moved inside the lodge for refreshments and a dance. I saw my parents in animated conversation with a very pregnant LeAnn, the twins at her side, pulling faces for the camera. And there was Wade, looking tall and handsome, completely surrounded by some of the female staff writers from the magazine. Then Jenny moved to the piano and William's father faced the group, microphone in hand, to announce that he'd like to dedicate a song and the first dance to his son and new daughter-in-law.

Looking every inch the gentleman cowboy, dressed in his best suit with a bolo tie and cowboy boots, Tom proceeded to sing "The West, a Nest, and You." Now, as I had then, I found a few tears slipping down my cheeks as we listened to my father-in-law's rich tenor voice. I watched as William took me in his arms to begin the dance, and the camera followed us around the dance floor. At the song's end, my husband drew me close for a long kiss amid cheers and applause. All except for the twins, whose faces were screwed up in obvious distaste at such a display.

Lying on their tummies, watching the kiss on video, the little boys were giggling and pulling similar faces at the sight.

"Gavin and Quinn, you better shut your eyes," William told them, "because I could use another one of those kisses from my wife right about now." He proceeded to kiss me, with cheers and applause from those around us.

When the video ended, Jenny announced that pie would be served just as soon as she whipped the cream.

I was getting up to offer my help when LeAnn approached me, her infant daughter sleeping soundly in her arms.

"Would you mind holding little Beckie while I help Mom in the kitchen?"

"I'd love to."

LeAnn handed me the baby and smiled as I gingerly adjusted the infant's position.

"Am I doing this right?"

"You're a natural." She gave me a wink, then headed for the kitchen.

I eased my way carefully to the couch and slowly sat down, trying not to disturb the sleeping infant.

William grinned at my ultracautious efforts. "If that baby can sleep through all the noise and hullabaloo around here, I doubt you sitting down is going to wake her."

"You're probably right." I gave my husband a sheepish smile.

Rebecca Ann chose that moment to open one eye and scrunch up her tiny nose. Then her eyelids fluttered and she settled back into blissful baby sleep.

"Oh, William, just look at that darling little face," I whispered. "Isn't she amazing? And so perfect . . ." I touched my lips to the baby's velvety cheek, breathing in the sweet newness of this little miracle person, and suddenly felt what could only be described as a deep maternal yearning.

My gaze lifted from Rebecca Ann to my husband's handsome face. "I want one of these," I said softly.

William slipped an arm around my shoulders and there was a definite gleam in his gray-green eyes. "Then let's go make one. I'll be more than happy to help get things started."

My insides quivered at the prospect and I smiled into his eyes. "Right now? You'll miss the pumpkin pie."

He leaned closer and nuzzled my ear. "Right now, all I want is you. Let's go home, Mac."

I gave him an assenting nod and lifted my lips to meet his kiss.

Nine months later, William and I brought our firstborn son home to Hearth Fires. William Thomas Evans Jr. was bright-eyed and wide awake as his father helped me up the porch steps. William bent his head to kiss me, then the downy head of his two-day-old son. Love and pride were shining in his eyes.

As we went inside, I could almost feel the old home smiling and offering a welcome to yet another generation of the Evans family. And I knew that in the days and years to come, Hearth Fires would have many more stories to tell.

About the Author

Dorothy McDonald Keddington is a native of Salt Lake City, Utah, now residing in Sandy. Writing has been a love and motivating force in her life since early childhood. She is the author of eight romantic-suspense novels, two musical plays, and the gripping true story *A Square Sky,* coauthored with Sayed Ahmad Sharifi. *Jayhawk* and *Return to Red Castle* are among her novels that have been perennial favorites with readers for several decades, often being passed down from mother to daughter to granddaughter. Mrs. Keddington has taught creative writing for community schools and privately, and is a popular speaker for civic and cultural events throughout the Intermountain region. In addition to her work as a novelist, Mrs. Keddington is a professional genealogist, specializing in Irish and U.S. family history.